GRACE

DANA K. RAY

GRACE, The Beginning of The Luciano Series
Dana K. Ray

Copywrite 2018 by Dana K. Ray. All rights reserved.
Cover Design by Dana K. Ray and Alan Davis

ISBN-13: 978-1724681645
ISBN-10: 1724681648

No part of this publication may be reproduced, stored in or introduced in a retrieval system or transmitted in any way, or by any means, electronic, mechanical, photocopied, scanned, recorded, or otherwise without prior written permission of the author except as provided by the USA copywrite law.

This is a work of fiction. Names, descriptions, characters, places, and incidents included in this story are the products of the author's imagination or are used fictitiously. Any resemblance to actual events or persons, living or dead, is entirely coincidental.

To the editor I met twenty plus years ago. You read my first manuscript, then encouraged me to pursue another dream.

In your face! LOL!

ACKNOWLEDGEMENTS

To God for continuing to give me the movies in my head!

To all my friends and fans who continue to encourage me with their love of my books!

To Tom, Madison, Keaton, Lydia and Collins for their love and patience as I continue to pursue my writing!

To Irene Onorato, Linda Robinson, and Beatrice Fishback whose writing and editing skills are outstanding. Without your help I could've never gotten this far.

ONE
Kansas City, Missouri

SONNY SAT ON the concrete loading dock and kicked the wall with the heels of his black Converse tennis shoes.

Antony, his older brother, randomly threw rocks at the broken windows of the five-story building. Each time he brought his long, slender arm back, his muscle flexed and the coiled snake tattoo peeked out from under the sleeve of his white T-shirt.

Antony glanced at him. "Would you forget about the tattoo? It ain't a big deal."

"Sure seems like one to you and Papa."

"So? You chickened out."

Terrified was more like it. The tattoos were meant to be an outward sign to others and a covenant of loyalty between the brothers.

Antony hadn't so much as flinched while the cluster of needles penetrated his skin. Sonny went pale. Their father shook his head and yelled something about how good Sonny would look in a dress. Being the brunt of his father's joke hadn't hurt half as much as the disappointment on Antony's face.

Antony hurled one last rock, shattering the remaining glass on a second-floor window. He raised his fists in triumph, jumped up, and sat next to Sonny. "It's not the tattoo Papa's mad about, it's the way you keep dogging on his business."

"Papa's seen *The Godfather* one too many times. The only thing he's got in common with the mob is that they come from the same country."

"If Papa heard you say that he'd beat the crap outta you." Antony lowered his voice to imitate his father. "I've worked my butt off to get to where we are today."

"Work? That's a laugh. He's a mafia Don wannabe. It doesn't bother you that he hurts people?"

"He helps some of them. Heck, he just loaned Jimmy Crank enough money to save his bar."

"And what happens when Jimmy can't pay him back?"

"Hey, if the slime ball can't pay back the money he should've never borrowed it in the first place." Antony cupped his hands in a praying position. "Papa is just trying to help the poor souls in the neighborhood."

Poor souls. That's how Papa had explained it, but Sonny knew his older brother was neither that naive nor that caring.

"You should've seen old man Kuehler when Papa told him he'd better pay or else," Antony said. "He peed his pants right there in front of him."

"If Papa would've caught you watching again, you'da done more than that."

"I can take anything Papa dishes out."

And Papa dished out a lot. His punishments were swift and severe. Mama never denied that the boys deserved correction, It was the method she couldn't condone. Nor prevent.

"Carlo's right. It'll be me and him taking over the family business. You ain't got the stomach for it." Antony grinned. His arrogance and Italian heritage reeked through his golden brown skin and coal black hair. His soul lay buried deep behind his dark brown eyes. Sixteen-years-old and he already had great confidence for what his future would hold.

"Not if Mama has her way."

"Oh, come on. You really think her religion will change Papa?"

Sonny shrugged. "She's right, though. If he doesn't go legit, he's going to end up in jail."

"No, he won't."

"How do you know?"

Antony threw his shoulders back and stuck his chest out, imitating their father. "Because I'm Lorenzo Luciano. Nobody can touch me."

Carlo and Dimitri Romeo walked across the concrete parking lot toward them. They were the sons of Gino Romeo, Lorenzo's partner. Decked out in jeans and sleeveless T-shirts, they proudly showed off their identical tattoos, a knife with a single drop of blood dripping from the blade.

Carlo's tattoo sat arrogantly on solid muscle. Dimitri's clung to fat, but no one would dare tell him that to his face. Dimitri had a fast right hook and calling him overweight would get you a black eye, a bloody nose or one less tooth.

Carlo flicked his half-smoked cigarette beneath Antony's feet. "We got company, again." He pointed to the far corner of the loading dock.

* * *

Antony jumped from the wall and followed Carlo. Leaning over a sleeping man, Antony's gold crucifix swung freely from his neck. The mixture of body odor, urine and booze hovered over the drunk. His body jerked then relaxed with a loud grunt.

Carlo grabbed the brown paper sack from the old man's clutch. Laughing, he poured out the last of the vagrant's cheap wine then threw it against the wall.

Startled, the drunk tried to stand but Carlo brought up his boot and thrust it onto the man's back, sending him face down onto shards of glass.

"Beat it and don't come back." Carlo sadistically laughed. "I ain't telling you again."

Antony ignored Sonny's piercing eyes. Guilt was something he prided himself in not feeling. He ran his hand over his freshly cut hair then wiped the clinging sweat across his jeans. The cynical grin was meant to camouflage his inner fears.

"How many times you gonna beat that old man?" Sonny yelled. He leaned forward and rested his elbows on his legs. A few strands of black hair fell forward allowing the sweat to run down and drip to the concrete where they immediately evaporated. His white T-shirt clung to him, the perspiration soaked through.

"'Til he obeys," Carlo snapped.

"Why you sweatin' over this drunk, Carlo?" Antony kicked at the old man's shoes.

The drunk stumbled to his feet, his eyes glassy, his face gashed and bloodied.

"Get outta here," Antony yelled.

"He ain't hurtin' nothin'," Sonny said. "Just leave him alone."

"Sheesh, Sonny, you're such a wus." Carlo chucked a rock at the drunk's back as he staggered away.

Sonny's eyes met Antony's. When no protective words came, Sonny looked away.

Carlo squinted, the sun piercing his blue eyes. They looked strange against his thin black hair. "Let's go score some smokes."

"Lay off Kuehler's store," Sonny said. "You keep walkin' out with his merchandise he'll never be able to pay Papa back."

"Yeah, maybe he'll be taught the same lesson Benny was taught." Carlo laughed.

Antony had talked Sonny into going down to the warehouse to see how Papa handled Benny's gambling debt. They'd peeked through the wooden slates that boarded up the basement windows. Sonny had been successful in fighting the tears but couldn't stop the churning in his stomach and ran to the bushes to puke.

Antony followed, quietly laughing. When some of Sonny's lunch landed on his new shoes, Antony's laughter stopped and his heart turned cold. He said nothing. He didn't have to.

Dimitri smacked Sonny's leg with the back of his hand. "Hey, idiot, you listening?"

"What?"

"Heard your father shook ol' man Kuehler down again." Dimitri ran a plastic comb through his black, feathered hair then slipped it in his back pocket. "Antony says Kuehler peed his pants, right there in front of your ol' man. You blow chunks, again?"

"No." Sonny tucked his gold crucifix under his shirt.

"Where's your shadow?" Dimitri asked.

"Lay off Clay, he's got no one else."

"Lucky he's got you now."

Carlo lit a cigarette. "I heard when they found Clay's dad laying in the tub, his eyes were practically bugged outta his head. Heart attack? No freakin' way." Carlo put his hands around his neck and made a face.

"Least our Mama took him in," Sonny said.

"Your Mama," Dimitri rolled his eyes. "The saint."

Sonny and Antony shot Dimitri severe looks.

"I was just yanking your chains." Dimitri conceded. "Be cool."

"Put a sock in it." Carlo reached under his shirt and pulled out a small snub nose thirty-eight special. "Look what I got."

"Papa's gonna kill you," Dimitri shook his head. "You know what happened the last time you lifted one of his guns."

"Yeah, well that was klutz's fault." Carlo jerked his head at Antony. "Thought your papa taught you better."

"How was I supposed to know it was loaded? Besides, who's the one impressing the chicks with this?" Antony pointed to the scar on his arm where the bullet had grazed him.

"Good thing you got that to impress them, 'cause you ain't got nothin' else." Carlo laughed then tucked the gun back into the front of his pants. "Let's blow this rat hole."

Antony rolled his eyes then looked up at Sonny. "Come on."

As they walked across the parking lot, Carlo jumped Antony, putting him in a headlock. Antony grabbed Carlo around his waist, wrestling to free himself. When Carlo loosened his arm, Antony pulled his head from Carlo's grip, laughing.

"What's that?" Carlo pointed to a thick silver ID bracelet that hung on Antony's wrist.

"Just something Mama gave me." It was one of the rare times Antony didn't tell the truth.

"It better not be from Elisa."

"You calling me a liar?"

"Giving you fair warning."

"Whatever," Antony pulled out a cigarette. He'd allow the smoke to calm his racing heart. Carlo and Antony were like brothers. They shared everything, except Carlo's cousin, Elisa.

"You look like a girl wearing that thing. Got a bracelet to match your necklace." Carlo turned to Sonny who was following behind them with Dimitri. "Sonny, you get a bracelet, too? Not like you need anything else to make you look like a girl."

Dimitri laughed.

"Shut up," Sonny said.

Antony winked at Sonny before playfully punching Carlo in the arm. "Lay off him."

Carlo and Antony continued to joke about Kuehler's misfortune as they all walked to the story.

* * *

In his fifteen years of life, Sonny had seen more of his father's evilness then he cared to. Mama's fresh talk about the church birthed something in Sonny that he had never felt before.

Mama's voice rang in Sonny's ears. She had read from Psalms that morning. Antony blew her off but Sonny stayed to listen. It was David she talked about that morning...*fear and trembling have beset me...Oh, that I had the wings of a dove! I would flee far away and be at rest...*

* * *

The four boys ran back to the loading dock. Antony pulled out a pack of stolen cigarettes, ripped it open and lit one. "What a rush."

Carlo leaned over trying to catch his breath, "Man, did you see ol' man Kuehler's face? That was so easy." Carlo laughed.

"You lied." Dimitri caught his breath, grinned coldly at Antony, then turned to Carlo. "He lied to you, man. Ask him about his girlfriend."

Antony breathed deeply, trying to thwart off the anger that consumed him. Dimitri was instigating a fight and he had the ammunition. The bracelet had flipped over at Kuehler's store and Dimitri had seen the inscription.

"Girlfriend? What's he talking about?" Carlo's lips pursed together as he glared at Antony.

"Nothing."

"Check out the bracelet." Dimitri pointed.

Carlo grabbed Antony's wrist, flipped the bracelet over and read the words engraved on it. "Love always, Elisa." Carlo's face grew redder. "I told you to break it off."

"I'll date who I want."

"She's my cousin. I know how you are. Use and abuse. Isn't that your motto?"

"You taught me everything I know."

Carlo's face hardened. Seconds later, he brought his fist back and punched Antony in the jaw, splitting open his lip. "I told you to leave her alone."

Antony shoved Carlo. "I'll see her if I want to." His anger was just as fierce as Carlo's, and if Carlo wanted to fight, Antony would gladly oblige.

Carlo threw another punch only this time, Antony was ready. He raised his left arm, catching Carlo's then brought his right fist around with a vengeance, plummeting it into the right side of Carlo's eye, blackening it.

"Hit him back," Dimitri yelled.

"Shut up," Sonny shouted.

Carlo quickly recovered and drove his right fist into Antony's gut. Antony backed away. One side of his mouth went into a slight grin as he wiped the blood that oozed from his lip. His chest pounded.

Sonny stepped between them. "Stop it!"

"Shut up." Carlo grabbed Sonny's arm and thrust him into Dimitri. Both boys fell to the ground. A shard of glass ripped open the skin on Sonny's elbows.

Carlo pulled out the snub nose thirty-eight and pointed it at Antony, his eyes wide and sinister. "Elisa is not a piece of meat."

"Cool it, man, I'm not using her. It's different with her. I promise." Antony's eyes darted between the gun and Carlo. "Come on. You don't want to do this."

Sonny came from behind and threw the weight of his body against Carlo. They both fell to the ground.

"Get off of me," Carlo yelled.

They wrestled, randomly throwing punches.

Dimitri caught Carlo's arm but it was yanked away so fast Dimitri fell back to the ground.

Antony tried to separate Carlo and Sonny. "Will you two stop it? This ain't cool."

Antony dodged the arms that flew through the air. He turned to Dimitri. "Go get Spence."

Spencer Romeo was Elisa's older brother and at this time of day could always be found playing poker on the third floor of the abandoned factory.

Dimitri turned and ran.

Carlo sideswiped Sonny across the face with the gun. Sonny grimaced, scrambling to get away but Carlo grabbed his leg and dragged him back. "You wanna fight, punk? We'll fight."

"Leave him alone." Antony grabbed Carlo and tried to pull him off of Sonny but Carlo shoved him so hard he fell backward.

Sonny punched Carlo and the boys rolled. Carlo ended up on top, the gun at Sonny's chest. Sonny grabbed Carlo's wrist, bending the gun away from him.

Antony reached for them. A deafening shot rang out. He froze, his heart pounding furiously.

The blink of Sonny's eyes brought Antony to his knees. He rolled Carlo's body off Sonny then pressed his finger against his neck, half expecting to feel a pulse. His eyes met Sonny's. "He's dead."

Sonny's face paled. "The gun, it just went off." He shook Carlo's shoulder, his brain still processing Antony's words. "I didn't mean to. Papa's gonna kill me."

"Oh, man," Antony raked his hand through his jet black hair, grief and anger raging. "I was handling Carlo, why'd you jump in?"

Sonny's eyes met Antony's. "Because he had a gun to your chest."

"And you thought you'd protect me?" Antony gave Sonny a deep eye roll. He looked down at Carlo, Papa's warning rang in his ears. *Two things will kill a friendship. Money and love.*

"Stupid," Antony said to Carlo's lifeless body, "I told you I loved her."

In fact, he'd told Carlo over and over again but he never listened. Carlo would just yell something about Antony using his cousin before he'd start throwing punches. It had put such a strain on their friendship that Antony had even tried to cool it with Elisa, but he couldn't. He was driven to her with a force he couldn't understand, let alone fight.

But Carlo killing him over a girl? No way. "Carlo would've never shot me," he said more to himself than to Sonny.

"Well, excuse me for thinking he would."

"You don't get it, do you? You not only killed Carlo, you destroyed our future."

"Papa's gonna kill me," Sonny whispered. "Isn't he?"

"No, he won't," Antony said confidently. "Gino will kill you first."

The small amount of blood that had returned to Sonny's face quickly drained away. It wouldn't matter that Gino Romeo was

Lorenzo's partner or that he owed Lorenzo for saving his life on numerous occasions. All that would matter was avenging his son.

Antony couldn't let that happen. Loyalty to family was more important than life itself. Sonny had protected him, and now he would have to do the same.

Pulling his T-shirt off, Antony threw it at Sonny. "Give me your shirt."

"What?"

"Your shirt, give it to me."

Sonny shook his head. "I can't let you do this."

Antony grabbed Sonny's shirt and ripped it over his head. "Put mine on. Hurry."

Shadowy figures ran down the stairwell of the abandoned factory. "I'll tell them I did it." Antony pulled Sonny's shirt on and cringed as the blood soaked shirt stuck to his chest.

"But…" Sonny said.

"Let me take the heat," Antony said in a softer voice, trying to be tender even though it wasn't his style.

"I can't let you do that."

Antony's attempt at compassion quickly evaporated. "Put it on, now, before I beat the crap out of you." He anxiously watched Sonny pull the shirt on. "And keep your mouth shut."

The last thing he needed was for his brother to ruin his act of nobility. Not that he was doing this for bragging rights since nobody would know about his sacrifice except Sonny. He was doing this simply because that's what brothers do.

Antony leaned over Carlo's body as a group of boys emerged from the doorway, jumped off the loading dock and gathered around them.

He looked up at Spencer, Elisa's brother. "It was an accident."

Spencer knelt over his cousin and stared into Carlo's empty eyes before looking at his chest where the bullet had ripped through him, exposing hamburger like flesh. Blood pooled on the concrete around Carlo's body. Spencer looked back at Antony. "You killed him?"

Antony hesitated. What was he doing, second guessing himself? Sixteen and branded a killer wasn't exactly in his plan but he had to protect Sonny. He finally nodded. "He found out about me and Elisa. You know how crazy he gets. He came after me with a gun."

Antony grabbed Spencer's arm. "It was an accident."

Spencer ripped his arm away, sniffing hard. Romeo blood ran fiercely through his veins, but Antony knew if he could convince Spencer it was an accident he might have a chance. A chance at what he wasn't sure of, except maybe, escaping death at the hand of Gino.

"Spence," Antony waited until their eyes met, "You know Carlo and I were like brothers."

Spencer faintly nodded. "I know." He pulled out a cigarette and lit it. "Gino's gonna kill you."

"You gotta help me. Not just for me but for Elisa."

Their eyes locked and for a second, unspoken words shot through the air.

Antony hoped Spencer could read his eyes and see how much he loved Elisa.

Spencer's eyes narrowed, reminding Antony that regardless of his feelings, or his sister's feelings, family extracts first loyalty.

He gave Antony a small, almost unnoticeable nod.

Relief engulfed Antony. If nothing else, he could die knowing that Elisa would be assured of how much he loved her.

The faint sound of police sirens grew louder. Dimitri Romeo shoved his way through the boys then fell to his knees next to Carlo, his only brother.

"I'm sorry, man. It was an accident," Antony said to Dimitri whose tears couldn't mask his hard, vengeful eyes.

Dimitri looked around the crowd, his eyes stopping on Sonny who was backing away, his face white, shirt clean, and his arms, splattered with blood.

Antony mentally kicked himself. He hadn't noticed the blood on Sonny's arms until that moment. His jaw tightened as Dimitri looked back at him. Had Dimitri seen through the lie? Regardless, he'd stick to his story, knowing that it would only be a matter of time before Carlo's death was vindicated. Accident or not, the family must be respected and defended by any means possible.

TWO

THE LITTLE ITALIAN bistro served one of the best steaks in Kansas City. It was Lorenzo Luciano's favorite.

He sipped on his drink. Martina Romeo drummed her long red painted fingernails on the round table. He wanted to pound her hand or break the fake nails off. Anything to stop the annoying clicking.

She pulled out a cigarette, tapped it on the table then placed it between her lips. "You have a light?"

Lorenzo reached into the inside pocket of his grey suit jacket, pulled out a monogrammed gold lighter, and obliged Martina and her cigarette.

Martina's face was emotionless, but there was no denying she looked good in her tight fitting, hot pink strapless dress. She nodded at Lorenzo, blowing smoke into the already clouded air, glancing at her husband, Gino, as he casually spoke to a man at the bar.

Gino approached the table, kissed Martina on the cheek before sitting down. He poured the last of the fourth bottle of wine into her glass while Lorenzo raised his glass of whiskey to toast.

Rachel, Lorenzo's wife, tugged at his arm, leaned in and whispered, "You're drunk."

"I am not." He lied then planted a kiss on her clear, high glossed lips. "To a job well done." Lorenzo gulped the drink and slammed the tumbler on the table. The warmth of the alcohol enhanced his excitement. He puffed on the thick Cuban cigar then clicked his fingers at the bartender, pointing to the empty glass.

Raking his hand through his thick black hair, he pushed the cigar to one side of his mouth, clenched it between his teeth, and grinned. "One more job like that and we'll own this town."

Gino's eyes narrowed. "The ladies don't want to hear business talk."

Lorenzo licked his numb lips, staring at Martina as she ran her long red fingernails up Gino's neck, gently fiddling with his short brown hair before resting her arm on his shoulder. Gino kissed her but she immediately backed away. "You'll smudge my lipstick."

"Oh, we can't have that." Gino pulled a cigar from his suit pocket, ran it under his nose, and sniffed deeply then lit it. "What'd this dress cost? Look at Rachel. She looks good and I'll bet she didn't spend a fortune."

"I've seen Rachel at Saks. She can drop a wad as fast as I can. Can't you Miss Goodie-two-shoes?"

"I won't be sucked into one of your cat fights."

Lorenzo grinned and reached under the table for Rachel's hand.

Rachel looked over at him. Her ivory skin came alive against her dark brown hair and maroon suit dress. Her eyes searched his, a small smile on her face. He was unsure what it meant. He couldn't read her anymore. At least, not like he used too.

Did Rachel want him to defend her in front of Martina or were her eyes asking him a much deeper question. Was she still proud of him or disgusted?

You know how I feel about your job, were words she had said to him the last time he came home excited about his newest business acquisition and pile of cash.

You knew what you were getting into when you married me, he had shouted back before going straight to a bottle of whisky.

Something had changed since Father Cannon took over the parish. Her once-loving eyes became judgmental, although her words were never condemning. He appeased her by going to church, even took the flack from his friends, but it didn't seem to make her any happier.

He smiled as he thought about the generous donation he had made to the parish. It wasn't that he believed any of the garbage the Father preached, but he knew it would make her happy. Gino had gotten Martina a fur coat.

Lorenzo brought Rachel's hand to his lips and kissed it. Leaning into her, he whispered, "Let's skip dinner and take the Romeo's home." He pulled away, raising his eyebrows seductively.

"Would you stop?" Her face reddened.

"What? I can't want to be with you?"

"It's not that..."

"Is he hitting on you?" Martina crushed the cigarette in the square transparent ashtray. Smoke escaping her mouth as she spoke, "Poor dear."

Lorenzo's eyes narrowed. "Watch it, Martina."

Martina batted her fake eyelashes against her black and silver, overly shadowed eyelids. "I just know how she is. She's turned into a prude."

"Better a prude then a trollop," Rachel snapped then gasped, bringing her hand to cover her mouth.

Martina's eyes widened, her neck instantly turning red. She turned to Gino. "You gonna let her talk to me that way?"

Gino puffed on his cigar, indifferent to her plea.

Martina flew to her feet, "Well, I never..."

"Don't suffocate in all that make-up," Gino yelled as she made her way to the bathroom. He eyed Lorenzo. "Tell your wife to lay off."

Lorenzo wrapped his arm around Rachel and leaned into her, "Cool it."

Rachel nodded.

*   *   *

Lorenzo welcomed the fresh air after enduring the smoke-filled bistro.

The Romeo's, stiff and tight lipped, climbed into the backseat of his black Audi Coupe.

Lorenzo stood with the car door open and waited for Rachel to get in. She grabbed his tie, pulled him to her, and kissed him with such passion he blushed and found himself praying the boys would still be gone when they got home.

"Lorenzo!" a man from the bistro yelled. "Phone call."

He waved in acknowledgement then gave Rachel a second kiss. "Be right back."

Minutes later, Lorenzo jogged to the car and wiped the beads of sweat off his forehead. His heart pounded so hard he knew it would burst out of his chest at any moment. He didn't know what a heart attack felt like, but he swore he was having one.

Gino's going to kill him. He slid under the stirring wheel. His hands shook as he put the keys in the ignition and started the car.

Rachel's face grew serious. "What is it?"

Looking in the rearview mirror, he saw the fight in the restaurant had finally ended and Gino was getting a long overdue thank-you from Martina for her fur coat. She didn't seem to care that her lipstick smeared all over Gino's face.

Giggling, she attempted to wipe it with her finger, scratching Gino with her long dragon nails. He jerked his head back and touched the blood that seeped from the scratch. The loving moment passed and another heated argument erupted.

Lorenzo leaned over, clasped his hand on the back of Rachel's neck, and pulled her to him. "There's been an accident," he whispered in her ear. "Carlo's dead."

"Oh, no."

"Don't say anything. We'll tell them when we get to the hospital."

Nodding, Rachel clasped her hands together and stared straight ahead. He knew by her closed-eye posture she was praying. When he stopped at a red light, he glanced over. How could he tell her one of their sons was responsible? It would substantiate her biggest fear—that his lifestyle would destroy their family.

He turned his attention back to the road. The alcohol effects boosted his urgency. The Romeo's argument erupted again and bellowed from the backseat. In a few minutes their anger would turn to heartache, their lives forever changed in an instant.

Lorenzo glanced back in the rearview mirror. Gino's eyes were hard and cold, even to his wife. He had to get his boys away before Gino found out which one pulled the trigger.

"Once they're safe, I'll take care of the one who did it myself," Lorenzo whispered.

Rachel took his hand. "Did you say something?"

"No." Lorenzo lifted her hand to his lips and kissed it.

Taking the same curve he'd driven a thousand times, he looked back over at Rachel. Tears escaped from her eyes. The setting sun illuminated behind her giving her an angelic appearance. He forgot about his anger and pain, and for a moment he was lost in her love.

The wheel jerked his attention back to the road. Alcohol numbed his perception and the idea that he might be taking the curve too fast floated out the window as quickly as the love between Gino and Martina had.

Screeching tires drowned out the Romeos' heated argument.

Lorenzo's euphoric haze vaporized instantly as the Audi skidded off the road and rolled twice, the metal crumbling beneath its weight.

Pain shot through Lorenzo's back and neck as the roof and side of the car compacted against him. Rachel's limp body fell toward him. He caught her as shards of glass flew through the air and ripped open his skin.

The car finally landed on flattened tires and stopped.

If Gino or Martina had screamed he hadn't heard.

He cradled Rachel's limp body in his arms and sobbed, then lost consciousness.

*　　*　　*

The interrogation room was hot and uncomfortable. Antony rubbed his eyes and looked down at his brother's shirt he was now wearing. Carlo's dried blood had soaked through it, stuck to his chest, and was making him itch. He slid his hand underneath and peeled it away from his skin.

The officer walked back into the room. "Can I get you something to drink?"

Was he serious? Maybe he should order a burger and fries. He rolled his eyes, crossed his arms, and slouched deeper in the chair. "I don't want a drink. I want you to call my father."

"We did."

"That's what you said two hours ago."

The officer pushed the tape recorder closer to Antony. "Tell me how it happened, again."

Recount the story. Antony knew the drill. The pig wanted to see if his story would change. Antony wouldn't do it. Once was enough. He wouldn't say another word until his father came with a lawyer.

A plain clothed policeman walked in, whispered something in the officer's ear then left. The officer stood and reached for Antony's arm. "You need to come with me."

Antony pulled away. "I ain't going anywhere with you."

"Come on." The officer grabbed Antony's arm and led him through the precinct, then outside to an opened door of a police car.

Antony stopped. He'd heard about things like this. Just last week the news reported an incident of alleged police brutality. In their attempt to get a confession, a perp claimed the cops took him back to the scene and roughed him up.

"Where you taking me?" Antony asked even though he knew he couldn't refuse.

"Get in."

"Don't I at least have the right to know? Or a right to an attorney?"

"Just get in." The officer pushed Antony's head down and propelled him into the car.

Antony stared out the window. Silence filled the car. Who cared if the police beat him up? It'd be nothing compared to what Gino would do to him. After shooting him in the head, Gino would sink him in the Missouri river so Mama would be spared the pain of ever knowing what really happened.

Caressing the silver ID bracelet, he thought of Elisa. What would she think when she found out he accidentally killed her cousin? Could he risk telling her the truth? He blinked away the tears and his chest fluttered. His best friend was dead.

The huge cross that sat on top of St. Mary's hospital came into sight. Antony pounded on the metal cage that separated the front and back seat. "What are we doing here?"

The officer said nothing and his face was unreadable as he got out of the car.

Antony figured Carlo's body must still be at the hospital. The cop would force him to stare at it until he talked, but it wouldn't change anything. He'd never tell the truth. He'd protect Sonny even if it meant jail or death by Gino's hand.

Elisa walked out of the hospital. He had to give the pig credit. Having her there would make it tougher to keep quiet. He pounded on the window. "You gonna let me out?"

When the officer finally opened the car door, Antony climbed out and held his arms out.

The cop shook his head. "No cuffs."

Antony shoved his hands deep in his pockets and stood motionless. He could handle being rejected by his father or hunted by Gino, but losing Elisa was not an option.

Elisa ran to him and wrapped her arms around his waist. Relief engulfed him. He held her and buried his face in her thick auburn hair. "I thought you'd hate me. I didn't mean to. When Carlo heard about us he went crazy."

"I know, Spence told me." Elisa sniffed hard. "I'm sorry about your parents."

Antony pulled back. "What?"

"The cops didn't tell you?"

Antony gently cupped her cheeks, his eyebrows wrinkled. "Tell me what?"

"They were on their way…" Elisa's eyes filled with tears. "There was an accident."

Antony's heart pounded. He rushed past her and ran into the waiting room where a group of men stood in a circle whispering to each other. He recognized most of them as his father's business associates. Their mumbling stopped as they glanced at him, then lowered their eyes and turned away.

A man leaned into Vince, Lorenzo's right hand man, and whispered something. Vince nodded and walked toward him in his navy suit. Proof that a hired thug could clean up, at least on the outside. His black shoes clicked loudly on the linoleum. He motioned for Antony to follow.

Antony walked down the corridor of the hospital wing. The smell of sterile alcohol coated the air. Sporadic paging of doctors would momentarily silence the muffled chattering of the nurses.

Vince stopped outside a door and turned to him. "There's been an accident."

"I heard. How bad?"

"Lorenzo just got out of surgery, and they're taking him to recovery. Doctor said his spinal cord was severed in his lower back." Vince placed both hands in his pockets. "They say he'll never walk again."

Antony's chest tightened and his stomach knotted. He wanted to run away from the stench of illness and death that swirled in the air, but his feet had become lead weights and he couldn't move.

"And Mama?"

"Your mother…well…" Vince lowered his eyes. "They tried to save her but couldn't."

"She's dead?"

Vince's nod made Antony's feel like he'd fall over. Darkness engulfed him and he fought desperately to focus. The harsh words he said to his mother about her religion danced in his head and taunted him. Her loving touch he so often pushed away would never come again. Her innocent smile, her soft voice, her kind words, all gone.

"No." He fought the tears and took deep breath in an attempt to fight off the pain, at least for the moment.

Vince touched his shoulder.

Antony brushed it off, squeezed his eyes and brought his fist to his face, but the tears forced themselves out. He kicked a chair and sent it screeching down the corridor, sending the noisy hospital wing into dead silence.

He walked through the waiting room, glaring at the group of men. "Where's Sonny?"

Elisa came up behind him. "He's in the chapel."

Antony turned to her.

Tears rolled down her cheeks. "Is there anything I can do?"

Antony brushed her tears away, cupped the back of her neck, and gave her a kiss then walked to the chapel alone.

White votive candles flickered in small red glass containers under a large wooden crucifix. Jesus' head lay forward in death. His brow was pierced with a crown of thorns, his hands and feet affixed to the cross with nails.

Antony glared at it. He wanted to scream but kept silent. He'd never had time for God and God had never had time for him. A fact his mother assured him wasn't true.

Sonny sat crying on the front row, his head buried in his hands.

Tears fell down Antony's cheeks. He wiped them away, walked down the aisle and sat next to Sonny.

"This is my fault," Sonny said.

"No, it's not."

"Vince said Papa was bringing Gino and Martina to the morgue to see Carlo." Sonny sniffed and wiped his nose on his arm. "They were in the car."

"And?"

"They're dead." Sonny hunched over, his crying intensified.

Antony couldn't deny that solved one of his problems, although it didn't lessen the pain.

"Papa's gonna kill me," Sonny said.

"I can handle Papa. You can't."

"Mama, she's…"

Antony rested his hand on Sonny's back and gently rubbed it. "I know. She's gone."

"She's in heaven, isn't she?" Sonny looked up at the crucifix then over at Antony. "You believe that don't you?"

Antony turned back to the crucifix. "I hate her God."

THREE

SOFT ELEVATOR MUSIC played in the hospital waiting room. It was supposed to be soothing, but after the last week, the music was grating on Antony's nerves.

Sonny slouched in a chair and stared aimlessly at the white wall, his eyes bloodshot and hazed. Lorenzo lay in his room, still unconscious.

Antony feared the stench of disinfectant would never leave his system. He stared out the window and followed a ray of sunlight down to a small courtyard where a man sat in a wheelchair. An older woman sitting next to him appeared to be reading aloud. A plaid blanket hung over the old man's legs but didn't conceal the urine bag that hung on the side of the chair. The sight made him shudder.

How could he face his father, the great Lorenzo Luciano, sitting helplessly in a wheelchair? Would he be able to perform basic bodily functions, or would he rely on a urine sack and an adult diaper?

He shook the thought of it out of his head and rubbed the back of his neck.

Elisa walked into the room. Her hair was pulled back in a ponytail.

Antony reached for her hand and wove her fingers between his. "I thought you were getting something to eat."

"I was on my way but the nurse stopped me. She said your father was waking up."

"Thanks."

Sonny sat in a motionless stare. The news of their papa hadn't fazed him.

"Hey." Antony grabbed Sonny's arm, forcing him to stand. "Didn't you hear? Papa's waking up. Come on."

Moments later he and Sonny stood next to Lorenzo's bed. The room was white and the smell of sickness floated in the air. Machines in the corner made disturbing noises, and tubes and wires emerged from Lorenzo's body.

Antony stepped closer and stared at his father. Except for a few scrapes and bruises, Lorenzo looked no different than he had many nights coming home late from a bar fight.

Lorenzo's eyes fluttered making Antony jump.

"Go ahead and talk to him." The nurse checked the IV. "He's awake."

"Does he know about my Mama?" Antony whispered.

"Yes. I'll give you guys a few minutes."

Sonny stepped forward and gently touched his father's shoulder. "Papa?"

Lorenzo groaned, turned his head, and opened his eyes. He spoke in short grunts, "Which…one…who killed Carlo?"

Sonny lowered his eyes. "It was—"

"Me, Papa. I did it," Antony said. "He came after me with a gun."

Lorenzo's eyes blazed with hatred. "You killed your mother." The beeps on the heart monitor quickened. "Get out, I don't ever want to see you again."

"Papa, he would've killed me."

"Get out!"

"Papa, no," Sonny said. "You don't understand."

"Don't defend him," Lorenzo yelled.

The nurse hurried back into the room. "Keep your voices down." She marched to Lorenzo's side, the rubber on her white loafers squeaking under her weight. She checked the machine and Lorenzo's vitals, then shook her head before turning to Antony and Sonny. "You boys need to leave. He needs to rest."

Antony grabbed Sonny's arm and pushed him back to the waiting room.

* * *

Antony stood at the window in the waiting room staring into the darkness. He wasn't surprised Papa blamed him for Mama's death, but it never occurred to him that he would be put out on the streets, especially since they didn't have to worry about Gino's retaliation. The streets didn't scare him half as much as leaving Sonny did.

He looked over at his brother folded up in a chair, softly snoring. Mama had been his life. She was soft, gentle, and caring while Papa was unsympathetic, cruel and callous. He wondered what would happen to Sonny's tender heart without Mama around for balance and him around for protection.

Maybe he could reason with Papa. It was a long shot but he knew he had to try, not for his sake but for Sonny's.

He stood in the doorway of his father's room. A single light over the hospital bed dimly lit it.

Lorenzo waved him in.

"I'd like to explain," Antony said.

"Come closer, boy," Lorenzo's voice was airy and raspy.

Antony hesitatingly took a couple of steps toward him.

"Vince told me the police believe your story. That it was an accident."

"It's the truth."

"They won't charge you?"

"So, they say."

Lorenzo's face was emotionless, unreadable.

"Come here, boy." Lorenzo waved him closer.

Antony stepped closer to his father's bed. He wasn't sure how much strength his father had, but given the chance, his papa would use every bit of it on him. "It's not my fault Mama's dead." He tried to sound strong and confident.

Lorenzo grabbed Antony's wrist, his grip tight, and his eyes cold. "It *is* your fault. She was my soul mate, *mi vida* and you killed her. I will never forgive you."

"But I didn't—"

"Go ahead and test me, boy. It's what you're good at." Lorenzo closed his eyes for a moment then opened them, his breathing shallow. In a pain-filled voice, he said, "You think because I'll be confined to a wheelchair you won't get what you deserve for killing her?"

Antony tried to pull away, but it only made his father's grip tighten.

"I hate you." Lorenzo's eyes were fierce. "I don't ever want to see you again. If I do, you'll pay."

Antony's chest heaved and he fought tears. He would not give his father the satisfaction of seeing his pain. When Lorenzo released him, he backed away, sniffing hard.

Lorenzo glared at him. "Get out."

Antony turned. Sonny stood in the doorway. He brushed past him, knowing Sonny would follow.

"I'm outta here." Antony welcomed the fresh air outside the hospital. "Have a good life."

"Please, don't leave. I'll tell Papa the truth."

Antony stopped abruptly, spun around, grabbed Sonny's shirt under his chin, and stared into his tear-stained eyes. "You keep your mouth shut or you'll both be on the streets, too."

With wide eyes, Sonny gave a confirming nod. A single tear rolled down his cheek.

"You'll be fine." He pulled Sonny into a hug, "I gotta go."

Elisa pulled up next to them in her white Mazda, killed the engine and got out. "What's going on?"

Antony gave her a quick kiss, ignoring Sonny's piercing eyes. "Can you drop me off at home? I have to pack."

"Pack? You're leaving?"

"I have to."

"What about your mother's funeral?"

"Papa just ordered me out, says it's my fault Mama's dead." Antony raked his hand through his hair. "I can't stay, not even for the funeral."

Her tears softened his heart. He took her in his arms and kissed her. "I love you. I always will, but I have to go."

"Go where? What are you going to do?"

"I'll be fine." He gave her a reassuring smile.

"Do you have any money?"

"Mama always kept a wad of cash in an old purse in the closet. She told us it was there for emergencies. I think she'd consider this one." He forced a grin, glanced at Sonny then quickly away. "It's not much, but it'll hold me over until things cool down. I gotta go."

"Hey?" Elisa's voice sounded like it was about to give way to sobs. "I thought you needed a lift?"

"You sure?"

Elisa smiled, forcing tears to escape her eyes. She held the keys up and jiggled them.

Antony grinned. "I love you."

"I know." She wrapped her arms around him. "You're coming back, aren't you?"

Antony locked eyes with Sonny. His brother's hands were buried deep in his pockets and his face was streaked with tears. After a long, painful moment, Sonny dropped his head, turned and walked back to the hospital.

Antony looked down at Elisa. "For you? Of course, I'd come back."

It was a promise he had every intention of keeping.

FOUR

Ten Years Later

VICTORIA LOOKED AT her watch and sighed. She had opened Francesca's early for Mrs. McClain and took special care when she chose the elegant gowns that hung around the private dressing room. An hour and a half later, none of them satisfied the wife of the most renowned cardiologist in Los Angeles.

Francesca's was the fastest rising clothing store in the heart of Woodland Hills. It attracted a large, prestigious clientele and catered to the rich and famous. Four years of experience and a college diploma had helped Victoria move from one of many fashion consultants to Vice President of Fashion and Retail, which was an ornate way of saying Assistant Manager. Her fattened paycheck and thirty-percent discount, allowed her to trade in her fifty dollar dresses for designer labels such as Ralph Lauren and Chanel.

"I don't know." Mrs. McClain stared at herself in the three-way mirror. Her stomach rolls were squished into a girdle and hidden in the current red sequenced dress.

"I think it's gorgeous." Victoria shifted her weight to her other knee, trying to straighten out the hemline. "It's a one of a kind."

Mrs. McClain wasn't sold on the five thousand dollar dress.

Victoria stood, gave her black skirt a tug, then flattened it out. She'd topped it off with a simple white blouse with a small amount of sequins to set it off.

She looked through the opened double doors of the oversized private dressing room. Customers and tourists filtered into the store.

Beautiful Barbie like sales associates walked around the racks of clothing, ready to pounce on any customer deemed wealthy. Victoria looked at the rustic elevator. It had an old iron gate and was operated by an attendant who stood ready to escort customers to the second and third floors.

Silently, Victoria prayed Fran would call the elevator to the fourth floor offices, come down and help Mrs. McClain make a decision, but she knew that would be a miracle only God could perform. Fran was no dummy. Important meetings always came up when Mrs. McClain walked in. Victoria couldn't blame her. As the owner of Francesca's she had earned the right to hide.

She turned her attention back to Mrs. McClain. "I promise, you'll knock 'em dead at the party." It sounded good, but frankly, Victoria was tired of trying to convince this plump size twenty that she looked like a size five.

Mrs. McClain wrinkled her nose at the dress then gently tossed her obvious out-of-a-box blond hair off her shoulders. She placed her hands on the side of her face and moved her skin up and away. "Do you think it's time for another face lift?"

Victoria sighed. Catering to the wives of millionaires exhausted her. She tucked her thick auburn hair behind her ears and smiled. "Didn't you just have one last year?"

"Uh, huh." Mrs. McClain stepped closer to the mirror, this time examining her nose.

Victoria wished she was going over last month's sales figures, plucking her eyebrows or getting a bikini wax. Anything would be better than this.

Mrs. McClain backed away from the mirror and placed both hands on her extra-wide hips. "What else do you have?"

Victoria looked through the gowns she had personally picked out for Mrs. McClain, but each one had already been deemed a disaster.

A deep voice came from behind them. "Mm-hmm, you look good in red."

Victoria turned and took in a quick breath. The six-foot-two man leaned against a high-back chair. His tanned, slender face showed a slight shadow even though it was only ten in the morning. His black hair was cut short and his dimples deepened as he grinned.

He walked closer to the wide eyed, dropped jaw, Mrs. McClain.

"If I may say…" He rested his hands on her shoulders and turned her back to face the mirror. "The way this dress shows off your exquisite God-made features, well, it truly takes my breath away."

Mrs. McClain turned three shades of red. "You think?" she spoke in an airy, I'm going to pass out, voice.

He took her left hand, slowly spun her around, and took in every inch of her oversized body. "Yes, I do." He kissed her hand and looked up into her heavily shadowed, obviously fake, eye-lashed eyes. One side of his mouth awry with a grin. "If you didn't have this rock on your finger, I'd ask you to lunch."

Mrs. McClain giggled like a sixteen-year-old then pulled her hand from his. "Victoria, I'll take this one."

Victoria mouthed *thank you* to the stranger as Mrs. McClain strutted into the dressing room. "Mrs. McClain, Lauren will ring that up for you."

"Thank you."

Victoria walked toward the man. "You saved her from another trip to the plastic surgeon."

"I do what I can."

"May I help you with something?"

"I need a suit. Fancy, but not a tux. Something that reeks of money."

Victoria led him through the double doors of the private dressing room, up the stairs to the second floor and motioned toward the men's department. They stopped in the center of a three way mirror surrounded by suit jackets and slacks.

"You look like an Armani man to me. Any particular color?" Victoria asked.

"What color would you suggest?"

She raised an eyebrow and grinned. He wore all black, t-shirt, leather jacket, jeans and boots. "How about black?"

"You're good at this." He winked as he pulled off the leather jacket. His t-shirt clung to well-defined muscles on his chest and arms.

She studied the red snake tattoo.

"I got that when I was sixteen." He flexed his bicep. "Not bad, huh?"

Heat filled Victoria's face. It wasn't often that a customer entranced her. Brad Pitt came in once. She could barely speak, but somehow had managed to sell him a suit and not look like a total idiot in the process.

The stranger took her left hand and shook it. "I'm Tony. You're Victoria, right?"

"Yes." She pulled her hand from his.

He turned and exposed a chrome plated Colt 40 that hung from a holster attached to his belt.

"You a detective or something?"

"Or something." He grinned.

Victoria walked to a rack of Armani suits and took a deep breath as she tried to slow her pounding heart. She picked out a black suit jacket with thin gray pinstripes, walked behind him and slid it up his arms onto his shoulders.

She looked at him through the mirror. "What do think of this one?"

Tony turned from the mirror to face her. "What do *you* think of it?"

With a cock of her head, she rubbed her chin, "Hmm, solid black might be better."

Tony took off the jacket and handed it to her.

She returned with a black button down shirt, an all-black Armani suit and a black tie. "Try these. The dressing rooms are right there." She pointed.

Tony took the clothes and disappeared.

"You live in Los Angeles?" Victoria leaned against a rack.

Tony opened the dressing room door and struggled with the tie. "I never could get these right."

"Let me help." Victoria kicked off her shoes, pulled her skirt up just above the knee, and climbed onto the wing-backed chair that sat outside the dressing room. "Come here."

Tony's eyebrows wrinkled as he walked closer.

She turned him around so his back was to her, reached over his shoulders around to the front, and began to tie the tie. Her chin brushed against his shoulder, and the crisp refreshing fragrance of his cologne tickled her nose. "My dad taught me like this when I was a little girl. I can't tie them any other way."

*   *   *

Antony's heart raced as her breath warmed his neck. He couldn't deny that she had intrigued him long before today and he knew just about everything about her. She and his brother Sonny met at the store soon after her mother had disappeared.

"There." She rested her hands on his shoulders.

He turned and looked up at her as she buttoned the top button of his shirt then put the finishing touches on the small Windsor knot.

The picture he'd received from his contact at the police department hadn't done her justice. Her body was perfectly proportioned, accented with naturally tanned skin. The soft shimmering beige shadow enhanced her deep brown eyes. Her cheekbones sat high and her lips were full.

If she had been snobby he would have guessed she'd spent thousands to look that way, but there was something much more attractive about this woman then her physical beauty. He sensed an overall goodness about her. Her touch was gentle, her eyes soft and caring. She wasn't superficial like a lot of women he'd known.

Antony placed his hands on her waist and lifted her off the chair, back onto the floor, unable to let go. She was magnetic and he was drawn to her with a force he couldn't fight. He forgot about Sonny and what this woman might mean to him. He went with his desire, pulled her to him, and kissed her, long and hard.

Victoria momentarily struggled then relaxed in his strong arms and kissed him back.

He pulled away and cupped her cheek in his hand. Her face flushed and he could feel her heart pounding. He looked deep into her eyes, waiting for permission to kiss her again.

"We can't," she whispered unconvincingly.

"Why?"

"I'm sorry." She backed away. "Oh my goodness. I can't believe I did that. I'm so sorry. I've never…it's just…"

"I'm irresistible?"

The lines on Victoria's face deepened. "I'm seeing someone."

Antony nodded. That someone was his brother. He turned to look at himself in the mirror. "You're not normal are you?"

Victoria frowned.

"I only mean, I've been in town one day and have been propositioned by two women, one guy and asked to star in a low budget movie. You know, nowadays, most girls don't care if they're dating someone else."

"I'm the last of a dying breed." Victoria smiled. "The kiss… I shouldn't have."

He placed the tip of his finger on her lips. "Don't." He reached around her and grabbed the suit jacket off the chair. He slid it on and turned to the mirror, eyeballing himself. "Not bad."

"Not bad? I think it looks great. You have to buy this suit."

"You're assuming I can afford this?"

"In LA, you never assume anything."

"I'll remember that." He looked down at the slacks and lifted the excess fabric off his boots. "You do alterations?"

"Of course."

"How soon can you have them done? I need a suit for tomorrow."

"We can have them ready by five."

"I'll take it."

By the time the shopping trip was over, Antony bought three suits and spent twice as much as he'd planned, but he left the store with a grin on face. At the moment, Victoria was Sonny's girl, but he could easily change that.

*   *   *

Victoria sat in her office. The walls were a soothing cream color, decorated with random pictures of fruit and flower vases. They reminded her of cheap hotel art but Francesca swore they had cost her a small fortune.

Last month's sales figures lay scattered on her desk, the numbers blurred together. Guilt was eating away at her. What kind of woman was she to let herself be drawn into a stranger's embrace? How could she so easily have forgotten Sonny?

She pulled a single rose from the dozen Tony had sent her and breathed its sweet aroma. Closing her eyes, she pictured his muscular godlike body, his alluring smile, seductive eyes, and firm lips. The moment they had touched her lips, her heart had sprinted like a scared rabbit. *Stupid.*

With a shake, Victoria shrugged off her momentary lust, laid the rose down, grabbed a bottle of water and walked over to the wilting fern. Brown prickly needles lay on the floor and surrounded the base of the pot. She sighed and poured the water onto the dirt. "Sorry, guys."

She tossed the bottle in the trash, picked up a framed picture of Sonny and smiled. Why was she letting this stranger capture her thoughts when she had Sonny?

Sonny might not be Hercules, but he'd give him a run for his money. Italian in every sense of the word. Sonny's temper was swift, but short lived. His deep faith in God came from his mother's example, but nobody could extract Sonny's allegiance like his father. Sonny said that true patriotism was loyalty to his father and the brother she'd never met.

A quick knock sounded on the door, and Sonny walked in with a rose covered gift bag. She smiled, replaced the picture and walked toward him. "I was just thinking about you."

"You were?" He raised his eyebrows and placed the bag on the coffee table that sat in front of an ivory sofa. "What exactly were you thinking?"

She walked her fingers up his white button down shirt, grabbed his yellow paisley tie, pulled him to her and planted a kissed on his lips, allowing his love to wash away the images of the stranger.

"I should stop by more often." He kissed her neck, ear then found her mouth again.

She loosened his tie and unbuttoned the top button of his shirt then backed away.

"I brought you something." As he leaned over the coffee table, some hair fell across the left side of his forehead. He reached into the bag and pulled out a beautifully wrapped box and handed it to her.

"What's this for?"

"Because I love you." He grinned. "Open it."

Victoria ripped the floral paper off. She held the white box inscribed with gold letters that spelled Reuge—the Rolls Royce of music boxes.

She lifted the lid and her eyes widened. She sank into the maroon chair and pulled out the elegant music box. The wood was scalloped in a stunning burl walnut. Victoria traced the inlaid lilies designed with mother-of-pearl, a tear rolled down her cheek. "It looks just like the one my mother had."

Sonny knelt next to her, took the box and opened it.

Inside, it was adorned with red velvet. The glass allowed her to look directly at the gears as they changed movements, creating the tune of "Edelweiss," which floated softly and elegantly into the air.

"How did you get this?" She wiped the tear away.

"I found it after you told me about your mom's."

Victoria took the box from him and held it. "We could never find mother's after she disappeared." Victoria stared at the gears as the music continued to play softly. "The police said it was a sign that mom had left us but my dad never believed it. He died convinced something else happened to her." She turned to him. "This is the nicest thing anyone has ever done for me. Thank you."

He hugged her. "I love you."

"I love you, too."

He took the music box and placed it on her desk.

"Let's go grab some lunch?" Victoria wrapped her arms around him. "I'm supposed to meet with Fran, but I could change it."

"I can't." He tucked her hair behind her ears. "I've got to meet Papa at the shipyard. He's buying a new vessel and I have to go over it before he'll sign the papers."

She turned back to her desk. "Edelweiss" had slowed down and was now unrecognizable. She closed the lid and ran her fingers over the high gloss finish. "We still on for six?"

When he didn't respond she turned back to him.

"I can't. I'm sorry. Papa says when I'm done at the shipyard he wants me in his office to go over some new deal. You know how he is."

"I know." Victoria looked back at the music box so he wouldn't see the disappointment in her eyes.

"Tomorrow night, I promise. I have a surprise."

"What?"

"I can't tell you." He pulled her close. "Then it wouldn't be a surprise."

"Oh."

"I should go. You know how Papa gets when he's made to wait." Sonny backed away and raised an eyebrow. "Wait a minute. You wouldn't know that, would you? You've never met the man."

"And I'm in no hurry."

"I can't understand why. He's an eccentric old fart with a temper that boils over more times than I can count."

"Keep talking like that and I'll never have a reason to meet him."

"You'll have a reason to meet him very soon." He raised his eyebrows. "A very good reason."

Heat filled Victoria's face. She knew he was talking about marriage. He'd hinted at it for the last couple of weeks. Sonny said he knew the minute he met her that she was the one. He claimed it was love at first sight.

He pointed to the roses. "Beautiful flowers. Who sent them?"

"A client."

"A client? Should I be worried?"

"You *have* canceled another date." Victoria tossed her hair off her shoulders and batted her eyes.

Sonny grabbed her arm and pulled her close. "You love me, don't you?"

She gave him a long kiss, then pulled away just enough to see into his eyes. "You know I do."

Sonny kissed her forehead, cheek, and lips. Her hand rested on his chest. His heart pounded as furiously as hers.

"You've got to get back to work," she whispered.

"Yeah, I know."

She forced herself to back away from his strong arms, loving eyes and irresistible lips.

"Okay, I can take a hint." He walked to the door, stopped and looked back at her. "Tomorrow night, just you and me."

"Okay." She took a deep breath to slow down her racing heart. "Sonny?"

One side of his mouth went into a deep grin. "Yeah?"

She picked up the music box and hugged it. "Thank you."

Sonny walked back to her, placed his hand on the back of her neck, and pulled her close. "You're welcome." He kissed her.

FIVE

AFTER FORTY-FIVE MINUTES on the 101, Antony drove into Ventura and sat in his car in front of a ten-story, blue glass structure. Two sides looked like giant stair steps up to a glass domed roof. Each rooftop had a patio and he swore it sounded like the echo of a tennis ball smacking against a racket.

At the front of the building, a courtyard held a circular water pond with a large fountain in the center. Blooming wild flowers reflected beautifully off the glass. Etched in large letters was the word Renato.

Antony let out a long whistle. "Not bad, Papa." He grinned. "Thank you, Aunt Cecilia."

The reflection of his black, two door, BMW kept him from seeing inside the building. "Must be a two-way glass of some sort."

He pulled forward and at the end of the building was a view of the Pacific. "Sonny. I'll bet your office is overlooking the ocean, right next to Papa's."

Antony gripped the steering wheel and floored it. His tires squealed as his anger soared, mad that Sonny lived the high life while he had lived on the streets. Sonny got a free ride to Stanford while Antony scraped through Kansas City's community college. To earn money, he'd missed more days than he could count.

When Sonny accidentally shot Carlo, Antony knew his brother was only trying to protect him, however absurd that was. *Like I needed protection.* He laughed at the thought of it.

His anger diminished as fast as it had risen. He had to take the blame. He'd protected Sonny since he could walk and that was something he had never begrudged. He wouldn't stop now.

Opening the map app on his phone, he got his bearings, and drove a few more miles until he found Aunt Cecilia's old estate. It was Lorenzo's now. Safely tucked away in the hills of Ventura. An eight-foot brick wall with two large black iron gates encompassed the property. He drove slowly by the gate, and craned his neck to see inside.

"Soon, I'll be back to take my place," he said, more to assure himself.

Antony hoped his father would welcome him, especially since he was returning with money, a reputation and a host of degenerates that owed him favors. He had lived the life his father had taught him, ruthless and uncaring.

He shook away the memories of the past and drove back to Los Angeles. Hitting Pete's number on his phone, he put it to his ear. "It's me…yeah, I'm in town…I got a favor to ask you."

"You can't just use me for information," Pete said.

Antony rolled his eyes. "It's not that big of a deal besides, you owe me."

Pete was quiet for a few seconds and Antony knew he was reliving the night in Kansas City when a gang of lowlife punks surrounded him, a rookie, decked out in full KCPD uniform. Antony had stumbled upon them and with some fast-talking and a couple of gunshots, the gang had fled.

"And I pay well," Antony added.

"True." Pete laughed. "What is it?"

"I need the make and plates on Victoria Stone's car."

"Hey, I already got you her picture, address, employer and cell number."

"I know, and this will be the last time I ask you for any more info on her."

"Sure."

"Man, I'm a good guy, remember?"

"Oh, yeah, I forgot. Hang on."

Minutes later, Pete came back on the line, and Antony scribbled down the information. "Thanks man."

"Hey, Antony. My brother come out here with you?"

"Of course. Wouldn't go anywhere without him." He sensed Pete smiling.

"Take care of him."

"You know I will."

Antony pulled into Francesca's parking lot, looked for the red Z-28 and found it parked near the back. He looked up at the two-story building. Perfect. The sun shone on the west side which had forced them to close the shades.

"This is too easy." He grinned.

He parked the Beemer next to the Z-28. When the lot was empty of people he climbed out of his car, pulled the hidden Slim-Jim from inside his coat, slid it between the driver's side window and door, and popped the lock.

After a quick glance around the lot, he opened the car door, leaned down and pulled the hood release. At the front of the car, Antony lifted the hood, yanked a wire then dropped it. From start to finish it took him almost a minute. He was getting rusty.

He shut and locked the door, got in his Beemer and drove around to the front of the building, parked his car and walked into the store.

A beautiful woman with long blond hair approached him. She held out her hand. "Lauren Bauman."

"Lauren." He took her hand and shook it. "Nice to meet you."

"The pleasure is mine." She looked him up and down. "Mm-hmm, you look good."

"Thank you." He grinned and handed her his receipt. "My suits?"

"Yes, your suits. I'll go get them."

He couldn't help but look as she strutted by him. He laughed, leaned against the counter and waited.

Lauren returned with a black plastic garment bag. Antony tossed the suits over his shoulder. "What time does Victoria usually leave?"

"Victoria has a boyfriend." Lauren frowned.

"I know." Antony winked which brought a smile back to her face.

Lauren scribbled something on a piece of paper. "She gets off at five." She took Antony's hand, placed the paper in it and curled his fingers around it. "If you want a good time this is my phone number, and I don't have a boyfriend."

"Then I'll call you."

"I look forward to it."

Antony raised an eyebrow, slipped the number in his pocket, turned and walked out.

He tossed the suits in his car, walked over and leaned against Victoria's car and waited.

* * *

Victoria put on her sunglasses as she went out the front doors of Francesca's. The wind picked up her hair and blew it around her face. She grabbed it and tucked it behind her ears then stopped. Her heart quickened at the sight of Tony leaning against her car.

She clutched her keys and shook her head as she approached him. "You shouldn't have sent me flowers."

"I would've chosen words like 'thank you.'" He grinned. "And you're welcome."

Heat filled her face. "I do appreciate it but—"

"The boyfriend?"

"Yes."

"You're so sure I want to date you?"

Victoria pursed her lips and pushed him aside so she could unlock the door. "What then? A one night stand? That's much more flattering."

Tony laughed, his dimples deepening. "I'm only looking for a friend to eat dinner with. Nothing else. I promise."

Victoria looked up at him. He was too tempting. "I can't, really."

Tony shrugged and opened the car door for her. She put the keys in the ignition and tried to start the car but it wouldn't turn over. She rolled down her window. "Did you do something to my car?"

"You think I'd do that? I'm not *that* hard up honey. Lauren is ready to pounce."

Lauren was always ready to pounce, but she'd let him figure that out on his own. She turned the key, again. Nothing.

"Pop the hood," Tony said. When she hesitated he leaned in and rested his hands on the window frame. "Trust me and pop the hood."

Victoria pulled the hood release then got out of the car. Tony removed his leather jacket and handed it to her. "Hold this."

She draped the jacket over her arm while Tony lifted the hood and looked down at the engine. The sun glared off the chrome of his gun and momentarily blinded her. She moved forward and watched him lean in. He jiggled wires and looked very serious.

"You know what you're doing?" she asked.

"Yeah, I do."

Her stomach knotted. Sonny was everything anyone could possibly want in a man—tender, handsome, romantic, and madly in love with her. Despite her love for Sonny, she couldn't deny a connection to this complete stranger.

"What do you do?" She leaned against the side of the car.

"I'm a business man."

"That carries a gun? I don't think I want to know your business."

"It's nothing illegal." Even the laughter in Tony's voice was sexy. "Try starting your car now."

Victoria walked back around to her opened car door, tossed Tony's jacket onto the passenger's seat and got in. A businessman that carried a gun? A private eye, maybe, but she always pictured PI's as sloppy dressers who lived in their car with a camera as they tried to catch an unfaithful spouse. A bodyguard was a possibility. Some of the hottest female stars had some pretty good-looking ones.

Tony peeked his head around the hood. "Hey, you gonna try to start it?"

"Yeah, sorry." She tried to shake the thoughts of him out of her head.

"Victoria!"

Victoria turned as Sonny approached the car.

"What are you doing here? I thought you were meeting with your father," she said.

"I'm supposed to be." The lines on his face were hard. "But I got a call from Lauren. Said she saw you kissing some guy in the dressing room earlier."

"What?" Victoria's eyes widened. Lauren? Figured. She'd take Sonny or Tony. Heck, she'd take them both if given the chance. "It's not what you think." Victoria got out of the car.

"So, you were kissing him?"

"It wasn't like that."

"Then tell me what it was like." His face, hard. "I suppose that's him fixing your car?"

"Yeah, it's him." Tony's voice shot from under the hood then he dropped it, and wiped his hands on his jeans. "And I kissed her."

Sonny's eyes widened. The veins in his neck stood out. "What?" He stared at Tony. "I can't believe it. What are you doing here?" Sonny's face grew hard. He pointed his finger at Tony as he walked closer. "You know what I should do to you?"

Victoria stepped between them. The tabloids would devour this. Sonny Luciano fighting over a woman in the parking lot of Francesca's. They'd add something about an alien baby she was pregnant with just to beef it up. "Wait a minute."

"Stay out of this, Vic." Sonny's eyes locked with Tony's. Both men half grinned.

Tony wrinkled his eyebrows. "Before you try anything, you'd better take a good look at this." Tony pulled up the sleeve of his t-shirt and flexed his arm. The snake tattoo rippled on his muscle.

"Still proud of that tattoo, huh?" Sonny asked.

"Still crying 'cause you chickened out?"

Sonny smacked Tony's arm then they embraced. "It's good to see you."

"You, too." Tony's hand wrapped around the back of Sonny's neck. "You look good."

"What are you doing here?"

Victoria shook her head. "What a minute. You two know each other?"

"This is my brother, Antony." Sonny smiled, his arm around him. "I haven't seen him in years." Sonny turned back to Antony. "Man, I missed you."

"Me, too."

"I tried to find you after we left. Where were you?"

"Around." Antony pulled Sonny back into a hug and gave him a firm pat on the back.

"*Brothers*?" Victoria's heart raced. Her question brought both men to face her. Her eyes jumped back and forth between the two. Now she could see the resemblance. Both had the same thick black hair, perfect nose and strong chin.

Besides Antony being a couple inches taller than Sonny, the only difference was their eyes. Sonny's reflected his soft and gentle personality while Antony's were undeniable hard.

Sonny turned back to Antony. "Where're you staying?"

"Hotel. I'll start house shopping next week. Thought I'd buy something up in Ventura."

"You seen Renato's?"

"Yeah, quite a set-up."

"You ain't kiddin'. Papa runs it like he ran the streets," Sonny said.

"I hear he's grooming you to take over?"

"Yeah, but now you're here."

"You think it's gonna be that easy?" Antony placed his hands in his pockets. "You really think Lorenzo's going to let me walk in and take my rightful place?"

"We'll make him. How'd you stumble on Victoria?"

She smiled politely but listening to the brothers' banter made her cringe.

"I heard Francesca's was the hottest place in town to get suits." Antony leaned into Sonny and lowered his voice. "I also heard the women there weren't bad either." He raised his eyebrows at Victoria.

Sonny's face grew serious. "You kissed her?"

"I wanted to see where she stood. You know I have to watch out for my little brother. You'll be happy to know she pushed me away and told me about you."

Victoria's face filled with fire as she glared at Antony, but he grinned at her. She crossed her arms and looked away.

"I did walk out of there with Lauren's number." Antony laughed.

"You and every other guy in town." Sonny grabbed Antony's arm and turned him to her, oblivious to her irritation.

"Vic, let me tell you all you need to know about my brother. He never lies. At least not to anyone he cares about. He's as loyal as a dog."

Both brothers pointed at each other and said in unison, "Only to those he cares about." They both laughed then Sonny added, "And he always, I mean always, gets what he wants."

Antony nodded. "It's true."

"You had dinner?" Sonny asked.

"I was just trying to convince Victoria to join me but she insisted she couldn't go because she had a boyfriend."

Sonny wrapped his arm around her shoulder and pulled her close. "Ah, not even your sleazy tactics can steal this one."

"Sleazy tactics?" Victoria gritted her teeth.

"Not sleazy." Antony stared at Victoria. "I'll admit, I'm attracted to her. Heck, who wouldn't be?" He turned to Sonny. "But I know my place."

Sonny tightened his arm around her. "You were under the hood. Did you do something to her car?" His eyes narrowed but he smiled.

Antony sighed. "Okay, I pulled the starter cable only in an attempt to convince her to join me for dinner."

"You lied to me?" Victoria was hurt and infuriated by the simple fact. "Guess I see where I stand."

"I didn't lie to you."

She shifted her weight to her other leg. "I asked you if you had done something to my car."

"She's got you pegged already." Sonny laughed.

Antony stepped back. "You asked me if I'd done something to your car and I answered, you really think I'd do that?"

"It's the same thing. A lie." Victoria crossed her arms.

"Technically," Sonny shook his head, "he didn't lie."

Antony's wink made her inwardly cringe.

"Let's all go get something to eat." Sonny turned to Antony. "Then, we go see Papa."

"You two should go eat by yourselves." Victoria said quickly. Too quickly because Antony's grin deepened.

"Vic." Sonny frowned. "We want you to come. Don't we, Antony?"

"Sure we do." Antony's dark eyes flashed with pleasure.

Her heart pounded. She looked up at Sonny. "You haven't seen each other in years. You don't want me hanging around."

"You sure?" Sonny asked.

"Yes, I'm sure. You two go and have fun."

"Okay." He gave her a quick kiss. "I'm going to call Papa." He pulled his cell phone out and walked toward his car.

"Don't tell him I'm here." Antony yelled. "I want to see his face when he finds out."

Sonny grunted out a laugh. "Like I'd tell him that on the phone. I'll be right back." He pointed to Victoria's car. "Put it back the way you found it."

Victoria waited until Sonny was out of ear shot then looked over at Antony, her arms crossed. "Is it fixed?"

"Yes."

Victoria's balled fists tightened. "You're Sonny's brother."

"Yeah."

"You said your name was Tony."

"Some people call me that." He laughed. "Okay, I did that because I didn't want you to know who I was."

"So you could test me. And I thought you really cared."

Antony reached into her car and grabbed his jacket. "I knew you were Sonny's girlfriend. At first, my intention was to just check you out, but then I met you." He looked down at her and slipped on his jacket. His face softened. "I knew at that moment, I wanted you for myself."

Victoria rolled her eyes and turned away from him.

"It's the truth." He grabbed her arm and forced her to turn back. His face grew serious. "I felt a connection. I know you felt it, too."

Yeah, she felt it but wasn't sure if she'd ever admit it. "Why do you carry a gun?"

"Because of mine and my father's past."

"If your father's past was so bad why doesn't Sonny carry one?"

"I know my brother. He's packing."

"No, he isn't."

"You ever check under his pant leg?"

Victoria stared into Antony's eyes. Past the dark intrigue, they were truthful. "Why wouldn't he tell me?"

"He probably doesn't want to scare you off."

She wondered if Sonny's past was darker than he had led her to believe. Regardless, she needed to know what Antony's intentions were.

She looked into his eyes. "Are you going to tell Sonny that—"

"You kissed me back?" Antony took a step closer. "Or that you're attracted to me?"

"Yes," she said, ashamed that she had feelings for him at all.

He touched her arm. "You're trembling. Why?"

"I'm cold." She lied.

Antony nodded, half his mouth tipped wryly. His eyes softened and face relaxed. "I think you really like my brother." He slipped on his jacket. "And by the look on his face, he loves you."

Her heart pounded.

He leaned in. "Don't worry," he whispered in her ear. His hot breath sent chills through her. "Your secret is safe with me."

She bit her lip and looked up into his alluring eyes. "So, you won't tell him?"

He backed away. "Like my brother said, I'm loyal to those I care about. And if Sonny is anything like he used to be, you'll be in my arms soon enough."

"You sound sure of that?"

He cocked his head. "Oh, I am."

She looked past him to see Sonny approaching.

"Papa's mad but we're set," Sonny said. "Antony, you want to go to the hotel and change first?"

"Are you saying I don't look good enough to meet Don Luciano?"

"Tell me you're not going to start that again."

"What? Feed the ol' man's fantasy that he'll run the mob someday?"

"Run the mob?" Victoria took a small step back.

Sonny turned to her. "Papa used to dream about running the streets of Kansas City like Michael Corleone in The Godfather."

As if he sensed her uneasiness, Sonny took Victoria in his arms. "But he was never in the mob."

"I didn't think so." She tried to brush off the absurdity.

"You okay?" Sonny asked.

When she only shrugged her shoulders and slightly frowned, Sonny tilted his head. "Is something else upsetting you? Is it the kiss? I'm not mad at you. Antony is just, well, he's Antony. We'll talk about it later."

"I'm okay. It's just been a long day." She sighed and wondered if Antony would keep their secret.

Sonny kissed her. "I love you."

"Me, too." Her heart slowed to a steady, content pace. "Have fun."

Sonny walked to the silver Lexus. When he climbed in she stared down at his pant leg. With the bending of his knee, the navy trouser rose and she caught a glimpse of a small Derringer strapped to his ankle. Her eyes met Antony's.

He rested his arm on the hood of the car, his fingers in the shape of a gun. He raised his eyebrows, smiled and climbed into the car.

Exasperated, Victoria got in her own car and left. She gripped the steering wheel and wondered if it was possible to love two men at once. What was she thinking? Love Antony? Hardly, she had just met him. Unlike Sonny, she didn't believe in love at first sight.

Maybe what she felt for Antony was purely lust? Yes, that's what it had to be because she knew what she felt for Sonny was love. They had a bond that was beyond anything she had ever felt before.

SIX

OVER DINNER, SONNY rambled on about the last ten years—Aunt Cecilia, Renato's, college and Victoria. Antony half-heartedly listened and tried to eat, but the thick filet tasted like rubber and he gave up. His stomach was in knots and his mind reeled about how his father would react when he saw him.

Sonny paid the check and drove them to Lorenzo's. He pulled the Lexus through the large iron gates and down the drive. "I'm moving out as soon as Victoria marries me."

Antony wasn't shocked at his brother's confession, although it posed a problem. Even in his worst times, Antony lived life to the fullest, never caring how his actions affected others. He had his own desires to consider and now those included Victoria.

"It's that serious, huh?" Antony asked.

"Yeah." Sonny grinned and threw the car in park. "Come on."

Antony followed Sonny up the porch to the front door.

Sonny turned toward him. "You nervous?"

"Me, nervous? Never." Unnerved was more like it, but he'd never admit it to his brother.

"You look like a million bucks in that suit." Sonny straightened Antony's tie then smoothed down his jacket. "Remember, play nicely with Papa."

Antony batted Sonny's hands away. "Only if he plays nice with me."

Sonny slid the key into the lock and opened the oversized wooden door.

Antony followed him down the darkened hallway. He squinted as he tried to get a glimpse inside.

Sonny opened the door to the second room on the left and motioned for Antony to go in. "Papa's office." He flipped a light on. "I'll be right back."

Antony buttoned the jacket of the black Armani suit then rolled his head back and forth. *Relax.* On the outside, he looked like he just walked out of GQ. On the inside, his nerves were shot.

After a quick scan of the room, Antony smiled. His father hadn't lost his taste for antique handguns. They hung proudly on the wood paneled walls. A large gun cabinet stood between a multi-stoned fireplace and a wet bar. He stepped closer and took a long look at a 1918, 9 mm Lugar. It must have cost a fortune.

At a large wall unit that sat across from a mahogany desk, he opened one of the doors and flipped the power on the three TV monitors that sat inside. Each showed a different area of the grounds—the iron gates in the front, the garden in back, and front porch.

"Surveillance." Antony flipped the monitors off. "Seems I'm not the only one concerned about the past."

He walked over to the desk and ran his fingers along the edge when Sonny burst back into the room.

"Man, I still can't believe you're really here." Sonny pushed a manila folder toward him. "I've been saving this for you."

"What?"

"Check it out."

Antony opened the folder. It was Aunt Cecilia's Will.

Sonny chewed on his thumbnail. "Go to page eight. I've highlighted what I want you to read."

Antony gave a presumptuous laugh, backed up and sat on the black leather couch. "This is unbelievable." He looked up at Sonny. "She left me twenty-four percent of Renato's?"

"Yeah. I found a copy of the will last year. I tried to track you down, but you're a hard man to find."

"You learn how to hide on the streets." He glanced over the papers. Sonny was left twenty-five percent and Lorenzo fifty-one. Lorenzo had control, but there was no legal way he could stop Antony from stepping in. "Papa know you have this?"

"Of course not." Sonny leaned against the desk. "We'll use it if we have to. You're not walking out of my life again. We're brothers and we both know, family is all there is."

"Thanks."

The door flew open which brought both brothers to their feet.

"Sonny." Lorenzo's voice bellowed through the doorway. "You'd better have a good reason for missing our meeting."

Vince wheeled Lorenzo into the room then stopped to shut the door. If Vince was shocked to see Antony, he didn't show it. He was still the same emotionless hired thug. His black hair was short, but still as greasy as it had ever been.

When Antony was younger, he and his best friend, Carlo, used to make bets on whether it was from lack of hygiene or too much hair gel. Antony won. They found the jar of goo in Vince's apartment. Vince had gone ballistic, cursed them for breaking and entering, but it was worth it to have something on the guy that proved he really was human.

Antony's eyes fell on Lorenzo. It wasn't the first time he'd seen his father in a wheelchair, but it shocked him just the same. The first time was at a distance through tear filled eyes while he hid behind a tombstone to watch his mother's funeral.

Now, it seemed a shame to see his once well-built father sitting gaunt and haggard. His thick black hair was thin and graying.

"It's a good reason, Papa." Sonny pointed to Antony. "Look."

Any pity Antony felt for his father was crushed the moment Lorenzo turned toward him. His father's eyes were cold, calloused and uncaring, like they'd always been.

Antony could only imagine what was going through his father's mind and he'd learned that fear of the unknown was worse than any reality. He gave his father a single nod. "Papa."

Lorenzo's eyes narrowed. "The prodigal son returns."

"Not exactly." Antony placed one hand in his pocket and took a step toward his father. "The prodigal son left with his inheritance. I left with only the shirt on my back."

Lorenzo glared at Antony. "After what you did—"

"We're not doing this." Sonny stepped between them. "Antony is home and that's all that matters."

Lorenzo's face hardened. He wheeled to his desk and opened the cigar box, pulled out a Cuban cigar and waited. Vince flicked the lighter and held it at the end of the cigar while Lorenzo puffed away. The room filled with smoke that hung in the air as thick as the bitterness did. "Is that why you came back," Lorenzo barked. "To get your inheritance?"

Antony clutched tightly to the manila folder. He could end the argument by demanding what was legally his, but he wanted his father's acceptance, his respect, and his forgiveness. Part of him needed it.

"As you can see, I did quite well for myself. I don't need a handout from you, but you taught me that the only thing that matters is family. You can't deny I'm your son anymore because I won't let you. I'm a Luciano. I lived on the streets you ran. I worked for the scums you once put out of business, but I made it and I want what's due me."

"What's due you?" Lorenzo bellowed. "What exactly do you think is due you?"

"My place in this family."

"You lost that privilege the day you killed your mother."

Sonny's eyes widened and his face reddened.

Heat raced up Antony's neck. He squeezed his fists to the beat of his pounding heart. "You were driving the car. You were probably drunk. If anyone killed Mama—"

"Stop it," Sonny shouted. "Antony's back and he's not leaving."

"Forget it, Sonny."

"No, I won't forget it." Sonny voice raised. "You have every right to step in. Every *legal* right."

Antony shot Sonny a severe look. "I said, forget it."

Sonny grabbed the folder out of Antony's hand and shoved it at his father. "Antony owns twenty-four percent of Renato's. If you don't want to work with him, fine, he'll work with me."

Antony raised an eyebrow. His brother's boldness was something he'd never seen before.

Lorenzo grabbed the folder from Sonny's hand and threw it on the desk. "You may own twenty-five percent," Lorenzo glared, "but I own fifty-one and I'm in charge, not you."

"I know, but legally he has the right—"

"Legally?" Lorenzo bellowed so loud the windows rattled. "Are you two threatening me?"

"Nobody's threatening you." Antony shook his head. "This was a mistake."

Sonny grabbed Antony's arm. "No, you're not leaving." He turned to Lorenzo. "Papa?"

Lorenzo puffed on his cigar and looked like the whole thing was an inconvenience.

Sonny ran his hand through his hair. "Antony also has a seat on the board."

Antony cocked his head. "A seat on the board?"

Sonny ignored him. "He'll work at Renato's. You don't even have to see him."

Silence blanketed the room. Lorenzo pulled the cigar out and shot a fierce glare at Antony. "Do you know anything about the business world?"

"I graduated from college, if that's what you're asking."

Lorenzo's eyes narrowed. "If you want to work for my company you will do it on my terms."

"Fair enough. What are your terms?"

"You will work here."

"And where will you work?"

"I'll be breathing down your neck every second of the day until I feel I can trust you."

It wasn't ideal but livable. "Where's Sonny's office?"

"I have a small one down the hall and one at Renato's." Sonny looked over at Lorenzo. "He'll need an office at Renato's, too."

Lorenzo's eyes hardened, but Sonny didn't stop. "You've always said the employees have to know who's in charge and Antony is a Luciano and that fact warrants respect."

Lorenzo nodded then glared at Antony. "But you'll work where I can see you."

Antony gritted his teeth. He thought he was done answering to anyone, but he'd concede. It was the means to the end. To take his rightful place as firstborn. To take everything that was due him.

Antony tightened his jaw. "Thank you."

Lorenzo waved his hand for Vince to take him away. "I want both of you at breakfast tomorrow. Eight o'clock. Don't be late."

Vince pushed Lorenzo out of the room. Sonny closed the door behind them then turned to Antony. He smiled. "We did it."

Antony sat on the couch. "Yeah, we did it."

"What's your problem?"

"I have to work next to him, every day? Thanks."

"Don't blame that on me. Papa doesn't trust you."

"And I love how you stood up for me," Antony said.

"I was supposed to stand up for you? You ran out on me when I needed you most."

"I was ordered out."

"Come on, Antony. Papa was on heavy medication. He didn't know what he was saying. Besides, Aunt Cecilia would've brought you to California with us in a second. She wouldn't have cared what Papa said."

Antony rubbed his forehead then drug his hand over his face and sighed. "You don't get it, do you? I gave up everything for you." His mind churned up the past. Banned from his mother's funeral. Torn away from Elisa, his home, the life he knew and any chance of ever being respected by his father.

"I never forced you to lie." Sonny sat on the corner of the desk.

"No, you didn't." The statement was true. It was his love and loyalty to his brother that forced him to lie. "But you never told Papa the truth."

Sonny brought his eyes to meet Antony's. "I was scared back then, you know that."

"And now?"

"Would it matter?" Sonny stood tall.

Antony sighed. "No. It would just cause more problems."

Antony couldn't imagine what their father would do if he found out they had lied to him for years. Lorenzo preached loyalty. It meant more than money, power or life itself.

"Why didn't you come home sooner?" Sonny asked.

"I did." Antony stood and walked to the window. Luminescent lights lit the vast green lawn. Tree branches rustled in the breeze and cut through the darkness. The image of the large two-story brick house in Kansas City came to his mind. He'd only been gone six months when he decided the streets were worse than anything Papa could dish out.

"I went home, but strangers were living in our house." Antony stared out the window.

"I told Elisa we were going to Aunt Cecilia's. Didn't she tell you?"

"I didn't talk to her." After going by the old house he'd gone to Elisa's, but before ringing the bell, he peeked in the window and saw her in the arms of another man. "She'd already moved on."

"I'd have never guessed that. Have you talked to her at all over the years?"

"A few times. She married some low life punk from the streets a few years back."

"Thank you for agreeing to Papa's terms."

"No problem." Antony knew obedience was the only way to earn his father's respect and maybe, he could earn his father's love.

SEVEN

VICTORIA CURLED UP ON the couch and sipped a cup of hot, decaffeinated tea. The latest Vogue lay opened on her lap, but she wondered how things went with Sonny, his brother, and father. Despite her love for Sonny she couldn't deny she was attracted to Antony.

Victoria tossed the magazine on the coffee table, angry that her mind kept returning to a man she hardly knew, let alone her boyfriend's brother. Somehow, she had to rid her thoughts of him.

The doorbell rang.

She set the tea on the coffee table, walked over and glanced into the peephole. Antony. She chewed her lower lip and contemplated opening the door. Or not. Maybe she should just ignore him. It was almost eleven o'clock. Any normal person would be home asleep, or at least heading in that direction.

His deep voice drifted through the door as he knocked again. "I came to apologize."

She silently prayed for peace, took a deep breath and opened the door. He leaned against the doorframe with a satisfied grin on his face and a plastic bag in his hands. Her heart pounded out of sheer panic. Or anger. She couldn't decide which.

Either way, she'd play it cool. "What are you doing here?" She looked around him and down the hallway. "Is Sonny with you?"

"No. He's at home tucked safely in bed." He held up the white plastic bag. "I brought you a peace offering. It's dinner."

"I ate hours ago."

The smile never left his face. She sensed defeat. "Here," he pushed it toward her. "You can save it for lunch tomorrow."

When she took the bag, he turned to leave.

"The cocky, self-confident man I met hours ago is gone?" When he said nothing she added, "I at least expected one of your tasteless come-ons."

He turned back to her, the left side of his mouth curled up into a smug grin. "I never beg." He reeked of the cockiness she thought he'd lost.

Their eyes locked and as hard as she fought it, she couldn't hide her feelings.

A smile spread across his face, but he said nothing, just stared into her very being with his dark, alluring eyes.

Heat filled her face and she tried to look away but couldn't. "I guess it wouldn't hurt for you to come in for a minute."

"You're sure?"

She opened the door wider and motioned with her hand.

Antony grinned, walked in, and took the plastic bag from her hand.

He went straight to the kitchen, as though he knew the layout of the small apartment, not that it was hard. It was only 1100 square feet with two bedrooms, one bathroom, a living room and kitchen.

He eyeballed the cupboards.

"What are you looking for?" she asked.

He gave her a quick glance before opening a cupboard door. With a smile, he pulled out two plates. It took him two tries to find the silverware.

"I'm not eating anything." She sat at the small round table. "It's almost eleven. I told you, I already ate."

He grabbed two glasses and placed them by the plates then opened the fridge. After a minute, he looked over at her. "You got anything besides diet soda?"

"Water."

His eyes narrowed. He reached into the fridge and emerged with two cans of pop. "Caffeine free?"

She gave him a shrug. It took him two trips to carry it all to the table. If he hadn't been so arrogant, she would have helped him. He placed a plate in front of her.

"I told you. I'm not eating."

"You won't be able to resist." He winked.

Heat flushed her face. "I can resist."

One side of his mouth curled into a grin. "We'll see about that."

He pulled the first container out of the bag and opened it. The room filled with the aroma of a mushroom covered filet mignon. Her mouth watered and she knew there was no way to resist all her favorites.

Cutting the twice-baked potato and steak in half, Antony slid them on her plate along with some mushrooms. The rest went on his. He reached into the bag, pulled out two pieces of garlic bread and placed one on each of their plates. Popping open a can of pop, he poured it into their glasses, clasped his hands in a praying position, looked over at her, and raised an eyebrow.

"What?"

"Try it." He smiled.

She conceded, cut a small piece of the medium rare filet, and placed it in her mouth. It melted. "What's in there?" She pointed with her fork to the last container.

"Double chocolate fudge cake."

She cocked her head. "All my favorites? How did you know?"

"Sonny told me." He slid a piece of filet into his mouth.

Sonny. How quickly he could make her forget. "How did it go with Sonny? He's told me a lot about you."

"All good I hope."

"Mostly." She laughed.

His grin widened. "Really. What'd my ol' brother said about me that wasn't good?"

Antony could make her blush at the drop of a hat. She took another bite. "Nothing I'd repeat."

"What?"

"Let's just say he's warned me about your type."

"My type?" He laughed. "What type is that?"

"Egotistical. Narcissistic. Self-indulgent."

He raised an eyebrow. "I think I'd use words like confident, loyal, and loving life." He pointed his fork at her. "And I'm capable of self-sacrifices, if necessary."

She gave him an uneasy nod. "How did it go with your dad?"

"Papa is Papa. He hasn't changed a bit in the last ten years."

"Why did you run away?"

"Run away? Is that what Sonny told you?" He rolled his eyes. "I never ran away. I was ordered out by my father."

"Why? What did you do?"

"You assume I did something?" He grinned.

"Lorenzo keeps Sonny on a short leash. I didn't think he'd let you go without a good reason."

"Let's just say I chewed through my leash." He opened the second soda and refilled their glasses. "So, why haven't you met Lorenzo?"

"He sounds like the kind of man I don't want to meet."

"You know about his past?"

"Some of it."

"And that bothers you?" When she couldn't look him in the eye he added, "I think there's another reason you haven't met him. I'll bet it has nothing to do with Lorenzo, but has everything to do with Sonny."

Was she that transparent? She shifted uneasily and reached for the cake instead of answering, but he quickly pulled it closer to him.

"Tell me how you feel about Sonny." His face was serious.

"Why would I talk to you about him? I hardly know you."

"Yet, here we sit, alone, in the middle of the night with you dressed in nothing but a thin layer of cotton."

As much as she would've liked to throw him out, she couldn't. He had a force about him that drew her to him, no matter how hard she tried to resist.

"Sonny told me he plans on marrying you," Antony said.

"Sonny said that the first day we met."

"Let me tell you a little secret about the Luciano's. We get what we want."

"And what do you want?"

His eyes seemed to probe deep into her soul. "You know what I want."

A shudder ran through her. She knew what he wanted, and with some persuasion, he might just get it. She gave her head a gentle shake to thwart off the thoughts of him.

"Why I haven't met Lorenzo, huh?" She drummed her fingernails on the table, hoping the gentle change of subject would lessen his desirous look.

Antony opened the container to the double chocolate cake, and cut her off a piece. She thanked him with a slight nod then took a piece of the rich, chocolate on her fork and slid it into her mouth.

"Mmm." She relaxed in her chair. "There's nothing as good as double chocolate."

He grunted a laugh. "Sonny hasn't remembered anything I taught him."

Victoria threw him a fierce look.

"Or maybe," he grinned. "You haven't given Sonny the chance?" When she refused to answer, he sat back in his chair.

His deepening dimples frustrated her more. Was she supposed to just blurt out that she was a twenty-four-year-old virgin by choice? Really, it was none of his business. Besides, unlike Sonny, he wouldn't understand her faith and her belief that sex outside of marriage was wrong.

"I love Sonny." There, she had said it aloud.

"Enough to marry him?" Her silence egged him on. "I didn't think so."

"I'm just not sure about getting married right now. I just finished college and I'm starting my career."

"Your career? You went to college to sell clothes? Don't get me wrong, you're great at it but—"

"I don't just sell clothes."

"Didn't you sell me three suits?"

Heat made its way up her neck. "Yes, but I'm the Vice President of Fashion and Design."

"Assistant manager?"

She laughed. "Okay, assistant manager, but someday I'm going to own a store just like Francesca's."

"That's what you want to do with your life? Run a retail store?"

"Yeah and produce my own line of clothes. I draw dress designs, you know."

"You'll have to show them to me someday. Maybe I'll invest. I'm always looking for good business ventures."

She smiled. "Thanks, but if anyone would invest, it'd be Sonny."

He raised an eyebrow. "That would make you a harder sell to Lorenzo."

"Excuse me?"

"My father's a hard man. He'll grill you because he'll think you're after the money and by the looks of this place and your high ambitions, the money wouldn't hurt you."

"I'm doing quite well on my own, thank you. I don't need the Luciano money, and that's not why I'm with Sonny."

"I didn't say you were. I'm only preparing you to meet Lorenzo. Telling you things Sonny doesn't like to admit. You're a non-denominational Christian who comes from a family of cops. It doesn't mix well with devout Catholics and loan sharking."

"From what I gather, the only thing your father is devout about is his business and the power and money it brings." She put the last of the double chocolate cake in her mouth. "And I didn't think he did the loan sharking anymore."

"Oh, he does. He's just become more civilized in his old age." He pushed his empty plate away. "But in the end, with you on Sonny's arm, he'll accept you."

"And if I was on yours?"

"Is that a proposition?"

"No. You just seem to think that your father hasn't missed you over the years."

He laughed. "He hasn't."

"How do you know?"

"I just saw the man, believe me, I know. He'll tolerate me because I own twenty-four shares of Renato's and a seat on the board."

She nodded.

His eyebrows rose. "You knew about that?"

"Yeah, Sonny told me. He really did try to find you."

Antony stood, walked to the kitchen window and stared out onto the parking lot.

Victoria picked up the plates, went into the kitchen and placed them in the sink. "What did you do in Kansas City?"

He looked over at her. "Things."

"Like what?"

"Why?"

"Well," she turned the water on and let it run over the plates. "You mentioned the mob, and I just wondered."

"Papa ran his own little business of loan sharking in KC. When he left, I went to college."

She laughed.

"You don't believe me? I did." He turned, crossed his arms and leaned against the counter. "I did some jobs I'm not proud of, but they paid for school."

"Illegal things?"

"I did what I had to, to survive."

She nodded, pulled out the coffee pot and a can of decaffeinated coffee. "You want some?"

"Sure."

When the coffee finished brewing, she filled their cups and proceeded him to the living room where they sat on the couch.

"Tell me about your mother," he said.

Victoria smiled. "My mother was wonderful. She ran herself ragged driving my sister and me to everything. Cheer, gymnastics, soccer… You know, all those after school activities. She never complained about it although I know it had to get on her nerves. She liked being our friend. Don't get me wrong. She was our mom, and she'd ground us and yell like any other mother would. But I always knew she loved me."

She sipped on the coffee, then leaned over and picked up the music box. "Sonny gave me this today." "Edelweiss" played when she lifted the lid. "Mom had one just like it."

Antony nodded. "And then one day, she was gone?"

Victoria shut the lid and the room was silent. "Yeah, just like that." She leaned back against the couch and tucked her hair behind her ears. "And your mom?"

Antony set the cup down, leaned forward, and rested his elbows on his knees. "She was great. A little too religious for me, but I listened because I loved her. She'd protect us when we needed it."

"Protect you?"

"From Lorenzo. He had a temper. Then, she was dead and everything changed." He rubbed his hands together.

"I'm sorry."

He nodded. "You ever wonder where your mom is? If she's still alive?"

"What did you do, have me investigated?"

He laughed. "Yeah. It's a habit of mine. I like to know what I'm walking into."

She should have been angry, but for some odd reason she wasn't. It seemed to be his character to walk cautiously, and she couldn't begrudge him that. "When you had me investigated, what did you find out? About my mom, I mean?"

"That the police said she was either kidnapped, killed, or she ran off to get away from you guys."

She stood and walked to the window, her arms around her stomach. No matter how many times she heard the story, it cut through her just the same.

Antony stood and walked toward her. "I also heard," he looked into her eyes, "that your dad always thought she was kidnapped and she was still alive."

She nodded. Tears filled her eyes. She looked down, but he placed his finger under her chin, bringing her eyes to meet his. "What do you think?"

"I don't know," she whispered.

"Yes, you do. What do you think happened to her?"

"She loved us, Zoë and me. If she left, there was a good reason. I always thought she was blackmailed. You know, by someone out for revenge for my daddy arresting them. Maybe that's why she left."

"Could be wishful thinking."

"I know, maybe." She wiped the tear that fell down her cheek. "I'd give anything to know the truth, but my daddy investigated every angle before he was killed. I'll never know what happened to her so it's something I try not to think about."

He rubbed her shoulder. "I'm sorry I brought it up. I didn't mean to upset you."

She took a deep breath. "It's okay."

He looked down at her, his eyes filled with love. She thought he'd kiss her, but he didn't. He smiled. "I guess I should go. It's getting late and I still have to find a hotel."

She looked at the clock and couldn't believe it was after midnight. *I could invite him to stay because there is a spare bedroom and a lock on her door.* She laughed.

"What's so funny?"

"Nothing." She decided he should go. He was too tempting. Sonny respected her faith and knew his limits, Antony would test them. It was a test she feared she'd fail.

His eyes danced as though he knew exactly what she was thinking. His grin deepened as he picked up the two cups and took them into the kitchen sink then walked to the door.

She followed him. "Thanks for dinner."

He opened the door then turned back to her. She looked up at him with a smile.

"Thanks for inviting me in. See you around."

"Sure." She closed the door behind him.

EIGHT

WITH ARMS CROSSED, Sonny leaned against his car in the driveway of his father's house. Clay stood next to him in the same stance. Both men were in navy suits and white shirts. Sonny wore a yellow tie and black designer shoes. Clay wore steel-toed cowboy boots, and his red tie was loosened the shirt unbutton at the top.

"Just showed up, out of the blue?" Clay asked.

"Yeah. I love my brother, but I can't help wonder why now?"

"I was thinking the same thing. You want me to do some checking?"

"Please."

Antony drove into the driveway, killed the engine and climbed out of his car.

Sonny stood straight and smiled. "Glad you made it."

"Did you really think I'd be late my first day?" Antony gave Sonny a gentle punch in the arm. He turned to Clay and held out his hand. When Clay took Antony's hand, he gave it a firm shake. "Clay, nice to see you."

"You too."

Sonny looked at his watch. "Let's to go."

They walked into the house, down a hallway and into the living room. "Come on." Sonny turned to Antony who had stopped and was looking around.

"I can't believe it." Antony ran his hand along the wing back chair. "This is the furniture from the KC house?"

For the first time in years, Sonny looked around the room with genuine interest. He had forgotten how special the décor was, and how tightly the past was woven in its history. "Papa brought everything he could from KC. Look," he motioned outside the

French doors. "He even had Mom's garden dug up and brought here."

Antony walked to the French doors, his hands deep in his pockets.

"Sorry. It must be weird."

"Yeah, weird." Antony turned. "The last time I went back to the house, it was empty. Always wondered where everything went."

"Buongiorno. Breakfast is ready," Consolata said with her thick Italian accent.

They walked into the dining room. Antony's eyes were drawn to the large crystal chandelier hanging from the ceiling. "Is that the one Mom got in Paris?"

"Yes," Lorenzo's voice bellowed from the doorway as Vince wheeled him to the table that was filled with eggs, bread and jam, and different kinds of pastries.

Sonny couldn't understand why his father was still so angry at Antony. He had just assumed that the years would have softened his heart. He gave Antony a head nod as they sat down.

Vince and Clay sat and only after Lorenzo took the first pastry did anyone else begin to eat.

"So," Antony sipped some coffee, "what's on the agenda for today?"

Sonny poured himself a cup. "I think after you get settled in your office, I'll give you a tour of Renato's. We can go down to the shipyards then around town to show you some of the businesses we're looking at purchasing."

The brother's eyes met then both turned to their father.

Lorenzo took a bite of cannoli then set it on his plate. He gave Sonny a single nod.

Antony scooted his empty plate to the center of the table. "What, that's it? I can just go with Sonny?"

Sonny pursed his lips and stared at his brother. He had hoped this would be easy, but it appeared Antony's heart hadn't gotten any softer either. The last thing he wanted was an argument and it looked as though Antony was going to start one.

Sonny took a deep breath. "So, Antony, what kind of work did you do in KC?"

"I did some work for Vito. You remember Vito, don't you, Lorenzo?"

The left side of Lorenzo's mouth went up into a grin. "Vito? It's been years. He took over?"

"Yes." Antony sipped his coffee.

"You worked for him?"

"Yeah, I did."

Lorenzo scanned the men at the table, his prideful ego lifting his lip in a sneer. "I made Vito. If I'd never left, he'd still be slumming it on the streets."

"He never ran them as good as you did."

It was obvious Antony was trying to get their father to accept him, but it was the way he was doing it that Sonny didn't agree with. He was playing into Lorenzo's fantasy of the mob.

"Antony, besides Vito, did you do any other work?" Sonny asked.

Antony nodded. "Yeah, I worked at a bank. Did some small business loans."

"Good." Sonny turned to Lorenzo. "Thought I'd give him the Hamburg deal."

Lorenzo glared at Antony. "You think you can just walk in and take over a deal you know nothing about?"

Antony raised his chin in defiance. "Give me the deal, I can work it."

"You haven't changed a bit," Lorenzo shouted. "Still think you can do anything."

"I can." Antony grinned and raised his coffee mug to Consolata. "I'll make you more money than you could ever want."

"Maybe living on the streets did you good." Lorenzo shoved a bite of toast and jam in his mouth.

Antony's eyes narrowed as he turned to Vince. "I can see you are still loyal to Lorenzo, but Clay, what exactly do you do?"

Clay set his fork down. "I work for Sonny, at Renato's."

"Bodyguard?"

"Among other things."

Antony nodded, a grin on his face.

Sonny frowned. "What?"

"I'm just wondering, if you are so legit why do you both still have bodyguards?"

Sonny wiped his mouth with the cloth napkin. "I don't really look at Clay as a bodyguard. He's my assistant. We went to college together, and he graduated with a better GPA then me. You can trust his judgment."

"You carry?"

Clay opened his jacket and exposed a holstered gun.

Antony leaned back in his chair. "What kind of deals do you do that would make you still need to carry?"

"The kind you'll love to be in the center of." Clay laughed.

Lorenzo dropped his napkin on his plate. "Antony, I'd like to see you in my office. Alone."

Sonny met Antony's eyes, sensing trouble he wasn't sure how to avoid. His fear was twofold. Antony held his secret. With Lorenzo pushing him, he wondered how long his brother would keep it.

Antony stood and gave Sonny a nod. "Be right back."

Clay looked over at Sonny as the room cleared. "You think he's going to say something? He's not that dumb."

"No, but depending on his agenda, we could all be on the streets."

Clay shook his head. "You don't think he just came back to come back? Your dad did always say family was all there is."

Sonny tossed his napkin on the table. "I'm hoping he came back to be with us, but we both know Antony. He always looked out for himself first."

"Yeah," Antony's voice came from the doorway. "That's why I always stuck up for you, took the beatings, took the blame, and lived on the streets."

Sonny stood, his heart pounding. "I thought you were meeting with Papa?"

"I stopped to use the restroom, and I couldn't walk away and have you two wondering." He moved into the room and rested his hands on the back of a chair. "I'm here because I was sick of working the streets and being around the lowlifes that I was forced deal with. What I don't get is why, after all these years, do you think I'm here to tell Lorenzo the truth?"

Sonny turned to Clay. "Could you excuse us?"

Clay nodded and left.

Sonny looked back up at Antony. "You don't understand the guilt that eats away at me. Part of me wants Papa to know the truth, but I know he will kick us both out on the street, so he can't know. I want to trust you, but I haven't seen you in years. Then all of a sudden, out of the blue, you show up."

Antony nodded, "You want to know why I showed up? I'll tell you why. It's nothing you and Clay won't find out when you guys have me investigated." He winked. "I don't hold it against you, I've already done the same."

Vince walked in. "Lorenzo is waiting."

"I'll be right there." Antony waited until Vince was gone then looked back at Sonny. "I did a job for Vito and things went bad. I was arrested and spent some time in jail. Makes you think, you know, sitting in that small cell. So, here I am."

"What happened?"

"A guy I was trying to collect from turned up in a dumpster. Did six months before the charges were finally dropped. Missing evidence." He grinned. "Good thing I had people that owed me."

Sonny didn't ask if the guy was dead. Working for Vito, hurting someone was inevitable. Maybe he was making too much of this. "Glad nothing came of it. You'd better get in there before Papa gets mad. I'll wait for you in your office."

"My office." Antony grinned. "Sounds good."

Clay walked back into the room as Antony left.

Sonny waved for Clay to follow him to Antony's new office. "Did you hear all of that?"

Clay nodded.

"Then you know where to start. Find out about the job, what exactly happened to the guy and the evidence." He turned to Clay. "People owing Antony favors is good, but find out if Antony owes anyone favors. I'd like to know if anyone is going to come collecting. Thanks."

Clay disappeared.

* * *

The dead guy in the dumpster was forced out of Antony's memory as quickly as it had entered. He wasn't one to dwell on the past, especially something he couldn't change.

He walked into Lorenzo's office, and sat only after his father motioned for him to. "What can I do for you?"

Lorenzo pulled out a cigar, ran it under his nose and sniffed hard before biting off the end. He pulled a lighter out and puffed as the tobacco crackled in the flame. "Worked for Vito, huh?"

"Yeah."

"I taught him everything he knows."

"Figured as much." Antony brought his leg up and rested it on his knee.

Lorenzo leaned back in his wheelchair. "This may work out real good." He tossed a folder at Antony. "I want a piece of land and the only problem is there's a company on it that doesn't want to sell. Sonny hasn't got the guts to get it for me. Whines about putting people out of work."

Antony grabbed the folder. "No problem."

"Not even going to look at it?"

"Nope."

Lorenzo snorted a laugh. "That sounds like you."

"I know how to take orders."

"As much as I'd like to trust you, I will never forget what you did or forgive you for it."

Antony sat staunch. "I never figured you would."

Lorenzo continued to puff on the cigar. The room filled with smoke that hung stagnant in the air. "I want to know everything you are doing. Every deal, where you eat, even when you take a crap. Your life is mine until I decide I can trust you."

Antony nodded. At least working for Lorenzo and owning shares in the company, he'd be lining his pockets, too. "After Sonny takes me on his little sightseeing tour I'll get on this." He held the folder up. "I'm assuming you don't want Sonny to know what I'm doing."

"There's a guy that will work with you—"

"I work alone." Antony stood. "I won't have a stooge hanging around. You either let me prove myself to you or get Vince to do this." He handed back the folder.

Lorenzo eyeballed him for a few seconds before nodding. "All right, you work alone. If you need someone, I will offer you protection."

"A bodyguard?" Antony opened his coat and exposed his Glock holstered on his belt. "Only protection I need."

Lorenzo nodded. "You can go. Your office is there." Lorenzo pointed to a doorway that connected to another office.

Antony walked through the door and shut it. Sonny sat waiting on the black leather couch. Not a moment to himself. He might really have to tell someone he's going to the bathroom.

Sonny looked up as Antony tossed the folder on the desk.

"What's that?"

"I don't know. Bedtime reading I guess." He ran his fingers along the red oak desktop then sat in the black leather chair. It was like a dream. He was home where he belonged, working for his father.

He knew he would never receive his father's forgiveness, but maybe he could earn back some respect. He brought his feet up onto the desk. "You got the name of a good realtor?"

"Yeah, what for?"

"I can't stay in a hotel forever."

"Why not stay with me?"

"And you live where?"

Sonny laughed. "You already know."

"You're right, I do." Antony laughed. "I figured Lorenzo would make me stay here, too, but I guess he doesn't want me around that much. Thank God." He grabbed the folder and stood. "Let's get going."

"I'll get you that name. You want to drive?"

"Yeah." They walked down the hall and ran into Clay. "Here." Antony pulled a card from his pocket. "It's my contact at the KCPD. Save you some time getting that info for Sonny." He gave Clay a wink.

He jiggled his keys as he walked to his car, opened the trunk, and tossed the folder that Lorenzo had given him into it then dropped it shut. "Let's go."

* * *

Victoria rushed through the crowd in the garden. She saw Zoë and waved. The sun was bright and the smell of freshly cut grass permeated the air. She grabbed a chair in front of the stage where a few chairs sat behind a podium.

Zoë joined her wearing her police blues. She was tall and thin with long, from a box, blond hair. A few strands fell over her face, but didn't hide the faint purple and yellow colors left over from the two black eyes.

They hugged then Zoë sat down.

Victoria pointed. "Looks good. Does it still hurt?"

Zoë gently touched her new nose. "Not too bad." She turned sideways so Victoria could see her profile. "It does look good, doesn't it?"

"An amazing job. And the handsome doctor?"

"He wasn't that handsome." Zoë laughed. "But check him out." She motioned with her head to a stocky man with dishwater blond hair cut in a buzz.

"Are you two…?"

"Well…" Zoë's face turned red. "He's my partner. He looks good in uniform, doesn't he?" Zoë giggled.

"You two are seeing each other, outside the police car?"

"Shh, that could get us both disciplinary action." She smiled at Martin who glanced her way and gave a two-finger wave, then turned back to Victoria. "You sure you don't want to be on stage and grab the plaque honoring daddy?"

"No, you should have it. You're the one following in his footsteps."

"Okay. So, what's new with you? How's Sonny?"

"Good. You'll never believe who I met."

"His father?"

Victoria shook her head. "His long-lost brother, Antony." She grinned.

"And?"

"Seems like a nice guy. Good looking. You'd like him." Heat filled her face just thinking about him.

Zoë's eyes widened. "Oh, you didn't."

"Didn't what?"

"Victoria. You kissed him?"

Victoria stared at her. "Why on earth would you think that?"

"By that look. I'm your sister. I know you." Zoë nudged her with her shoulder. "You can tell me. It's not like you and Sonny are married."

"But it's his brother." She shook the thoughts of Antony out of her head. "And you know, I can't stand girls who go out on their boyfriends."

"Then maybe you and Sonny should cool it, at least until you sort out your feelings."

"My feelings?" What an absurd thought. "How did one kiss turn into me having feelings for the guy?"

Zoë laughed and pointed at her. "It doesn't. I just wanted you to admit you kissed him."

Victoria rolled her eyes and laughed.

"So, tell me about him. Is he how Sonny described him?"

"Kind of. I mean, he's tough, but he also has a heart, or at least he showed it to me."

An officer on the stage waived at Zoë. "That's my cue. Talk to you when this is over."

* * *

Victoria looked around. Sonny said he'd try to come, but with Antony showing up, she doubted he'd even remember.

After the short speeches were done, Zoë stepped up and received the plague.

Victoria stood with the crowd and clapped. She was greeted by officers who hugged and saluted her while Zoë stood on the stage talking to her blond hunk.

She slid her purse strap on her shoulder and turned to go.

Sonny and Antony sat in the back. They stood as she walked toward them. Sonny leaned in and gave her a kiss on the cheek. "We made it. Late, but we're here."

"Thanks. It was pretty neat, huh?"

"Yeah." Sonny took her hand.

"Oh, man, Vic, your sister looks good in a uniform." Antony grinned. "Better than her pictures."

She looked over at him. "You've seen her before?"

"Yeah, you know, when I had you investigated."

Victoria laughed. "You guys had lunch?"

Sonny shook his head. "You want to go get some?"

"Yeah." She waved at Zoë who whispered something to her partner then walked over. "How's it going?" Zoë leaned in and gave Sonny a hug. "And you must be Antony." She held out her hand.

Antony shook it.

"You were right, Sis. He is good looking." Zoë's grin deepened.

Heat filled Victoria's face. She held Sonny's hand as Antony's eyes met hers. Then he flashed his killer grin.

"Well," Zoë smiled. "Martin is waiting for me." She pointed toward the stage area where the policeman stood. "See you guys later."

Victoria knew a fight with Sonny was inevitable. "Sonny, you want to ride with me? Antony, you can follow us. How about Mikayla's?"

"Mikayla's? What's that?" Antony asked.

"Seafood and steak. Best in town." She squeezed Sonny's hand. "At least we think so."

Sonny nodded and dropped her hand.

"I'm there." Antony smiled. "Don't lose me. I don't know where it's at."

By the red that still flushed Sonny's face, Victoria knew he wished he could lose Antony, or at least get him to stay out of her life.

NINE

SONNY SWERVED IN and out of traffic, driving Victoria's car to the restaurant, checking every so often in the rearview mirror to make sure he hadn't lost Antony. Anger still burned in his stomach. "So, Vic, you told Zoë about Antony?"

"Yeah. Does it bother you I said he was good looking?"

He glanced at her. She had no idea who she was dealing with when it came to his brother. He knew Antony and the way he worked. "A little."

"Then of course he'd be good looking, just like you." Reaching over, Victoria intertwined her fingers in his.

Sonny smiled. "How can I be mad at a comment like that?"

He pulled the car into a parking spot, killed the engine, jumped out and jogged around to open her car door. Taking her hand, he walked to the front of the restaurant. "We'll wait here for Antony. I'm sorry I acted mad."

She gave him a kiss. "It's okay."

As Antony approached them, he clicked the fob making his Beemer chirp.

Sonny opened the door and motioned for them to go inside.

Mikayla's was painted in a bold white. Dark walnut cross beams adorned the ceilings and rich replicas of famous paintings hung on the wall. Monet and Rembrandt, Victoria's favorites, were among them.

The hostess grabbed some menus. "Same table, Mr. Luciano?"

"Yes, if it's open." Sonny squeezed Victoria's hand and they made their way to their favorite table. Located in the far corner of the restaurant, with two, three-quarter-high walls held a variety of wines and champagnes.

The waiter brought Sonny and Victoria their usual, water and Diet Coke, set them on the table and looked at Antony. "What can I get you to drink?"

"Water with lemon is good."

"So, what have you boys been doing all morning?" Victoria set the menu down and sipped her pop.

"Sightseeing." Antony rolled his eyes and sighed.

"You don't sound too thrilled."

"I'd rather get to work, but Sonny thinks I need to see everything."

"Just trying to get you familiar with what we're all about," Sonny said.

Antony took the drink from the waiter and they ordered their food.

"Do you really think I don't already know everything about Renato's? I've had you, your girlfriend, and your girlfriend's sister investigated. Believe me, I know everything possible about Renato's. I'm ready to get to work." Antony chugged his water.

"What are you so anxious to get started on? The deal Papa gave you? Is that Hanson Manufacturing?"

"I don't know. I haven't looked at it." Antony grinned.

"So, Antony," Victoria interrupted their impending argument, her perky tone suggesting it was intentional. "Are you going to look for apartments or a house?"

"Not sure, any openings in your place?" Antony playfully raised his eyebrows at her.

Sonny could feel the heat rise up his neck and leaned back as the waiter set their food down. "Thanks." He shook some salt and pepper on his grilled chicken. "What'd Papa say when he gave you the folder?"

"Not to tell you about it." Antony cut into his steak.

"And you're okay with that?" Sonny knew his brother hadn't changed.

"Yeah, I am." Antony took a bite. "You guys were right, this is one of the best steaks I've had." He wiped the napkin over his mouth, checked his phone then stood. "I'll be right back."

Sonny cut off a piece of his grilled chicken, but ten minutes with Antony had just about killed his appetite.

Victoria poured the dressing on her salad. "You should cut him some slack."

"What? And watch him make a deal that would put thousands of people out of work? I agree its prime real estate, but those people have families. It's not like we're hurting for the money."

"Yeah, but look at it from Antony's point of view. Your father told him to do something. He's just trying to get your dad to accept him. Why wouldn't he do anything Lorenzo asked?"

"How would you know anything about how my dad and Antony feel about each other?"

Antony walked around the table and sat. "Because we talked about it." He took another bite of the steak, gesturing with his knife as he talked. "And she's right. You think I'm going to walk in here and ignore an order Lorenzo gives me? I'm not giving him any reason to throw me out, again."

Sonny looked at them both. "When, exactly did you two have this little heart to heart?"

"Last night." Antony put the last bite in his mouth.

Sonny tossed the napkin on the plate.

Antony shoved the food to the side of his cheek, making it bulge. "Sorry, Vic. I thought you told him."

"I haven't had the chance." She set her fork down and looked at Sonny. "I was going to."

Figures. Sonny could tell the second he saw them together that Antony had his eyes on Victoria. He would have to play this very carefully because Antony was good.

Sonny put his arm around Victoria. "Here's my problem. We've worked really hard to keep Renato's legit. Papa has tried many things, but Clay and I have out maneuvered him and kept Renato's looking good. We've become an upstanding company, and the Luciano name isn't associated with the low life scum we used to be associated with in Kansas City. I want to know if I can trust you to keep it that way."

"You want to know if you can trust me?" Antony leaned back in his chair.

Trust was something Sonny always had confidence in with Antony, but years of working and living on the streets could change any man.

"I know nothing about how you lived or what you've done. So, yeah, I think I have a right to know a little bit about you before we just hand things over."

"What do you want to know?" Antony leaned into the table. "I've always been honest, you know that."

"Where did you live after Lorenzo kicked you out?" Victoria asked Antony.

"I hung with some friends for a while, a few days here, a few days there. I could never stay long because their parents were worried about who might come after me."

The waiter came and picked up their empty plates.

Victoria laid her napkin on the table. "And then, after you couldn't stay with friends?"

"I lived on the streets. Slept in dumpsters, doorways, abandoned buildings. I tried to go back to school, but first time I needed a parent I was done. I went to work, friends let me clean up at their place. I got my GED, rented a cheap dump while I went to college, and here I am."

"What kind of work did you do?" Sonny asked for Victoria's sake. Maybe if she saw him for who he really was he wouldn't be able to steal her away.

"Collection."

Victoria raised an eyebrow. "Collection?"

Antony grinned. "I didn't use the phone or anything. I used my charms and talents." He flapped open his coat exposing the Glock. "Collected every debt but one." His eyes turned to Sonny.

Man in the dumpster.

"Why?" Victoria took a sip of her drink. "You don't look like the kind of guy who would accept defeat."

Antony leaned into the table. "I don't, but the guy kinda died."

"Oh." Victoria leaned into Sonny.

Sonny tightened his arm around her and grinned at his brother. "You said you have people who owe you?"

"Yeah." Antony's eyes narrowed and he pursed his lips.

"Do you owe anyone? Is anyone going to come looking for you?" Sonny asked.

"Only one person I can think of, but he'd probably be looking for us both."

That deflated Sonny in a second. He took deep breaths to slow down his pounding heart. "You didn't talk to him over all these years? I heard he was still in KC."

"Yeah, I talked to him. We worked a few jobs together."

"Who?" Victoria asked.

Sonny looked over at her. "Just someone we knew." He looked back at Antony. "You think he'll come here?"

"I don't think so. We left on pretty good terms."

Sonny nodded.

Antony smiled at Victoria then looked back at Sonny. "Can Victoria take you back to Renato's? I'd really like to get started on that project."

Sonny looked over at Victoria. "I'll text Clay. He's got my car."

Antony stood and walked out of the restaurant.

Sonny never thought he'd be so glad to see his brother leave.

* * *

Victoria dabbed the napkin on the corner of her mouth. Sonny's face was still hard from the argument with Antony.

He looked at her. "So, what's going on with you and Antony?"

"Nothing."

The waiter brought the check, and Sonny handed him some cash. "When you and Antony talked last night, was it at your place?"

"Yes. He brought me dinner. It was after he left you and your father."

Sonny's face hardened.

"Are you mad?"

"Hmm." He pursed his lips. "First he kisses you then goes over to your place in the middle of the night. Wouldn't you be mad?"

Italians. Their tempers were so easily ignited. She took a deep breath and slowly released it. "I suppose, but you have nothing to worry about. I'm in love with you, not him."

Sonny leaned back in his chair and gently rubbed his bottom lip. "It's not you I don't trust."

"You don't trust Antony?"

He shook his head. "You don't understand him. When he sees something he wants, he gets it, and he has his mind set on you."

"It doesn't matter if your brother wants me, he won't get me, okay."

Sonny nodded.

She did love Sonny, but there was a connection to Antony she couldn't explain. How deep the feeling ran was something she'd have to examine later.

They sat in silence for a moment. Her mind wandered back to the conversation with Antony about her mother. The Luciano name alone could get her information that no one else could. She had asked Sonny to help before, and he wouldn't. Maybe this time he would.

"Can I ask you to do something for me?"

"Sure." He smiled and took her hand. "You know I'd do anything for you."

"Will you investigate my mother's disappearance?"

"We've been through this. I can't."

"Why? You have the resources. You investigate people all the time. Can't you see if you can find something that my dad couldn't?"

He shook his head and looked into her eyes, "I can't, hon. You know the cops investigated thoroughly. Your dad did everything he could. If they found nothing out, I won't be able to."

"You won't even try?"

He shook his head. "No, I'm sorry."

His answer cut through her entire being. Maybe he didn't love her as much as he professed. Her eyes teared up and she crossed her arms as the heat rose up her neck. "I can't believe you sometimes."

Antony came around the partition and grabbed his sunglasses off the table. "I forgot these."

Victoria blinked away the tears.

"You okay?" Antony asked.

She wiped her eyes and stood. "I'm just fine," she said, walking away.

* * *

Sonny stood.

"What's wrong with her?" Antony asked.

"Nothing for you to worry about."

"Did you get on her about me going over to her place last night? It wasn't her fault." Antony tucked the glasses into his pocket.

"It has nothing to do with you."

Victoria came out of the bathroom towards them. Her eyes were still bloodshot, but she seemed composed.

Antony leaned into her. "What's going on?"

"Nothing. I've got to get to work."

They walked to the cars.

Antony slid on his sunglasses, climbed into his car and took off.

Clay pulled up. Sonny turned to her. "I'm sorry. I didn't mean to upset you."

"It's fine. I guess you won't do anything for me, huh?" She turned from him.

He grabbed her arm. Trying to explain it again was useless, but he had to try. "Listen, you have to trust me. If I could do anything, I would."

"Sure. Whatever."

He pulled her into a hug but she was stiff. "I love you."

"I need to go." She took off.

He rounded the back of his car and got into the passenger side. "To the Hanson factory."

"Is that the deal your dad gave Antony?" Clay pulled out of the lot, onto the road.

"It's gotta be."

Sonny stared out the window. "Vic's asking about her mom."

"You didn't tell her anything, did you?"

"No, but it didn't go well." Sonny ran his hand through his hair and pushed the images of her mother out of his head. "I need to talk to Antony before he goes in to see Robert over at Hanson's."

"We'll make it."

TEN

ANTONY SAT IN the parking lot of Hanson's, opened the folder and read its contents. He looked around and tried to figure out why this was so important to his father. The land was prime, but what else would you put on it? Hanson's wasn't hurting for money although they could use money to update and expand.

He shook his head. Something else was behind this. Lorenzo kept trying to buy it and Sonny kept blocking it. Maybe it was Lorenzo's way of seeing whose side Antony was on.

He tossed the folder on the seat. Whose side was he on? He wanted to be accepted, forgiven, and even loved by his father, but doubted that would ever happen. But Sonny was his brother. He'd die for Sonny and proved it over and over again. But did that mean he should sit back and let Sonny take everything that was rightfully his?

The passenger side door opened. He pulled his gun before he realized it was his brother.

Sonny's eyes widened. "You do have people you owe."

"Just a reaction. Someone jumps in your car unexpectedly you'd pull yours, too."

Sonny grabbed the folder and handed it to Antony as he slid into the car.

Antony held it up. "Why do you want to save this company so bad, and why does Papa want it?"

"Did you just call him Papa? I haven't heard you call him that since you got here."

"Slip of the tongue. What's the deal?"

Sonny looked out the window then back at him. "It's more of a power struggle then anything. He barks an order, and you're expected to follow. I can't do it, not all the time.

This company's solid. There's no reason to buy it and put it out of business."

Antony nodded. "I looked around. It looks like good real estate, but what would Lorenzo want it for?"

"To prove to me that he can get it."

Antony nodded. Sounded like their dad. "So, why are you here? To try and talk me out of getting it?"

"No, I had an idea."

"What?"

"Ever since Papa has had his eye on this, Clay and I have been trying to get Robert to move the company."

"What have you offered him?"

"Any help we could, but he won't budge." Sonny rubbed his hands together. "I'm afraid that through our negotiations, Robert has figured out that I like the company and won't come in and take over."

"He found out you're soft." Antony grinned.

"Yeah, something like that. You have a presence. You act like, you, and he'll know you're not bluffing."

"Because I won't be. I'll do whatever it takes to get this company to prove to Lorenzo..." Antony shook his head. "I don't know what it'll prove to Lorenzo. I guess that I'll take orders."

Sonny hit his leg. "We won't have to take them all our lives. He'll have to step down sometime."

"I can't believe you said that. I thought you were so devoted."

"I love him, but I can't wait to run Renato's the way it was meant to be run."

"*You* run Renato's?"

Sonny grinned. "*We* run Renato's."

Antony nodded toward the factory. "I won't walk in there without walking out with something for myself."

"I didn't figure you would. That's where all those years of college come in." He handed Antony a piece of paper. "You decide what you want. Bill, in legal, give him a little bonus on the side, and he'll draw up any contracts for you without telling Lorenzo. Don't trust the others."

"Thanks."

Sonny opened the car door.

"Hey," Antony grabbed Sonny's arm. "About Victoria. What was that all about at lunch? I could tell she had been crying."

"It was nothing. I need to get back so Lorenzo knows you're working on this. I'll meet you at Renato's."

Antony nodded. He waited until Sonny left then climbed out of the car and walked into the office building.

He tapped on the receptionist's desk. "Antony Luciano to see Robert Hanson."

"Is he expecting you?"

"No." He smiled. "Just tell him Antony Luciano is here to see him."

He walked into the lobby with his hands in his pockets and waited.

Robert Hanson soon appeared. He was tall and thin. Younger than Antony thought he'd be. He held his hand out and Antony shook it. "Don't think I've ever met you. Robert Hanson."

"Antony Luciano. Lorenzo's oldest son."

Robert motioned for Antony to follow. They went into a large office where Robert sat down behind his desk. "What can I do for you?"

Antony shut the office door. "It's more of what I can do for you. Lorenzo came to me with this deal because my brother has gone easy on you. Renato's wants this land and we get what we want. The choice is yours on how we do that." Antony took his jacket off exposing his holstered gun. "May I sit?"

"Please do." Robert stared at the gun.

"I've had your company checked out. I've looked at the profit and loss statements and I would agree with my brother, you've got a good business here."

"Then why close it down?" Robert asked.

"Because my dad wants it, and he gets what he wants. The only thing you need to decide is if you want to save it or not."

"Save it?"

"I'm giving you two options. One, I come in and shut you down."

"Or?"

"You find another piece of land and we move your company."

Robert leaned back in his chair. "Same thing your brother wanted to do."

Antony stood and leaned into him, his face hard. "Only I don't have a heart. I'll shut your doors by the end of tomorrow, trust me." He placed his hands in his pockets. "Your choice."

Robert's face turned white. "How exactly do you think I could move my operation? You guys have never offered me enough money to move it even if I had agreed."

"You've been dealing with the wrong guys." Antony pulled a toothpick from his pocket and rolled it across his tongue. "I'm willing to help you, only I want a piece of the action."

"What?" Robert eye's narrowed.

"You can find some land." Antony walked to the edge of the desk. "You've probably already got a place in mind. Use the money Renato's gives you, and I'll invest the rest. Me, personally."

"What's in it for you?"

Antony laughed. "A piece of all this."

Robert stared at him. "How much of a piece?"

"60-40."

That brought Robert to his feet. "No way. Maybe 30-70."

Antony laughed. "I'm willing to give you enough money to not only move to a better location, but upgrade your equipment. Fifty-fifty split."

Robert walked to the window and stared out.

Antony could only imagine what thoughts were running through his head. Robert's grandfather started this company and he had kept it going through some very hard times and made it a success. The last thing he'd want would be to lose control.

And Antony would settle for 40-60, which he was confident would be Robert's next offer. He'd wait.

Robert turned. "40-60. I keep total control of operations. No interference."

Antony nodded, holding out his hand. "No problem there."

"This is between us. Not your father."

"Just us. I'll fund this with my own money, not Renato's. Deal?"

Robert nodded and shook Antony's hand.

Antony pulled out the contract his father had given him. "Here are the papers on the sale to Renato's."

"What about the other contract, between me and you. I'm not signing this before I sign the other."

"The other hasn't been drawn up, but you can trust me."

"I don't know you enough to trust you. I'll sign them both together."

Antony nodded. "I guess I can't fault you for that, but in the future, you can trust me."

Robert nodded. "Why do I feel like I've just made a deal with the devil?"

Antony slid his jacket on. "Trust and loyalty. It's all I require. I think you'll like me as your silent partner."

"Silent? I doubt that."

Antony laughed. "I'll see you later this afternoon."

* * *

Antony grabbed his cell and called Sonny as he drove to Renato's. "Deal's done. I need to meet with Bill and get another contract drawn up."

"I'll meet you in the lobby to give you the tour, that way it won't raise any suspicions on why you're going to legal. I'm sure Papa has spies everywhere. He'll be watching you for a while."

"Great."

"He shadowed me when I first started."

"I'm here. Be inside in a minute." Antony parked and got out. He stared up at the five-story building, shaking his head. Hard to believe he was finally walking into his place of destiny.

Sonny opened the front door. "Come on. I do have a job, you know."

Antony followed him, not really paying much attention to the tour until they got to legal.

Sonny tapped on the door of Bill Maxwell's office then stuck his head in. "Got a minute?"

Bill smiled. "Always, come in." He stood, walked around the desk and shut the door behind them.

Antony couldn't tell whether the young man's hair was styled or just messy, but his clothes were impeccable.

"Bill, this is Antony, my brother."

"The long-lost Luciano. I've got papers for you, accounts, your shares and holdings." He opened a cabinet and pulled out a large expandable file folder.

"Great." Antony took it. "Sonny tells me you're the go-to guy to write me up a contract."

"And you don't want Lorenzo knowing." Bill smiled. "Not a problem. What you got going?"

"Hanson's is selling. The contract from Renato's is good, and I'll be turning that over to Lorenzo today."

"You got him to sign it?" Sonny raised an eyebrow. "How?"

"I offered to invest my own money in the new location."

"What do you get?" Bill scribbled notes on a pad of paper.

"40-60 cut."

Sonny smiled. "Not bad. How'd you get so much?"

"I can persuade." Antony took off his jacket and laid it across the chair, exposing the Glock. "It's the best move you can make in negotiations." He laughed as Sonny shook his head.

"That'd persuade me." Bill stared at the gun, his eyes wide. "You get any control?"

"Nope, don't want any. Just the profits."

"You agree on a buy back?"

Antony shook his head. "Nope, didn't even discuss it. Didn't talk about much after the jacket came off."

They laughed.

"I'm gonna like this guy." Antony pointed at Bill. He turned back to Bill. "What's your fee?"

"Whatever you feel comfortable with. Cash, if you don't mind. You can pay me after I get this drawn up. I'm assuming you want it ASAP?"

"Please."

"How about if I run it up to your office when I'm done. Give me an hour?"

"Sounds good. You know where I'm located?"

Bill laughed. "Everyone knows, memo went out this morning."

Antony nodded, a grin on his face.

He followed Sonny out of Bill's office, up to the fifth floor.

"Here it is." Sonny motioned to the office door.

Antony stood for a moment as he stared at the oversized doors. "You sure this is mine? I figured Lorenzo would give me a hole in the wall."

Sonny opened the door and walked in. "If he had his way, you would be in the basement, but he knows the only way to get respect is to have you appear to be the long-lost son who finally saw the light."

"That's how he's portraying me?"

"It's nothing he ever talks about, but it was rumored to keep the overall image going. You've got to be in an office as big as mine, but not as big as his."

Antony stood in the center of the large office. High ceilings were surrounded by deep mahogany crown molding that accented the cream-colored walls. The wall-sized windows faced the ocean, which gave an unparalleled view of Anacapa Island.

"Diana is your secretary. She'll help you get settled in. Here," Sonny handed him a piece of paper. "It's the number of a good real estate agent for house hunting. I've got some meetings. If you need anything, let me know."

Antony nodded and waited until he left. He pulled out his cell phone and called Bosco. "I'm at Renato's, fifth floor. I'll let them know you're coming. You're checking the office first and I need cash. I'll text you the amount."

He slid his phone in his pocket and walked out of the office to a smaller desk where a slender brunette sat. He guessed she was in her late twenty's. "Diana?"

"Yes, Mr. Luciano?" She stood and smiled. "Mr. Luciano…I mean, your bother, told me I'd be working for you."

"I've got a guy coming up, Bosco. Let them know downstairs."

She nodded. "Anything else? Things you want to go over?"

"Later." He walked back into the office, looked around and shook his head. The office was bigger than the entire rat hole he lived in back in KC. He pushed his hands deep in his pockets, took a deep breath and slowly released it. He had finally made it.

ELEVEN

ZOË RELAXED ON THE couch of the two-bedroom beachfront house she'd bought with her share of Dad's life insurance money as a down payment. The only part of the house she could brag about was the beach. Someday, the fixer upper would show off her designing abilities.

It lacked in exterior and interior décor, but possessed some essentials—a flat screen TV with cable, a couch, and a bed. On the coffee table lay the plaque from the ceremony, two warm cokes and a half-eaten pizza.

Martin came out of the kitchen with a bottle of water. "We should take a walk on the beach."

"Later. Come sit." She patted the couch next to her.

He obeyed, put his arm around her, and pulled her to him. They kissed.

"This is much better than a walk on the beach."

He brushed her straight blond hair from her face. "Was that Sonny Luciano I saw you talking to earlier?"

"Yeah, my sister's dating him. I just met his brother Antony today. He came from KC. He's got a pretty good rap sheet. Nothing they could make stick, though." Zoë pulled away from him. "Why?"

"Just wondering."

She grinned. "You want to make detective pretty bad. Maybe his collar could help you along?"

"No, although that does give me an idea."

She playfully smacked him. "I won't let you use my family to further your career."

"They're not your family."

"Not yet, but Sonny's gonna ask Vic to marry him."

"Will she accept?"

"I don't know, probably. She claims to love him. I do know he can give her the security she craves."

"And you, what do you crave?"

"I have to tell you?"

Martin laughed, stood, and pulled her up. "Come on. We have to be on duty in a few hours. Let's take that walk."

Zoë sighed. "A walk on the beach. Wouldn't you know I'd pick a romantic. You know what the brass would do if they caught us together? Our partnership would be over. I'm thinking we shouldn't be outside at all."

"We can be friends and partners, you know. And if anyone gets suspicious you can go out with Antony, get some dirt on him, and help me make detective."

"Ha, ha." She walked to the door and took his hand.

He dropped it. "Not in public."

"Sorry." She smiled as they walked out the back door and onto the beach.

* * *

Antony leaned back in the leather chair behind the mahogany desk. The contents of the expandable file lay scattered about. The bank's legal papers bothered him. Papa's name was on every account. He'd have to get that changed.

Diana buzzed him. "Mr. Bosco's here."

"Thanks, send him in."

Bosco whistled as he looked around. "Man, you always said you were rich, but I guess I never really knew how much."

Antony gave him a firm handshake and slapped him hard on the arm. "I always told you to trust me, didn't I?"

"You know I do."

"I need the place swept."

Bosco laid a large duffle bag on the desk and pulled out a plastic briefcase that held a camera and a bug detector. After going over every inch of the room, twice over the phone, he gave Antony a nod. "You're clean." He put the equipment back and scooted the duffle bag toward him. "Your cash."

Antony counted out ten thousand. "Here."

"What for? We're square."

"Just take the money. Call it a bonus."

Bosco nodded. "What else can I do?"

He handed Bosco the name of the realtor Sonny gave him. "Give her a call and see what she's got. Line up some things to look at. Safe room, if you can find any with them."

"Got it." Bosco slid a hand in his pocket. "Boss, I got a favor to ask."

"What?"

"I not only owe you for my life, but also my brother's." Bosco cracked his knuckles. He ran a hand over his military buzzed hair, his arms the size of tree trunks. "I'm loyal, you know that."

"You talk to Pete since you got to town?" Antony asked.

"Not yet. Thought I'd wait and see what we got going."

Antony smiled. Bosco was devoted and would even forgo a relationship with his cop brother to work for him. "What's the favor?"

"My cousin just got done with a tour in Afghanistan and needs a job. I think he'd be good for you. Ex-special forces."

Antony was always on the lookout for good devoted men. "You trust him completely?"

"Oh yeah and he knows how to take orders."

"Bring him on board." Antony walked him to the door. "I'll call you later."

Bosco walked out as Bill emerged from the elevator.

"Come on in." Antony closed the office door.

Bill handed him the contract. "It's all there. Just need's signatures."

"Thanks. I got one more question." Antony grabbed some papers off his desk. "These accounts all have mine and Lorenzo's name on it. Does this mean he can get his hands on it?"

"Only in the event of your death. Otherwise, he can't touch it. But you can change who that reverts to."

Antony nodded. Last thing he wanted, dead or alive, was Lorenzo anywhere near his money.

"Here," Bill handed him a business card. "On the back is the name of a banker you'll like. He'll make you loans without Lorenzo knowing. Sonny likes him. You could ask him about changing those accounts."

"Thanks. It's nice to know who I can trust. Here." Antony handed him five grand.

Bill's eyebrows wrinkled.

Antony walked around the desk. "It's not enough?"

"Oh, no." Bill looked up at Antony. "Sonny's never paid this much, maybe I shouldn't—"

"No, keep it. Call it a sign-on bonus." Antony smiled and reached out his hand. They shook. "I like to know who I can trust and I'm glad I can trust you."

"You can, Mr. Luciano."

As Bill left, Antony slid the contract in with the other, returned the papers into the expandable folder then buzzed Diana in.

"Yes, Mr. Luciano?"

"It's Antony, please. Have a seat." He reached into the duffle bag and pulled out the other five grand, set it on the desk, and put the duffle bag on the floor. "I wanted to go over a few things with you, if that's all right."

She nodded.

"If you work for me then you don't answer to Lorenzo or Sonny. Understood?"

"Yes."

"Bosco can come and go as he pleases. I trust him with my life. He's kinda like Clay is to Sonny."

"I understand."

"This is for you." He handed her the money.

"Oh, Mr.—I mean, Antony, I couldn't."

"I want you to take it. It's five thousand dollars. I must be able to trust you, completely."

"You can trust me. I work for you, but you don't have to give me extra money."

"I'd like you to have it anyway." He scooted it toward her.

She didn't move.

He couldn't believe she'd turn down the money. Could a person be loyal without being paid off? It was a concept the people from the world he lived in wouldn't even consider. He had always paid for everything.

"You really don't have to do that. I've worked for your brother on many projects your father knew nothing about."

"What if there's a project I don't want my brother to know about?"

"Then I won't tell him."

"Okay." It still made him uneasy. He'd keep a close eye on her. "I'm taking this contract back over to Hanson's then I'm heading over to Lorenzo's so I'll see you tomorrow."

Diana pointed to his folders with her pen. "Do you want me to get you a briefcase? I can have the office supply send one over."

"Sure. Something in black."

She left.

He took the five thousand dollars, slid it into his suit jacket, grabbed the folders, and headed out.

* * *

Sonny rang the bell of the large tan stucco house and waited. A man opened the door, gave him a nod and led him into the living room.

An old four-by-six picture frame sat on the fireplace showing off two little girls, a man in uniform and a woman. Alias Amelia Cohan. Real name, Susanne Stone. Victoria and Zoë's mom.

"Sonny?" Her voice was soft as she walked into the room.

He replaced the picture he'd picked up. "Hello." He gave her a hug.

"How's Victoria?" she asked.

"Good. I saw Zoë today."

She smiled, motioning for him to sit. "How is she?"

"She looked good. There was a ceremony to honor Philip for his years in the police force. Zoë's working on becoming a detective." He stood and paced with hands in fists. "This is stupid. You're alive. You should be talking to them yourself."

He never figured finding her would cause him such heartache. All he had wanted to do was surprise Victoria and give her the one thing she wanted. Her mother. He had no idea it would lead him to lie to the woman he loved.

Susanne took a deep breath and slowly released it. "As much as I'd like to, I can't. You know that."

"I won't protect you forever without telling her."

"You can't say anything." Susanne walked to the window. "Why did you come here?"

"Victoria asked me to find you, again. She knows I can. I have the resources. It makes me sick to hide this from her. If she ever finds out, she'll hate me."

Susanne sat on the couch. "She must never know. You shouldn't even be here. If anyone followed you—"

"No one followed me." He wasn't stupid. Looking over his shoulder was a given with his father's past, even though he'd never admit that to anyone. "You're safe."

"For now. If they ever find me..."

"They won't. I won't let them."

"I don't know. If they find out I'm alive, they might go after Zoë and Victoria. I can't put them in danger. Everyone has to keep thinking I'm dead."

"I love Victoria. I can protect her, Zoë, and you."

"No. I won't put my daughters' lives on the line."

Sonny sighed. "Do you need anything?"

"I just need you to make my daughter happy."

"She loved the jewelry box. Thank you for giving it to me."

"She didn't recognize it as mine?"

"No, but she was surprised that I found one just like yours." He shook his head. "I hate lying to her."

"You have to, to keep her safe."

"I should go." He stood.

Susanne hugged him. "Thank you. Remind her how much I loved her." Her eyes filled with tears.

"I will. Really, my family can protect all of you."

"No. I'll live with the consequences. Someday, when I'm gone, you can explain it all to her."

"I'd rather you do that."

"I know. Thanks, Sonny."

He spun around and went back out to the car.

Clay got in and they left. "What'd she say?"

"She doesn't want them to know. Not yet, anyway."

"What's she think she's going to do? Hide all her life?" Clay shook his head.

"I don't know. She could. If Victoria finds out I know her mother is alive and didn't tell her, she'll hate me."

"She won't find out."

"I hope you're right."

TWELVE

AT HER DESK, Victoria pulled a red rose from the vase of flowers Sonny had sent. The arrangement of two-dozen crimson blooms looked regal and elegant next the wilting roses Antony had sent the other day.

The flowers were Sonny's apology for refusing to look for her mother. Frankly, she was tired of accepting it. It made no sense. It'd take one phone call from Sonny, throw around the Luciano name, and she'd have her answers.

She dropped the stem and paced. If she had any money left, she'd do it herself but she'd already drained her dad's life insurance money and savings on PI's. All of it gone.

The emptiness was something she tried to keep buried deep within her so she wouldn't feel this way. With a heavy sigh, she wiped away the tears, stepped to the window, and looked outside.

The tap on the door made her spin around. "Yes?"

Antony strutted in with a devilish grin. "I was going to call, but thought coming by would be better. Flowers?" He pointed to them. "Sonny forgiven?"

"I guess." She sighed and sat on the ivory leather couch.

He settled in next to her. "You don't sound convincing. You look like you've been crying, again. Was Sonny giving you a hard time about me coming over?"

"No, I mean, he wasn't happy about that, but that's not why I'm angry."

"Oh." Antony rested his arm on the back of the couch. "So you're angry with him?" He grinned.

"Angry. Sad. I just don't understand."

"Understand what?"

There was something about Antony that made her want to pour out her soul. He was genuinely concerned about what was going on, almost to the point of obsession, but not in a creepy kind of way. "Why are you so easy to talk to? I hardly know you."

He touched her shoulder. "This is what I was talking about. There's a connection. It was there the first time we met. You can't tell me you don't feel it."

She smiled. "I do feel it but it doesn't mean I can just stop loving Sonny."

"I wouldn't expect you, too. But even with you loving Sonny, we can still have this."

"A friendship?" She looked at his eyes. They wanted more than a friendship, but she believed he'd respect her boundaries.

"You know, I don't have any here."

"Here?" She laughed.

"Okay, anywhere." He winked, stood and removed his suit jacket. "You gonna tell me what my brother said that has made you so upset?"

Her gaze drifted down to his gun. Maybe he would help her. It was obvious he was attracted to her and he had the loyalty thing going, Sonny had assured her of that.

"What?" He grabbed a chair. "Does my gun bother you?"

"No, I was just thinking."

"I won't snuff out my brother no matter how badly he hurt you."

She gave him a playfully smack. "I wasn't thinking that."

"Then tell me."

"Your questions about my mom last night got me wondering again. What really happened to her? My father did everything he could to find out. I've tried. I hired a couple of not-so-good PI's. I asked Sonny for his help today. He's said no before and today wasn't any different."

"He won't help you?" When she nodded he looked puzzled. "If you were my girlfriend, I'd have already found her."

She sauntered to the window knowing she'd have to play this just right. A mix of flirting and heart felt sadness.

Sensing him behind her, she turned, took his hand and looked deep into his eyes. "Would you help me?"

He entangled his fingers in hers. A provocative grin deepening. "Are you using me?"

"Not using. Asking for a favor. Sonny said you're loyal to those you love."

"And you think I love you?"

"I didn't say that." She tried to blink away the tears. "But we are friends. There's that connection… Would you help me?"

He brushed her hair from her face. "This is really bothering you, isn't it?"

"I'd do anything to know what happened to her. I'll pay you back any money you spend. I promise."

He cupped his hand around the back of her neck and pulled her into a hug. "I'll find out what happened to your mother."

"You will?"

"Of course. And you don't have to repay me for anything." He backed away. "I'm assuming you don't want Sonny to know."

Their eyes met. "If you don't mind."

He raised his eyebrows. "Keeping a secret about you from him? I don't mind at all. It might come in handy someday."

Victoria looked into his eyes and detected softness beyond their hardened exterior. There was a heart in there when it wasn't masked by drive and determination. She knew he would go to any lengths to accomplish his agenda.

"I'll get on it." He winked.

"Thanks." She wiped the single tear that escaped and rolled along her cheek.

"I gotta go." He grabbed his jacket and slipped it on.

"How'd it go with that deal?"

"Getting the papers signed now, then I'll drop them off at Lorenzo's. Not bad for my first day."

"It didn't make Sonny too mad, did it?"

"We compromised."

"Good." She smiled.

"I'll let you know if I find out anything."

"Thanks, again."

* * *

Antony strutted through the store. Lauren stood near the door. Her flirtatious grin made his heart quicken. She was beautiful. A body perfectly proportioned, like a Victoria Secret model.

"Hey, handsome. Thought you were going to call me?" Lauren seductively licked her lips.

"I came by instead. What time you get off?"

"How about you pick me up in an hour." She looped her arm through his.

"Give me two. I'll come by your place. I've got a couple of things I need to finish up."

"You still got the address?"

He grinned. "Sure do. See you then."

Once back at Hanson's, Antony tapped on the receptionist's desk as she buzzed Robert.

Robert rounded the corner and extended his hand. "Antony."

Antony shook his hand, followed Robert into the office and closed the door. He slid both contracts on the desk and sat.

the papers and paced as he read them. The only ▃▃▃ the ticking of the clock. When he appeared ▃▃▃ ▃obled his name on the lines highlighted in ▃▃▃ ▃d them back to Antony.

▃ny stood. "You won't regret this."

"Why do I feel I will?"

Antony cocked his head. "I don't know. You've got a line of credit, a way to upgrade your company, and make more money than ever."

"Less your cut."

Antony grinned. "I'll only be around if you need more money than the credit limit I've given you. This will succeed if you want it to. If you need help moving things, let me know. Renato's has trucks, cranes, stuff like that. I could get some boys over here."

Antony held out his hand. Robert shook it.

"You'll learn to like me," Antony said.

Robert nodded.

Antony left and drove back to Lorenzo's. He tucked his contract in the glove compartment and grabbed the one for Renato's.

Inside, he gave two quick knocks on his father's office and walked in.

Lorenzo looked up from his papers. "What do you want?"

Antony tossed the signed contract on his desk. "He'll be gone in ninety days."

Lorenzo picked up the contract, flipped to the back page, and looked over the signatures. He leaned back in his chair. "How'd you do this?"

Antony pulled his suit jacket back, rested one hand on his gun and the other on his waist. "I know how to persuade."

Lorenzo grunted a laugh. "You're definitely my son."

Antony wanted to grin but he didn't. Anytime Lorenzo paid a compliment a fierce backlash would follow. He'd wait.

When Lorenzo said nothing, Antony put one hand deep in his pocket. "Anything else for today?"

"No. You start on that job Sonny wanted you on?"

"First thing in the morning. I figured this took priority. I'll get started on Sonny's project tomorrow. Here or at Renato's?"

"Renato's." Lorenzo stared at his laptop.

Antony left, relieved. It was much easier to work without Lorenzo breathing down his neck. He called Bosco as he drove to Lauren's. "Meet me on the corner of Frances and Ocean."

Antony pulled into the convenient store, scribbled down some information he already knew about Victoria's mom and climbed out of the car as Bosco pulled in.

Bosco got out of his black Chevy truck with a second man who got out of the passenger side. He had dirty blond hair, built like a tank with an oversized nose and a crooked smile. "This is Doc," Bosco said.

Antony shook Doc's hand. "Nice to meet you. Bosco tell you how I work?"

"Yes, sir," Doc said.

"I trust Bosco. You screw up, you're done."

"Understood."

"What do you have for us?" Bosco asked.

Antony passed Bosco the paper. "I want to find out what happened to this woman. Cops have investigated. Check with your brother." Antony ran his hand through his hair. "You have to do this very quietly. If she's still alive, there's a reason she's hiding. If someone's after her, I don't want to stir anything up, at least not until I know what we're in for. Got it? They've killed one cop already who got too close."

Both men nodded.

Antony turned to Doc. "You only answer to me. Ever. About anything."

"Yes, sir."

"You find us a place to crash?" Antony asked Bosco.

"That real estate agent's got you couple places to look at tomorrow. I told her you'd call and let her know what time. I went by and saw them. One looks like a good set up. With a few minor changes we could make it work. Immediate possession if we want it."

"Good, thanks." Antony jiggled his keys. "Well, boys, I've got a date."

Bosco laughed. "You work fast my friend."

Antony raised a brow and grinned. "I gotta go."

* * *

Victoria left the store with a new hope. There was no doubt in her mind that Antony would find her mom.

Sonny leaned against her car with another bouquet of flowers. Her heart pounded. She did love him despite his refusal to help her.

She took the flowers buried her face in them and took a deep breath. The aroma was sweet. "You didn't have to give me more." She leaned in and kiss him. "But I love them anyway."

"Can we go somewhere and grab some dinner?"

"You don't have to meet with Lorenzo?"

"I told you yesterday, tonight we were going out." He grabbed her hand. "Come on, I'll drive."

Sonny drove them up the coast, finally pulling into the driveway of a large house. He stopped at the gate, rolled the window down and punched in a code. The gates opened to show off a modern house with white square pillars and lots of windows. The gates closed behind them and he pulled into the drive and killed the engine.

"Whose place is this?" Victoria asked.

"Mine. I bought it." He jogged around, opened her car door, reached out his hand and helped her out. "I've been working on buying it for months, and I finally got it. I can't wait for you to see it."

She held tightly to his hand as he opened the front door and led her inside. The great room included the living room, dining room and kitchen. It was painted light beige that brought warmth to the room. The entire wall facing the beach was made of glass.

"Wow, this is amazing." She looked out the window to a magnificent view of the ocean. "You bought this?"

"Yep. It's all mine."

"Did it come furnished?"

He shook his head. "No. Your sister's handiwork."

It was obvious Zoë added the colors and touches Victoria liked. "She did a beautiful job. Are you moving out?" She couldn't imagine Lorenzo letting him go without a fight.

"Well, not yet. And this is too far away to drive to work every day. I have my eye on a place in town. I may put an offer on it. I'd like to take you by, see what you think."

"Okay." She knew why he wanted her to go. To get her approval. He told her the first day they met he was going to marry her someday.

"Come on." He grabbed her hand. "Let me show you the rest of the place before we take a walk on the beach."

He led her through two bedrooms and a bath upstairs, two bedrooms and two baths on the main floor and the unfinished basement.

Out the French doors, down a few steps and they were onto the beach. She kicked off her shoes. "You going to lose yours?" She scrunched her toes in the sand. "It feels so good." She leaned into him. "Put your gun in your pocket."

"I didn't know you knew about that?" He sat on the last step, rolled his pants up, and yanked the Velcro gun case from his ankle. He took his shoes and socks off, stood, and slipped the gun in his pocket.

"Why didn't you tell me about the gun?" she asked.

Sonny shrugged and grabbed her hand. "I don't know. It never came up, I guess. How did you find out about it?"

"Saw it the other day as you were getting in the car."

He nodded.

The water rushed in, covered their feet then rushed away. It was refreshing, washing away the tensions of the day. She relaxed and entangled her fingers in his.

He stopped and brushed his knuckles on her cheeks. "I love you."

"I love you, too." She meant it. Despite the feelings Antony could stir in her, Sonny was the love of her life. She kissed him.

"I'm sorry I can't help you with your mother."

She squashed the rising anger. What did it matter now that Antony would do it? "I'm sure you have your reasons."

"Trust me, please." He ran his fingers through her hair. "You know I'd do anything for you. I just can't do this, not right now."

"It's okay. Really." She forced a smile.

He looked down at his watch. "You hungry?"

"Starving."

"Let's go eat."

*　　*　　*

Sonny sensed something odd. She gave up too easily. He clutched tightly to her hand and wondered if his brother was behind whatever was going on.

He grabbed their shoes, walked up the stairs onto the deck, and opened the French doors. The great room was filled with candles and the dining room table was set. The smell of steak and baked potato's floated in the air.

"What? How?" Victoria looked around.

He smiled. Janice had out done herself. "I have ways."

"You had this done while we were on the beach?"

"Yeah. You like?" He walked her to the dining room table, pulled out a chair and motioned for her to sit. He lifted the lids that covered the food on the table. "Let's eat."

She nodded.

Sonny gazed at her. Victoria was so beautiful. He had known the minute he met her that he would marry her. Sooner than later, so they could get on with their lives. He wanted to shower her with everything she loved, kids, dogs, horses, and security.

Tucking her hair behind her ear, her face turned red. "You're staring."

"Sorry. You're so beautiful. I wish…" He'd begged her too many times. He'd be patient.

"Wish what? That I'd meet your dad?"

He grinned and put a bite of steak in his mouth.

"Okay."

"What?" His eyes widened as he swallowed. "You're ready to meet him?"

"I've met your brother. I guess it's time I met Lorenzo."

He jumped out of his chair, pulled her to her feet and held her. "You just made me the happiest man alive." He kissed her. "Let's plan dinner at The Towers. I'll let you know what night works for Papa."

* * *

Antony rang the bell to the apartment.

Lauren opened the door, pulled Antony inside, and kissed him.

"Whoa." He backed away. "Getting a little ahead of ourselves, aren't we?"

She laughed, closed her eyes and leaned back in. He grabbed her cheeks and waited until she opened her eyes. When she did, he smiled. "I'm hungry."

She raised her eyebrows. "Me, too." Her fingers wandered over his chest.

"For food." She was going to be hard to control, but he liked her spunk. She'd keep his mind off of Victoria and look good on his arm. "Let's go." He let go of her face and grabbed her hand.

She followed him to his car and got in.

He glanced at her as he drove. "Anyplace particular you'd like to go?"

"Back to my condo." She grabbed his hand and entangled her fingers in his.

"Anyone ever tell you guys like it when you play hard to get?"

"Ah, that's the way you like it, huh? Okay." She pulled her hand from his. "I can play that game." She pointed to a club. "There."

Antony pulled up to the valet parking. He climbed out of the car, tossed his keys to the attendant while another attendant helped Lauren out. Antony grabbed her hand and walked in.

Twenty-foot ceilings covered a dance floor on the main level, and loud music came from huge speakers mounted high on the walls. Strobing lights of varying colors flashing through the air.

He leaned into Lauren. "Do they have food here? I really am hungry."

"Yes, love." She patted his chest and turned to the hostess. "Hey, Georgiana. Got a lounge open?"

"It will cost ya."

"Not a problem." She smiled at Antony.

"How much?" Antony pulled out his money clip. He slid out a hundred and handed it to her.

"Follow me."

They walked into a luxurious room. It had a HiDef TV, couches, a table and a fireplace. "Here you go." Georgiana motioned with her hand.

"Thanks."

Lauren sat on the couch and patted the spot next to him.

He smiled, his hands deep in his pockets, thankful the music was muffled so they could talk. Although by the way she was eyeballing him, she didn't want to talk. He laughed.

The waiter strolled in. "I'm Jonas. There is a fully stocked bar there, both alcoholic and non-alcoholic or I can get you something else." He handed Antony a menu.

Antony opened it. "Bottle of Dom. Shrimp cocktail and stuffed mushrooms." He glanced at Lauren. "You eating anything?"

"Nope, got a shoot next week."

He turned back to the waiter. "I'll take a steak, medium rare, garlic potatoes. Thanks." He handed the menu back to him. When he left, Antony walked to the couch and sat.

"So, you model? Is that your dream job?"

"Yeah." She scooted closer to him, ran her hand over his cheek then to the back of his neck and pulled him to her.

"Hey, can you stop." He raised his hand. "Quit the come-ons and talk. I want more than a plastic face and someone to be with. There's gotta be more to you then that."

She leaned away from him with a puzzled look. "What?"

"You can talk, can't you?"

She rolled her eyes. "You just don't seem like the type who wants someone to talk to."

Maybe she didn't have anything but a plastic face. Better to find out now then later. If there was no depth, he'd still keep her around. It was better than being lonely.

The waiter walked in with the appetizers. Antony looked over. "Can you bring that over here?" He pointed to a coffee table. "Thanks."

"So, was modeling always your dream?" He dipped the shrimp into the cocktail sauce and ate it.

She took the glass of champagne from the waiter. "Yeah, I guess. I was your typical Beverly Hills kid. Blond hair, nose job by fifteen, cheerleader. Then my parents lost most their money in some bad investments."

"That had to hurt."

"Dad killed himself. Mom sent me out on my first modeling job. It was fun, so it just grew on me."

"How'd you start working at Francesca's?"

"Fran, the owner, saw me on the runway. Offered me work when I wasn't modeling. It pays the rent. My modeling money is my mad money."

Antony offered her food but she shook her head. "You gotta eat something."

"This champagne has enough calories to make me run an extra mile or two tomorrow." She curled her legs under her and scooted over to him. "So, how about you? What's your dream?"

"To work for my dad, make lots of money, and do whatever I please." He looked up as the waiter set his steak down.

"So, you work for your dad. Doing what exactly?"

"Anything he says," Antony said.

"Not quite doing whatever you please, huh?" She sipped on her champagne.

He ate a piece of steak. "Not yet, but when the ol' man dies, I'll run the place. And I'm lining my pockets while I do it."

"You own part of the company?"

"Yeah, set up pretty good. Can't complain about the money. Course, I didn't do too bad on my own."

"What'd you do?"

"Worked at a bank and on the streets. Collection jobs for a friend."

She raised an eyebrow. "Collection? Like gambling debts?"

"Gambling, drugs, loans, anything my boss needed." He wiped his mouth and pushed the almost empty plate away from him. "Man, that was good."

She took another sip of her champagne.

He pointed to her. "You're a cheap date."

She laughed. "We gonna dance?"

"We can now." He stood and dropped his napkin on the plate, grabbed her hand and led her out onto the dance floor.

THIRTEEN

SONNY KNOCKED ON Antony's office door then walked in. "I'm going to pick up Vic. You bringing anyone?"

Antony looked up from his folder. "Yeah, Lauren's coming."

Sonny raised his eyebrows. "Lauren? You've gone out with her?"

"Yeah, a couple of times."

"And how'd that go?" He hoped well. It wasn't that he thought Lauren was a good choice for his brother, but maybe she would make him happy while he got settled. Who was he kidding? He was hoping it would keep his brother's eyes off Victoria.

"We had fun. She introduced me to some people." Antony glanced through a file. "What'd Vic think of the beach house?"

"She loved it."

"You pop the question?"

"No, not yet. We'll see how it goes with Papa."

"You think he'll scare her off?"

"If you haven't scared her off, I doubt Papa will." Sonny laughed. "I'll see you in an hour."

* * *

Antony sat in the corner of the Italian restaurant across from Pete, Bosco's brother, and his contact at the police station. "So," he slowly spun the glass of water on the table. "What do you got?"

"I was like you. It didn't add up. Judging by every report I read, they had a good life. A happy family. Susanne wouldn't have left voluntarily. I don't think she's dead because it appears they just stopped the investigation without giving a good reason. I did some more digging and I kept coming across a name. Tabor." He handed Antony a file folder.

Antony opened it. "Tabor. He's a judge?"

"Look." Pete leafed through the papers, pulled one out, and pointed. "Look at this."

Antony read it. "Susanne was his court reporter."

"Yeah. These say some of the cases he presided over were a bit shaky. Maybe someone roped Susanne into going undercover to investigate Tabor."

"Tabor ever get charged with anything?" Antony asked.

"No."

"You think things got bad and they took her off to witness protection?"

"Wouldn't surprise me." Pete sipped his pop. "I think Philip was on to Tabor with some new evidence when he was killed."

"Would they use a court reporter like that?" Antony leafed through the papers.

"Feds or cops? Either would use anyone to get their guy."

"What's your gut telling you? Witness protection, or is she running scared?"

"Maybe witness protection. If she is they've changed her name."

"Can you find her?" Antony asked.

"I think so."

"You know I'll make it worth your while."

"I have no doubt about that. You've been very generous so far."

"So, Bosco took care of you?"

"Yes." Pete gulped the last of his drink. "I'll keep digging."

"Be careful. Philip was killed investigating this."

"Yeah, but they'd expect that. It was his wife missing. I'm not related, nor did I have anything to do with the case at the time."

"But, I need you around."

Pete smiled. "I'll be careful."

* * *

Victoria held tightly to Sonny's hand as they rode the elevator up to the twenty-fifth floor. Her heart pounded and she couldn't decide who she was more nervous to see, Lorenzo or Antony.

She had waited all week for word from Antony on what he found out, but he never called. She texted him a few times but all she got back was short flattering messages.

Sonny and Victoria stepped off the elevator into the private club with deep maroon walls trimmed in rich mahogany. He led her through the hallway, past a dance floor where a couple swayed while a man played the piano, then took her into a private dining room.

Victoria smiled even though she thought she'd throw up. Lorenzo sat in his wheelchair, and a strange, scary looking man sat in the corner.

Antony stood as they walked in.

Lauren smiled.

Sonny led her over to Lorenzo. "Papa, this is Victoria."

Victoria held out her hand. "Nice to meet you."

Lorenzo's face was expressionless. He looked at Sonny, back at her, then gave her hand a firm shake. "Nice to meet you."

She looked at Antony. "Nice to see you, again." Then at Lauren. "Hi Lauren."

Amazing. Lauren went out on two dates with Antony and met Lorenzo all in less than a week and it had taken her almost a year before she let Sonny introduce her to his father.

The man in the corner stood. "I'm Vince." His voice was reprimanding.

"Sorry. Vic, this is Vince. He works for Papa."

"Nice to meet you, too."

Victoria hesitated at the table with two empty seats between Antony and Lorenzo. Which to sit by? The lion or the tiger? Both would devour her, but the choice was easy. She stood at the chair next to Antony. Sonny pulled it out and she sat.

The waiter came, took drink orders, and gave them menus.

Victoria leaned into Sonny. "What are you getting?"

"Thinking about the lamb? How about you?" He pointed. "You'd like the Steak Diane. It's really good."

She nodded.

"So," Lorenzo's voice bellowed around the room. "You work in retail, Victoria?"

She tried to slow her pounding heart. "Yes, at Francesca's. I'm in management as the owner's assistant. I also go to shows and do purchasing."

"And she designs clothes." Sonny sipped his water.

"I'd like to have my own line of clothing someday. Lauren works there also, when she's not modeling."

The waiter showed Lorenzo the bottle of wine then poured a small amount into his glass. Lorenzo swished it around before taking a drink. He nodded at the waiter who proceeded to fill everyone's glass.

Lauren smiled, her face perfect. "I have a gig this weekend. Get to model some make-up for a magazine."

"That's great," Victoria said.

Lorenzo gulped the wine.

The waiter returned and went around the table, taking orders. Victoria grabbed Sonny's hand under the table.

Sonny gave it a squeeze and leaned into her. "You want to dance?"

"Yes." They stood.

"Where are you going?" Lorenzo asked.

"We're going to dance." Sonny dropped his napkin on the table.

"Later. I want to talk to you about the Whitesburg deal."

The lines on Sonny's forehead deepened and she wondered if he would back down.

"Papa, the ladies don't want to hear about our business."

"Antony can take them. We need to talk."

Sonny looked over at Antony. His brother winked at him. "I'd love to take the girls dancing."

"No." Sonny looked back at Lorenzo. "We can talk after I dance with Victoria." He pulled her along to the dance floor before Lorenzo could respond.

Antony and Lauren followed.

"Way to stand up to him, little bro." Antony took Lauren in his arms.

Sonny pulled Victoria close and wrapped his arms around her.

She rested her head on his shoulder and could feel his muscles relax.

"Sorry about that," Sonny whispered in her ear.

"It's okay. It's gotta be hard standing up to him. You did good." She looked up into his eyes. "You know, he can't run our lives."

"Our lives." Sonny's grin deepened. "That sounds so good. I've got an appointment to look at that house here in Ventura tomorrow. Can you come with me?"

"You're buying another one?"

"Yes. The beach house is for weekends and vacations. This one is close to work and will be a permanent residence."

"Sure, I'd love to see it." She snuggled closer into his arms and relaxed. They felt right, good.

When the song ended, they stopped and clapped softly. He leaned into her and gave her a kiss. "I should go see what Papa wanted. I'll be right back."

She nodded and watched him walk back into the private room.

"Want to dance?" Antony said from behind her, his voice alluring.

She turned and looked up at him. "Where's Lauren?"

"Powder room." Antony took her hand and led her out on the floor.

"Doesn't your father want to go over that deal with you, too?"

"Nah." He pulled her closer. "Want to know what I found out?"

Her eyes widened. "Yes."

"Nothing concrete, but I think your mom is in the witness protection program."

Victoria stopped dancing and stared into his eyes. "So, she's alive?"

Wrapping his arms back around her, he moved to the music. "I think so. They probably need her to testify, so they're keeping her hidden."

"Why would she leave us for that?"

"Witness protection? She'd have to, and she wouldn't want all of you guys to go into hiding. What a way to live, always looking over your shoulder. You would've hated it. Zoë and your dad would've hated it. I'm sure she didn't want to put you guys through that."

"Can you find her without tipping off whoever she's hiding from?"

The left side of his face went up into a grin. "I'm Antony Luciano. I can do anything."

His cockiness filled the entire room as he pulled her back to him.

A smile spread across her face and she leaned her head on his chest. She would see her mother again.

"You happy?" he whispered in her ear.

"Yeah." She pulled away and smiled up at him. "Thank you."

"That's what friends do, right?"

"Yeah," she said, laughing.

"What's so funny?"

"The only time you seem lacking in confidence is when you talk about being friends."

"I don't have friends. I have a couple of guys I'd trust with my life, but where I come from, anyone else could turn on you in a second." His face grew serious. "You won't turn on me, will you?"

"No, I won't."

"No matter what you hear about me or what you think I've done?" He cupped her cheek.

"No matter what you've done."

He nodded.

A hand laid on his shoulder. He turned and grinned. "Sonny."

She pulled away from Antony and looked at Sonny. The lines were deep on his forehead.

"You done talking to Lorenzo?" Antony asked.

"Yeah. Food's here."

Lauren stood on the edge of the dance floor, her arms crossed, tapping her foot like a spoiled school-girl.

"You guys go ahead. I want one more dance." Victoria grabbed Sonny's hand and pulled him close. His hands finally came around her. When she felt him begin to relax she looked up. "How'd it go?"

"Good. Stupid. There was nothing he wanted to talk to me about. Nothing important. He just likes to see if I'll obey his every order. Drives me crazy. What were you and Antony talking about?"

"Nothing, really. He was going on about loyalty and asked if he could trust me, stuff like that." She laughed, hoping he wouldn't pursue it.

"Sounds like Antony."

* * *

Sonny could sense something more was going on. Antony wanted her. Whether it was love or not, he wasn't sure. The only thing bothering him was that couldn't read Victoria.

He stopped dancing and looked at her. "I love you. You know that, don't you?"

She touched his face. "I know."

"Then why won't you tell me what you two were really talking about? It looked like a pretty deep conversation. Even Lauren was ticked. What's going on with you guys?"

"Nothing. We're friends, okay?"

He shook his head. He didn't believe it.

"That's what we were talking about. Being friends. He said he's never had a friend and he asked if I'd be one. Sounds crazy, I know, but he gets pretty intense. He was asking if he could trust me. I told him he could. It's no big deal, okay?"

Sonny nodded. His question shouldn't have made her mad unless there was something more to it.

She stopped dancing and put her hand on her hips. "Do you think I'm lying to you when I say I love you?"

"No, I trust you."

"Then act like it."

He took her hand and led her to the large window that overlooked the city. "I do trust you, but I can also see the way he looks at you. I believe he thinks he's in love with you."

"And what? You think I secretly want him instead of you?"

He looked away from her. It sounded stupid and childish, but he'd own up to it. "Yeah, part of me thinks that."

"I'll admit, he says things that are enticing, but I love you. I want to be with you." She kissed him. "Not him. I'm trying to fit into your family. He is your brother and wants a friend. Apparently, he has none."

"Okay." He put his hand on the back of her head, his fingers entangled in her hair and pulled her into a kiss.

"Ahem."

They turned.

Antony stood with hands in his pockets. "Sorry to break up the make-out session, but Lorenzo wants you two at the table."

"Okay." Heat filled Sonny's face. He grabbed her hand and ran his other through his hair. She was going to have to marry him soon. It was getting harder and harder to honor her wishes.

* * *

Victoria ate but couldn't help glancing at Lorenzo every so often. His eyes were hard and seemed to be glaring at her and Sonny. She wasn't quite sure what he was angry about. Sonny not obeying him and dancing with her or them not being around when the food came. Maybe he didn't like her. Perhaps he didn't like anyone.

Except for the giggles coming from Lauren as Antony whispered something in her ear, the table was quiet. The waiter finally picked up the empty plates and took desert orders.

Victoria opted for coffee while Lorenzo, Antony and Sonny went for the bananas foster.

"Lorenzo," she said. "Sonny told me you like to fish."

Lorenzo set the fork that held a bite of bananas foster on the plate. "Yeah."

"Where do you fish?"

He looked at her, his face hard. "I like the Delta for trout, but I prefer the ocean. Hook me anything that's big."

Victoria smiled and sipped her coffee.

"So, this thrift store you work at," Lorenzo slipped a bite of food in his mouth. "How long you been there?"

"Papa." Sonny protested but Victoria touched his arm.

"It's okay." Her heart pounded, but she took deep breaths to stay calm. She'd rather argue with him then have him glare at her in silence. "It's actually been compared to Chanel, Prada and Christian Dior. It's not a cheap place to shop."

"That's for sure." Antony grinned. "I bought three suits and spent over three grand."

"True, but you bought Armani and they look good on you, don't they Lauren?"

"Mmm hmm." Lauren's hand wandered the back of his neck. "They sure do. Course, anything would look good on him."

"So," Lorenzo took another bite of dessert. "How does one design a line of clothing?"

Her heart returned to a normal beat.

Sonny took her hand and squeezed it giving her an almost unnoticeable nod.

She sipped the coffee. "I draw the designs, pick out the fabrics and make them. If they're good enough, you have a runway show which will get the buyers to purchase them. Afterward, they put them in stores. I'd like to own my own boutique, like Francesca's someday. Maybe sell my line exclusively there."

"Might limit the profit." Lorenzo gulped the last of his drink. He wiped his mouth with the white napkin and tossed it on the table. "You gotta make a profit."

"True, I'll remember that." She looked around the table to see if anyone else would talk. No one did.

"We should be going." Sonny stood and took Victoria's hand.

Lorenzo nodded. "Why don't you guys get the car? I'd like to talk to Victoria alone for a moment."

Both Sonny and Antony's foreheads wrinkled.

Sonny shook his head. "We can all go."

"It's fine." Victoria waved them off. "Go get the car." She sat back down next to Lorenzo. When the room had cleared she looked at his hard, cold eyes. "What did you want to talk to me about?"

"You got money?"

"Not anything like you guys have. I work, and I live comfortably. Why? Do you think I'm after Sonny for his money?"

"Are you? Because I can fix it to where you'd never see a penny."

She clasped her hands together. "That would be fine, if that's what Sonny wants."

"So, you'd sign a prenup?"

"I'm not after your son for the money. I love him. As far as marriage? He hasn't asked, but if we decided to get married and he wants a prenup, I would have no problem signing it." Her grin deepened. "It might come in handy. If my clothing line sells like I hope, I may have more money than him."

Lorenzo tipped his head backward and let out a hardy laugh. It was a good sign. Maybe she had showed him that she wouldn't stand by and let him run her life. "Anything else?"

"Nope." He put his hands on the wheels of his chair.

She stood, grabbed the handles on the back and tried to help him.

"I got it," he barked.

Two steps forward and one back.

Sonny and Antony stood at the curb leaning against Lorenzo's car. Antony grinned at her while Sonny went to the door and opened it for them. Vince got out of the car and helped Lorenzo into the front seat then quickly folded the chair and placed it in the trunk.

Sonny took her hand. "You okay? What'd he say?"

"I'm fine." She gave Antony a wave. "Tell Lauren good night."

Antony nodded and walked to his car.

Sonny closed her door, jogged around to the other side, climbed in and took off.

* * *

Martin took the stairs two at a time up to the second floor offices of the police station. Pete sat in front of the computer screen at his desk. There were only a few detectives left, most had left for the day or were out on cases.

He pulled the chair up next to Pete, tossed a piece of paper on the desk. "I got this from a file Zoë had. It was the one Philip used."

"You must want to make detective pretty bad."

Martin leaned back in the chair. "Hey. I'm helping my ex-partner find out the truth. If I get a nice collar and a promotion out of it, then I'm all for it."

"Zoë know you have this?"

"No. I'll fill her in on a need to know basis."

Pete's face grew serious. "If you had ever pulled anything like this when we were partners, I'd have killed you."

Martin grinned. "Yeah, well, I owe you. You did get me out of some deep crap."

"Kept you outta jail."

"Kept me from making detective."

"That will all change after this." Pete held the piece of paper up. "When we're partners again, we'll be even."

They nodded at each other. It wasn't that Martin didn't enjoy being Zoë's partner, but since falling in love with her, things had changed. He worried too much about her getting hurt. He knew she'd never leave the force, but maybe not having to ride with her every day and see the danger she could get into would make it easier.

"So," Martin asked, "Is Sonny paying you for this info?"

"No."

"Victoria?"

"Nope." Pete punched the access code into the computer. "Well," he said with his finger on the enter key. "Here goes."

They both stared at the screen. When the file that said S. Stone came up they both smiled.

"Well," Martin said. "Open it."

Pete clicked on the file folder. It opened up. They both looked at the flashing red mixture of letters and numbers in the left hand corner of the screen. "Oh, crap." Pete stuck in his jump drive and copied the file to it.

"What?"

"You know what that means?"

"No." Martin stared at the flashing red file code.

"That means we just alerted the feds."

Martin ran his hand through his hair, his heart pounding. "How much time before they're on us?"

"Twenty-four hours, maybe forty-eight, if we're lucky." Pete pulled out a file folder, slid the jump drive into his pocket, shut the computer down and motioned with his head. "Come on."

Martin followed him out the door. They walked to his car. Pete handed him the file folder and the jump drive. "I need you to take this and research it. Feds will be all over me because they'll trace it back to my computer. I'm working for Antony Luciano. You answer to him and only him, you got it?"

"I don't answer to anyone."

"When I brought you in on this you agreed—"

"I didn't figure I'd be answering to some street punk with a rap sheet."

"He's not like that. The guy saved my life in KC." Pete shook his head. "He'll pay you well."

"I don't care about the money."

Red crept up Pete's neck. He ripped the folder and the jump drive out of Martin's hands. "Whatever. Just keep your mouth shut about what you know so far. I'll give this to Antony myself. You say anything about any of this, I'll make sure you never make detective, ever."

Martin's eyes narrowed. "I back up the badge. You know that."

"You can't trust anyone in there. I don't know who the feds have working on this. It's big so when they come to question you—"

"I know how to deal with the feds."

Pete nodded. "Thanks for the number. I'll fill you in on what I can when I can."

Martin sighed. Antony Luciano? He'd dug into his past. Killed two people that the cops knew about. One deemed an accident, one they couldn't pursue because of missing evidence. How convenient.

Antony had worked the streets with low life drug dealers and loan sharks. His father, a two-bit criminal, trying to go straight. Antony was scum.

But if he could close this case, the brass would love him. He'd finally prove himself. Every cop in his family wore the blue. He wanted to be a detective, possibly even work undercover. This could get him there.

And he couldn't forget Zoë. She never talked about it, but he knew she wanted to know the truth. He'd caught her digging into it, and forced her to stop. It was too dangerous for her to work on alone.

"Okay, give me the file." Martin stared into Pete's questioning eyes. "I'll work with Antony. He crosses the line he goes down. I'll take both collars."

Pete laughed. "I'm not asking you to break the law. Just help me out."

Martin took the jump drive and the folder.

Pete looked at him. "Whenever I text you about going out, meet me at Mikey's so we can talk. The more distance between us the better, but we have to keep each other informed."

Martin nodded. "I'll make dupes of these and put them in a safe deposit box."

"Good." Pete turned, stopped and turned back. "Thanks."

"No problem. That's what friends do."

* * *

Sonny pulled his car up next to Doc's at the gas station and rolled his window down. "Get in."

Doc obeyed, and Sonny rolled the darkly tinted window back up, shielding them from outside view.

Doc looked at him, his face hard. "What'd you need?"

"Information."

"And you think I'm going to give it to you?" Doc stared straight ahead. "Antony has been good to me."

Sonny glanced over at him. He knew he was the only one. From what Clay had dug up, Bosco had been with Antony since he hit the streets. Loyalty like that was strong. Doc only came on a few weeks ago. He might just be able to get the info he needed.

If Doc refused, the worst he could do was tell Antony. What did that matter? Antony admitted to investigating them, so why would his brother think Sonny wouldn't do the same.

"And you're okay with Antony's business practices?" Sonny asked.

"Your brother does what has to be done. It's hard to begrudge him that."

Sonny nodded. "I also do what needs done. I know he's got something going on, and I need to know what it is. So I can protect my family."

"Why would I tell you anything?"

"Because I've read your bio. You come from a long line of marines. You're all about integrity and protection. I love Victoria and would do anything for her. To keep her safe. If my brother is doing something that could jeopardize that, I'd like to know. I will pay you well and he'll never know."

"He'd know."

"If he does, you can come work for me."

Doc looked at him, his eyes narrowed. "Why would I trust you?"

"Why not? I've run a multi-million-dollar business for eight years. I've got no criminal background. My brother comes from the streets, collected debts for a loan shark and has been implicated in two murders. Yeah, he's so much more trustworthy." He shook his head. "Get out."

Doc hesitated.

Good, Sonny was getting to him. He softened his voice. "I really need to protect Victoria. I love her. If he's doing something that could hurt her, I need to know."

"You got my back if this goes bad?" Doc asked.

"Of course."

"We're investigating the disappearance of Victoria's mother, and we're getting close."

That explained a lot. The subtle glances of Vic and Antony over family dinners. She was searching for information. Antony didn't understand what her mother's reappearance could cause. His brother never thought ahead. He wanted Victoria and he'd do anything to win her.

"Thanks." Sonny handed him a stack of bills.

"You owe me if this goes bad."

Sonny nodded. "I need another favor." He ignored Doc's rolling eyes. "I want you to protect Victoria no matter what happens, you got it? If my brother finds Susanne, he has no idea the trouble it could cause. I'd feel better if I knew you were protecting her."

"I can when I'm around her, but if Antony calls me out on a job, I have to go."

"I understand that, but when she's around, you'll protect her?"

"Yes. And I expect to get paid."

"You will."

Doc nodded, got out of the car, and left.

Sonny waited a few minutes and took off.

FOURTEEN

SONNY HELD THE phone to his ear. "Yes, tonight. He really does want you to join us, again."

Victoria laughed. "He invited me?"

"Well, he said he didn't mind if you came."

"I never thought I'd be included in this weekly ritual."

He grinned. "Get used to it. So, I'll see you tonight?"

"Okay."

Sonny slid the cell phone back into his pocket when Clay came into the office.

"I met with Doc," Sonny said. "You're not going to believe what I just found out."

"What?"

"Antony is looking for Susanne, and he's getting close."

"Explains why Victoria gave up so easily."

Sonny paced the office. "I can't really blame her. She knew the Luciano name alone could find info that her father couldn't. I'd turned her down. Why wouldn't she go to Antony? It's apparent he'll do anything for her."

"She loves you," Clay said.

Sonny nodded. "Is he here?"

"No, but Diana said he's coming back."

"I'll wait for him in his office."

Sonny sat in Antony's chair behind his desk glancing through a folder when he heard the door unlock and open.

Antony's eyes narrowed and red crept up his neck. "How'd you get in here? I had this lock changed."

Sonny closed the folder and stood. "You forget. I'm a Luciano, too." He walked around the desk, took deep breaths, and tried to control his anger. "Call your men off."

The left side of Antony's mouth went up into a grin. "I'm not sure what you're talking about."

"You know exactly what I'm talking about. You're helping Victoria when I won't. Call them off."

Antony laughed. "Why would I call them off? I'm just doing what you won't do. Finding Vic's mom."

"Oh, it's Vic now?" Sonny paced the room. "You're unbelievable. You'd use this to try and win her from me?"

"You feeling a little uneasy in your relationship with her?"

He stopped and glared at Antony. "No."

"I'm doing a friend a favor." Antony's grin deepened. "You had your chance to help her, and you turned her down. What I can't understand is why?"

Sonny walked to the desk, picked up the phone and pushed it toward him. "Call your men off."

Antony shook his head. "No."

"You know her dad was killed trying to do what you're doing."

"I'm not scared." Antony sat down. "I figured living with Lorenzo all these years would've toughened you up."

"You have no idea who you're dealing with."

"Yeah, I do."

"No, you don't."

"My men are discreet. Don't worry about it."

"You don't understand." Sonny sighed. "I'm asking you, as my brother, call your men off."

"Has he threatened Victoria?"

"No."

Antony's eyes narrowed. "Then what are you scared of?"

"I'm not scared." Sonny shook his head and slid his hands deep in his pockets. "I've already found her."

Antony's eyes widened. "What?"

Sonny sat down. "I sent my men out to look for Susanne after Victoria's father was killed. I knew how much it'd mean for her to know the truth. I love her. Of course, I'd do anything for her."

"Then why haven't you told her?"

"I can't. Susanne has asked me not to. She's trying to protect her daughters." He ran his hand through his hair. "I talked with her again a couple of weeks ago, after Victoria asked me to find her. Susanne's still insisting I not tell her."

"So, you know where she's at right now?"

Sonny nodded. "Susanne doesn't want Victoria or Zoë to find her, or they could both be in danger."

"Then give them bodyguards, take Susanne to the safe house, anything. You have to tell Victoria."

"No. Susanne will go underground again if I go against her wishes. And I can't risk Vic's life. I'm asking you not to risk it either."

Antony leaned back in the chair.

Sonny pushed the phone at him again. "Call your men off."

"How'd you find her?"

"I have friends, too."

Antony pulled his cell phone out, hit a number and put it to his ear, "Hey, bring it in, I'll let you know." He hung up, looked at Sonny, "There, you happy?"

"No. You've gotten Victoria's hopes up."

"And what am I supposed to tell her?" Antony asked.

"Why didn't you come to me? Tell me what she was asking you to do?"

"I don't answer to you."

Sonny shook his head and looked out the window. He was glad Antony was back, but he knew he'd bring certain complications. He just hadn't expected those to involve his girlfriend. "Tell her you couldn't find her."

"She'd know I was lying."

Sonny turned to him. "And you won't lie to her?"

"No, and not just because I care about her. I am Antony Luciano. I can do anything. She knows I won't give up."

Sonny couldn't argue with that. "She may just think you found out she was dead."

"And that's what you think she should believe? That her mom is dead?" Antony shook his head. "Let me talk to Susanne. We can protect her."

"Then you're the hero."

Antony slammed his hand on the desk. "It's not about being the hero. Heck, you're already the hero for finding her. This is about Victoria knowing the truth."

"No matter what the cost?" Sonny did a quick pace of the room then stopped in front of Antony's desk. "Listen, you're not telling me anything I haven't argued with Susanne about. I offered Papa's safe room and living in our house. No one would ever find her there, but she wants no part of it. In fact, she almost ran off again after I found her. I assured her I wouldn't say anything to Vic or Zoë."

Antony leaned over the desk and rested his arms on it. "I can get Susanne to change her mind or we could just take her to Vic. You gotta convince her to come out of hiding or tell Victoria the truth."

"I'll try talking to Susanne. Give me some time."

"What can I do? I've got men."

Sonny shook his head. "Stay out of it. I'll let you know if I need your help." He looked down at his vibrating phone. "Vic's here. I'm bringing her to dinner tonight. You can tell her then."

"Tell her what?"

"That you're not looking for her mother anymore. You've hit a brick wall. Stall her. I don't want her to know anything, not yet."

Antony rolled his eyes before giving him a single nod.

Sonny turned and walked out.

* * *

Victoria stood in Sonny's office and stared out the window at the ocean. She wanted to run into Antony's office and ask him for an update, but she didn't want to arouse Sonny's suspicion. She'd wait.

"Hey." Sonny leaned in and kissed her. "I'm just about ready. I've got to take care of one more thing, then we can go."

"Okay. I'm going to use the restroom." She went into the huge bathroom that connected his and Antony's office. She heard voices coming from Antony's office. She leaned into the door and could hear Lorenzo.

"What the heck is this?" Lorenzo shouted. "You lined your pockets with Hanson money?"

A stream of Italian words came from Antony. Cuss words, she figured. "Got yourself a stooge, huh?" Antony yelled. "It won't take long to flush him out. I funded that factory with my own money. Not one penny from Renato's. It's a legitimate contract and my business. Has nothing to do with you."

"Everything you do is my business. I can't trust you," Lorenzo yelled.

"Oh, here we go again. Get a new record, old man. This one is getting old."

She heard a loud bang. Maybe a fist pounding on the desk then Lorenzo's voice. "You know why I can't trust you. You killed your mother. You killed Carlo. Don't roll your eyes at me. You can't deny it."

"I don't deny killing Carlo, but I did not kill Mama. You did that. I'm not going to rehash this with you. What happened, happened. I can't change it." His voice got louder. "Can we drop it?"

The handle turned and Victoria realized she hadn't locked both doors. She walked to the faucet and turned the water on as Antony opened the door.

He raked her over with a questionable gaze.

"Oh, you scared me." She smiled.

"Sorry. I didn't know you were in here."

"You okay?" She shut the water off and dried her hands. "Sounded intense in there."

Antony stepped closer to her. "Anytime he talks to me, it's intense. See you tonight." He winked.

"We'll talk?"

"Yes."

She let out a deep breath as he left. She went back into Sonny's office, pulled out her phone and Googled the names Antony Luciano, Carlo, Kansas City. Thousands of hits came up.

The KC Star article told about Antony accidentally killing his friend Carlo. Shot him in the chest while they wrestled with a gun. Lorenzo lost control of the car driving his wife and Carlo's parents, killing the three of them and paralyzing himself.

"That must be why Antony was kicked out. Lorenzo blames him for the death of their mother," she whispered.

Sonny came back into the office. She slid her phone in her pocket. He walked through the bathroom to Antony's office. "Vic and I are heading to the house. See you there."

* * *

Victoria sipped her water at the Luciano table. Things were strange. Lorenzo was in his normal I-hate-the-world mood. Sonny and Antony shot severe glances at each other. She wondered what was going on but doubted either one would tell her.

Lorenzo finally growled, "Sonny, I need to talk with you."

She guessed that to be the new normal. He'd done it the other times she was there. After dinner, he'd stolen Sonny for thirty minutes as his way of showing him or her, who was in charge.

Antony stood. "I'll give Victoria a tour of the garden."

She wanted to run to the garden to see if Antony had any information, but she waited for Sonny's approval.

Sonny leaned in and gave her a kiss. "I shouldn't be long. Enjoy the garden. It was once my mother's."

She squeezed his hand and nodded.

Antony led her out into the garden that was filled with roses, gardenias, and many other flowers too numerous to count. "Like Sonny said. This was our mom's garden at the old house in KC. The one I grew up in."

"Really." She looked around. "That must be weird, to see it after all these years."

"Very." They walked farther into it. Small lights lit the path as the house grew farther away. "Sonny said Lorenzo had it dug up and flown out."

"Didn't know you could do that." She looked back and couldn't see the house so she stopped. "Okay, enough. You're driving me crazy."

He turned to her, his grin deep. "I am?"

"Not like that." She playfully smacked his arm. "Have you found anything out? I haven't heard from you all week."

"And you've been missing me?"

She laughed at him. "Only what you can give me."

His eyebrows raised. "You have no idea what I could give you."

She shook her head and turned away from him, walking closer to the rose bushes. "You know what I meant."

* * *

Yeah, he knew what she meant. She wanted information and would do just about anything to get it. How could he lie to her? How could he squash her hopes like his brother did?

One option was to tell her the truth. That Sonny had known all these months and had been lying to her. But was that enough to make her change her mind and be with him?

Antony loved her and knew they'd be together someday. He wouldn't win her by hurting his brother. She had to want him as much as he wanted her, with her entire being.

The sweet scent of roses clung to the air. "Vic."

She turned toward him, her eyes flickering in the moonlight.

He stepped closer. Her face was soft and when she looked up at him, he succumbed to his desires, pulled her into his arms and placed his mouth over hers. His heart raced at the softness of her lips. Cupping the back of her neck, he pulled her into his very soul.

Antony felt her melt in his arms, and he was sure she felt the same way.

Victoria seemed to realize what was happening and pushed him away. "I can't."

He backed off. "I want to be with you." He held tight to her trembling hands.

"I can't. I'm with Sonny. I love him."

"You have feelings for me. Tell me you don't and I'll walk away."

"There's no denying the feelings I have for you," Victoria's voice was soft. "But—"

"But what?" Maybe it was something else. "Did you overhear Lorenzo and me fighting? You heard I killed Carlo, didn't you? You have to believe me, I didn't..."

"I know it was an accident." Her words were filled with love not condemnation. "I do love Sonny, but I think part of me loves you, too. But how can that be?" The tender sweetness of her expression pierced his soul.

"I'm not asking you to dump him. Okay, maybe I am." He winked. "At least give us a chance."

"I don't know. You confuse me." She took his hands. "Friends?"

He nodded and fought the urge to tell her the truth. That Sonny killed Carlo. That her mother was alive and Sonny was hiding her, but as much as he wanted to, he couldn't do it to his brother.

If a friendship was all he could have then he'd live with that, for now.

She turned from him.

He grabbed her arm, brought her back around, and gazed into her moist eyes. "I'm sorry. I didn't mean to upset you."

"It's okay. It's just hard to understand my feelings. I don't know how to explain them."

"Then don't try. I can't explain them either." The only thing he was sure about was that someday, they'd be together.

"Now," he rubbed his forehead then drug his hand down his face. "About your mom. I'm getting closer but I really don't have anything new to tell you. I'm sorry."

"Really? I was hoping..." She crossed her arms over her stomach. "Nothing."

He pulled her into a hug. "These things take time. Your dad was killed trying to find information. You know I have to do this slow and precise, so that I don't raise any suspicions."

This brought her eyes back to his. "I understand."

He touched her cheek. "You know I won't give up until you have all the answers."

She nodded. "Thank you. I can never repay you for this."

"I can think of a few ways." He laughed.

She reached up and kissed his cheek. "We should probably get back."

He motioned toward the house. "After you."

FIFTEEN

SONNY STOOD AT the French doors and watched Antony and Victoria stroll back toward the house. It broke his heart to see her wiping what looked like tears from her eyes. Maybe Antony was right, he should just tell her, but his fear of losing her the same way she lost her father was unacceptable. He couldn't put her in that kind of danger.

She smiled at him as she came inside. It looked forced. He took her hand. "You okay?"

"I should be going." She squeezed his hand and walked to the front door.

"Why?"

"I need to go."

At her car, he wrapped his arms around Victoria's waist and kissed her. Her response felt mechanical. Cupping her cheek, he stared into her sad eyes. "What's going on? Did Antony say something to upset you?"

"I'm just tired." She got in the car and left.

He hadn't thought she'd tell him what was going on, but it cut through him just the same. The secret was dividing them. The distance between them was growing, and he knew he had to tell her the truth. In the morning, he'd let Susanne know and take Victoria to her mother.

Antony came up next to him. "You happy now? I did what you wanted me to."

"What'd you say?"

"I told her that I didn't know anything new."

Sonny's brows furrowed. "That's it? That wouldn't make her run off like that about to break down in tears."

"You calling me a liar?"

"No, I just don't think you're telling me everything."

"Yeah, you'd think that." He pulled his phone out and read a text. "I gotta go."

Sonny waited until Antony pulled out of the driveway then got into his car and followed.

* * *

Antony's heart pounded. He had called the investigation off so why was he being summoned to the sports bar, by a number he didn't recognize. He called Bosco and Doc. "Meet me at Mikey's."

He glanced in his rearview mirror and recognized Sonny's car. He pulled into a convenience store, walked to Sonny's car as he drove in behind him and tapped on the window. "What's up bro?"

Sonny climbed out of the car. "Was about to ask you the same thing."

"Got business to take care of."

"With who? Victoria?"

Antony laughed and shook his head. "Man, you've gotten insecure over the years." His face grew serious. "This is business."

"What kind of business? Illegal?"

"No. Now go home."

"Not until you tell me what's going on."

Antony shook his head. "I can't because I'm not sure myself." Their eyes locked and he narrowed his. "Go home, now."

Sonny spun on his heels, got in his car and left.

Antony drove to Mikey's and waited for Bosco and Doc before climbing out of the car.

"What's up, boss?" Bosco said.

"Not sure. Meeting someone." He glared at Doc. "Sonny found out about the investigation. I've got an idea who leaked it and when I find out for sure, heads will roll. Now get in there and cover me."

Both men nodded. Bosco walked into the bar first. Antony waited a few minutes and walk in with Doc behind him.

The owner waved him over. Antony leaned closer across the counter.

"There's a man, asking for you. I put him in your usual spot," Mickey whispered.

"Thanks." Antony recognized the guy in the corner. He had stood on the stage with Zoë. A cop. When their eyes met, he gave him a nod that was returned.

Antony spoke over his shoulder in a low voice. "Doc, go sit." Antony went over to the cop and slid into the booth. "And you are?"

"Martin Tucker. I'm Zoë's partner." He extended his hand.

Antony shook it. "What can I do for you?"

"It's more of what I can do for you."

The waiter set down two glasses of water. "Can I get you anything, Mr. Luciano?"

Antony raised an eyebrow at Martin who shook his head. "We're fine, thanks James."

"You pay for good service." Martin grinned.

"It's nice to know who you can trust." Antony wondered how the cop got his number and the code that Pete had set up.

"Pete was my partner before he made detective."

Antony nodded.

"He said you saved his life."

"Yeah, back in KC. He was a young street cop. He didn't know much about the streets." Antony laughed. "Why are we here?"

"He needed an authorization number to get into a file," Martin said.

"And this involves me how?"

"The file was on Susanne Stone."

Antony's face remained emotionless. A trait he'd learned long ago. He took a sip of water and speculated as to how much Pete told him. "Why would that involve me?"

Martin leaned into him. "I know you're looking for Victoria and Zoë's mom. Finding Zoë's mom would be nice, but taking down Tabor is my goal. Pete needed a number to get into a file. Zoë didn't know what the number was for. I got it for him and now, I'm swimming in this as much as he is."

Antony nodded. "So, you got into the file?"

"Yeah, only problem is when we punched it in, it alerted the feds. They'll trace it back to Pete, so he's out. Looks like I'm your contact now."

Antony knew nothing about this guy, but if Pete trusted him, he guessed he should. Who was he kidding? It didn't matter what he thought, Martin was involved.

"I guess I gotta work with you," Antony finally said.

"You don't have a choice." Martin slid a folder and jump drive across the table. "This is for you. It's what we got from the file. I've made duplicate copies of these. I kept one and put the other in a safe deposit box at First National. The key." He laid it on the table.

"Have you looked at this stuff?"

"Briefly. I think you'll find it interesting. She was in witness protection, but escaped from the feds. Looks like they've got some pretty good leads on where she is, but it also says they're tailing some of Tabor's men. Says it's all going down here in Ventura. If the feds find her, they'll hide her. If Tabor finds her—"

"She's dead." Antony tapped his fingers on the table. "I can find her. How much time?"

"Pete said the feds would be all over him within twenty-four, maybe forty-eight hours."

Antony nodded.

"I want to bust Tabor. What will you do with Susanne when you find her?"

"You gonna have to know every detail? You can trust me."

"Trust you? You're a two-bit punk who's killed at least two people. I have no intention of trusting you." Martin's face was red.

Antony grinned. "Two that you know of." He took a gulp of the water, refusing to deny killing the guy in the dumpster even though he didn't do it. Letting people think he did only helped his reputation.

"So, how you going to find her and what're you gonna do with her?"

"I'll track her down and keep her with me."

"I want in on it."

"I'll call you when I have her," Antony said.

"Where will you take her?"

"I've got a line on a place. It has a safe room in the basement. The place doesn't have my name on it, so no one will trace her to me there."

"Doesn't your father have a safe room? His place is like Fort Knox."

"Yeah, but Susanne is Victoria's mom and Sonny is dating Vic. That'll be one of the first places they'll suspect."

"How you gonna find her?"

Antony's grin deepened. "I have ways."

Martin nodded and left without saying another word.

Antony looked down at his vibrating phone. A text from Bosco.

Sonny's in parking lot.

Antony gulped the water then marched out to Sonny's car. He stuck his head in the rolled down window. "You don't take orders very well, do you?"

"Nope. What were you and Martin talking about?"

"You have to take me to Susanne, right now," Antony insisted.

"No way."

Red crept up Antony's neck. He didn't want to use his trump card but he would if forced. "I have connections at the station. Things are going down that you don't know about, and if we don't get Susanne outta there in the next few hours, the feds or Tabor's men will be all over this."

"And I'm supposed to just believe that?" Sonny asked, rubbing his bottom lip.

Antony pursed his lips. "You know, I've never done anything but protect you. Why don't you just trust me?" He shook his head. "I don't have time for this. Susanne's life is in danger. If you don't take me to her, I'll go to Victoria and tell her the truth. Then, when they find her mother's dead body, you can explain to her why you didn't help me."

Sonny grabbed Antony's arm. "You wouldn't."

"Yeah, I would."

"Get in. I'm driving."

"Give me a minute." Antony walked to Doc and Bosco. He motioned for Bosco to come closer and dropped his keys in his hand. "Go to Victoria's." He scribbled the address on a piece of paper. "I'll let you know where to bring her."

Antony waited until Bosco left, then went to Doc. "You, follow me."

Doc nodded.

Antony texted Vic while he walked to Sonny's car. *Bosco is picking you up. He'll bring you to me.*

Is it about my mother? Did you find her?

Can't talk now. See you soon.

K

Antony slid into the passenger side of Sonny's car and hit his brother's arm. "Let's go get Susanne."

SIXTEEN

SONNY SLOWED THE car, grabbed his cell phone and dialed a number.

"Put it on speaker," Antony said.

Sonny nodded and obeyed.

"Sonny?" her voice was soft.

"I have to see you. Now," Sonny said.

"It's late."

"I know. This is important."

Antony covered the phone and whispered, "Have her meet us outside."

"But—"

"Just do it. She'll leave with us whether she wants to or not, and I don't want to have to fight her security guys if she doesn't want to go."

Sonny rolled his eyes. If Antony would let him explain, he'd tell his brother there was no need to hide. The men guarding her were Sonny's, but he'd learned from childhood that Antony like to call the shots. Whatever. He'd play it Antony's way. Let him feel like a fool later.

"Susanne?" Sonny said into the phone.

"Yes."

"Meet me outside. You'll see my car."

"Is everything okay? Something happen to the girls?"

"They're fine, but I need to talk to you."

"Okay. I'll be right out."

*   *   *

A tapping on the door drew Victoria to look through the peephole. "Yes?"

"It's Bosco."

She opened the door. "Come on in. I'm almost ready."

Bosco stood inside the small apartment.

"Did Antony tell you why I'm meeting him? Is it about my mother?" She slipped on her shoes.

"He didn't say."

She grabbed her purse. "Okay, I'm ready."

He opened the door.

She followed him to Antony's car and didn't bother to ask why he had it, because she doubted he'd tell her.

They sat but Bosco didn't move.

"What are we waiting on?" Victoria asked.

"Directions."

A text pinged on his phone. He looked at it and took off.

Victoria prayed he was taking her to her mother.

*   *   *

Antony climbed out of the car and walked to Doc who had rolled down his window. "Stay in the car."

Next, he called Bosco. "We're taking Susanne back to the house. You'll have to meet with the real estate gal tomorrow, and tell her we want to close with immediate possession. Cost is not an issue. Tell Victoria that no matter what, she has to be quiet. Make sure she understands that."

"You should tell her. Her mother's been gone for a long time."

Antony nodded and looked at Sonny who was pacing. "Okay, put her on the phone."

"Antony? Did you find her? Is she alive?"

"Listen," he said softly, turning so Sonny wouldn't hear him. "She's alive."

"Thank God. Oh, thank you Antony."

"Victoria, listen to me. When you see her, you have to be quiet."

"Okay."

"No, really, quiet. I need you to trust me, no matter what, okay?"

"Yes, yes, anything."

"Listen to me. No matter what you see, or no matter what I have to do, trust me."

"Anything, Antony."

"You'll stay quiet?" he asked, again.

"Yes, only whispers." He could tell she was crying.

He turned to see Sonny walking to him. "I gotta go."

"Who were you talking to?" Sonny asked.

"Just getting things ready."

"Ready? For what?" Sonny asked, his voice hard.

"For this." Antony motioned with his head as Susanne walked out toward them.

She clutched the sweater tight around her neck. "What's going on?"

Sonny touched her shoulder. "Thanks for coming out. This is my brother, Antony. He'll explain."

Antony nodded at her. "Nice to meet you."

He pulled her closer to the car Doc was in. He pounded on the hood and motioned for him to get out. "Look around. Make sure no one followed her."

Susanne's forehead wrinkled. "What's going on?"

"Listen," Antony turned back to her as Doc disappeared into the darkness with his gun drawn. "You have to come with us. Victoria asked me to look for you and when we got close, somehow, we tipped off the feds. We also found out that Tabor has men looking for you and they're close. They both have a trail to follow, but it won't take them long to trace it back to us. We need to get you somewhere safe."

"No. I won't come out of hiding. I can't go with you. I'll move again. The danger it'll put my daughters in—I just can't." She shook her head.

"You have to. I can protect you, Vic and Zoë."

"No." She looked up at him. "You don't understand. I won't."

Susanne turned to leave, but Antony grabbed her arm. "You're coming with us." He reached inside his jacket resting his hand on his gun. He'd threaten her if he had to.

Antony's car turned on the street and the lights went out.

"Who's that?" Sonny asked.

"Bosco," Antony said. The car stopped. "And Victoria." Antony grinned as Victoria climbed out and ran toward them.

When Victoria got to her mother she wrapped her arms around her. "Oh, my God, you're alive. I knew it. I always knew it. I love you. I missed you so much."

Tears rolled down Susanne's cheeks. "I missed you too, and I love you so much."

Antony gave them a brief moment then pushed them both toward the car. "Let's get out of here."

"I can't go." Susanne wiped the tears. "I can't."

"What?" Victoria pleaded with Antony. "Antony, no. She has to come with us."

"Shh, shh, shh." Antony looked at Sonny. Victoria apparently hadn't even noticed he was standing there. Antony leaned into her. "She'll go with us. Go with Bosco and get in the car."

"Not without her."

"Trust me."

She nodded and glanced back at her mother as Bosco pulled her back to the car. "I love you."

Antony grabbed Susanne's arm and pushed her toward Doc's car. He looked at Sonny. "Get in the car and follow us."

Doc jogged back. "No sign of anyone."

"Let me go or I'll scream." Susanne tried to get free from Antony's grasp.

In one motion, Antony wrapped an arm around her head, his hand covering her mouth. He lifted her up with his other arm, threw her into the car and jumped in behind her. Grabbing his gun, he pointed it at her. "Let's go," he said to Doc. The car lurched forward and took off down the road.

Susanne struggled. He pressed the gun into her side. "I'm serious."

When they were a good distance from the house, he replaced his gun. "Now you can scream all you want."

Doc glanced at him in the rearview mirror. "Sonny and Bosco are both following."

Antony grabbed his phone. It had been vibrating non-stop since they left. Missed calls. Sonny. Victoria. Sonny, again.

He dialed Martin's number. "Hey, I need you at 2020 W. Elm. I got her."

"You're fast," Martin said.

"I'm good." Antony laughed and tucked the phone back in his pocket. He ignored the vibrations.

*　　*　　*

Susanne looked at Sonny's brother. He looked genuinely good, but there was also an evilness about him. Maybe it was because he pulled a gun on her. She could understand why. Part of her wanted to stay with her kids, but she wanted to protect them more. "Where are you taking me?"

"Somewhere to keep you safe," Antony said.

"I'm supposed to believe that?"

He laughed. "Yeah. Vic asked me to find you. I always keep my promises."

"Even if it gets me killed?"

"No one will hurt you."

"What about Victoria?"

"I'll protect her," Antony said.

"How, exactly, do you plan on that?"

"I have my ways."

"Can you at least fill me in a little? This is my life, you know."

Antony turned to her, his head tilted slightly. "I've got bodyguards that will never leave your side. We're taking you to my place. It has a safe room. If you end up locking yourself in there, no one will be able to get you."

"A safe room?"

"You'll never need to use it. No one will even know you're with me, except for my guys, Sonny, and Victoria."

"What about Zoë?" Her heart was returning to a steady pace. She was beginning to think this might work. Something about this man reeked survival.

"Do you want me to tell Zoë? Her boyfriend is meeting us at the house."

"Her boyfriend?"

"He's a cop."

"Zoë has a boyfriend? A cop." She smiled. "Just like her father." She had always wondered if anyone would tame youngest daughter. Maybe a cop could. "Yes, I'd like to see Zoë. It wouldn't be fair to see Victoria and not Zoë."

"You know, they'll have lots of questions. You ready to answer them? Their dad was killed trying to find you. How're you going explain that to them?"

A shudder ran through her as her eyes filled with tears. "I don't know. I thought he'd let it go." She looked out the window.

Not going to the funeral had hurt, but being unable to comfort her daughters was something she thought she'd never get over.

She was beginning to feel more at ease with Antony. "I can't believe you pulled a gun on me."

"Kept you quiet." He laughed.

"Was it loaded?"

"It's always loaded."

"Sonny have a gun?" She now wondered if all the stuff she'd read on the Internet about the Luciano family was true.

"One on his ankle. Don't know if he could ever get it pulled out if he needed it."

"Would he ever need it?"

"Doubtful."

"How about you?" She was thankful he appeared to be honest "Would you ever need it?"

"Needed it tonight." He raised an eyebrow and grinned.

"Besides tonight."

"Might." He shrugged. "Never know."

"Sonny said he wants to marry Victoria."

"Yep." Antony looked toward the front of the car.

As the streetlights beamed through the car, Susanne saw a shadow of sadness pass over Antony's otherwise cocky expression.

"You love her?"

"Yes."

"Does she love you?"

"I think so."

"But she loves Sonny?"

Antony turned to her. "Yes, she does."

"You finding me. Will that change her mind about Sonny?"

He grinned. "It just might."

"Is she better off with you than with him?" When his eyes narrowed, she added. "I'm just thinking about my daughter. Not that you're bad or anything. I want what's best for her."

He said nothing as they pulled onto a street, and Antony stared at a parked car. "Drive slow," he said to Doc. "This may be Martin."

"Zoë's boyfriend?"

"Yes."

"It's him." Antony shot him a text.

They pulled up to the gates. Doc rolled his window down and punched in some numbers. They opened. Antony patted his shoulder. "How'd you get those?"

"Bosco texted them to me. Guess he figured you might need them."

They pulled up to the garage. Doc threw the car in park. "Give me a minute. He jumped out, punched the numbers in the keypads and five garage doors opened.

"I saw the For Sale sign." Susanne said. "You bought this place?"

"Yep. We close on it tomorrow."

"In your name?"

"No way. I'm not stupid. Bosco's real name. They'll never connect it with me or you to him."

She nodded. He was smarter than she thought. "So, when did you come up with all this?"

"In the last hour."

Doc climbed back in the car and drove it into the garage. Sonny pulled in next to him, along with Bosco and Martin. They all climbed out of their cars, and Doc shut the garage doors.

Victoria jumped out of the car, ran to her mother, and grabbed her hand.

Antony used his cell phone as a flashlight. "No lights until we're in the basement. Let's get Susanne settled."

SEVENTEEN

WHEN THEY REACHED the basement, Antony flipped on a light. Sectional cream couches, a pool table and a full wet bar filled a spacious room.

Bosco guided Susanne toward the left by her elbow. "I'll show you your room."

Susanne nodded, releasing Victoria's hand.

"I'll be there in a minute," Victoria said. "I want to thank Antony."

Susanne hugged her. "I love you."

"Me, too."

Antony couldn't help but feel sorry for Sonny. He looked defeated and sad.

Victoria finally noticed Sonny. She smiled, which released the tears that had pooled in her eyes.

He pulled her into a hug, whispered something in her ear then released her.

Victoria came closer to Antony, grabbed his hands and held them tight. "Thank you for finding her."

Antony pulled her into a hug and welcomed her embrace, but he felt Sonny's eyes pierce him. He ignored them, knowing he could have everything he wanted. But could he willingly break his brother's heart?

He wasn't sure. Sonny was blood. He'd given up Elisa, the life he'd known, the life he was supposed to have. But when would it stop? Did he really have to give up more? No. He wouldn't do it. If Victoria loved him, he'd have her.

Antony pulled away from her and cupped her face in his hands. "You know I'd do anything for you. I love you."

"I know. I think I love you, too."

He smiled, his heart pounding. "But you love Sonny."

"Yes."

Antony had to get away from Sonny's glare. He took Victoria's hand, led her to the stairs and they sat down.

She looked over at him. "What's wrong?"

He hesitated, knowing the truth could go both ways. She'd either hate Sonny for lying or love Sonny more for finding her. He'd bet on hate. He squeezed her hand. "Sonny found her first."

"What?" Her forehead wrinkled. "When?"

Antony looked at the floor. "I was close to finding Susanne when Sonny found out I was looking for her. Not sure how he did that, but you can bet I'll find out. He confronted me today and told me he'd already found her. I made him take me to her tonight."

"Look at me." When he looked her in the eye, she asked. "Really? Don't lie to me."

"You know I don't lie, not to those I love."

"Then you're not telling me the whole truth."

The left side of his mouth went into a grin.

"When did he find her?" she asked.

"You'll have to ask him."

"Do you know?"

"Yes, but you should ask him. He loves you."

"I know."

He cupped her face and wanted to pull her into a kiss, but he didn't. "If you want me, I'm here, but I don't know."

"Earlier tonight you were ready to whisk me away. What's changed?"

"I don't know." He turned away from her. "Maybe Sonny's better for you than me."

She laughed. "Is that a question?"

"A fact."

She leaned into him, entangling her fingers in his. "What changed?"

"If I tell you, you might hate me."

"I won't hate you. Friends no matter what, remember?"

He grinned because there was no sorrow in what he did. "When I grabbed your mom, she threatened to scream because she didn't want to go with us. I pulled my gun on her."

"You what?"

"Yeah. I held it at her waist. I would've never used it, but all I could think of was what it would do to you if you never saw her again. I couldn't live with that."

"I'm glad you did." She laid her head on his shoulder.

He wrapped his arm around her. "If you choose Sonny, can I still flirt with you and tell you how much I'm madly in love with you for the rest of your life?"

She laughed. "I'd have it no other way."

"You don't think my brother would mind?"

"Oh, yeah, he'd mind." She stood and grabbed his hand. "Thank you, for everything you did to get my mother here and for protecting her."

He gave her hand a squeeze and released it. "I'd do anything for you."

*　　*　　*

Victoria took a seat next to Sonny on the couch. She couldn't help but wonder what Antony was keeping from her and why he was protecting Sonny.

"So…" She rubbed her hands together. "Antony tells me you found my mother first."

"He told you that?" Sonny cocked his head.

"Did he lie?"

"No, I just can't believe he'd tell you. The guy wants you pretty bad. I can tell you have feelings for him."

"I do have feelings for him. It'd be hard not to. He acts like he worships the ground I walk on."

"Have you kissed him, besides that first day at the store?"

"Yes."

He looked away from her. "Tonight, at Papa's?"

"Yes," she said.

"That's why you left?"

"He confuses me."

"Do you love him?"

She wasn't about to answer that one. It would take her to a conversation she didn't have any answers for. "How long have you known where my mom was?"

"Does it matter?"

"Yes." Her eyes narrowed. "How long?"

"About a year."

She looked away from him, her jaw tight. "I can't believe it. You lied to me for a year?"

"I had to. Your mom insisted."

She looked back at him. "Before or after my dad was killed."

"After. You were so broken and hurt when you lost your dad. I knew finding out what happened to your mom would help."

"And you found her?"

"Yes."

"And never told me she was alive? I asked you to find her for me a number of times, and you flat out lied to me."

"I'm sorry."

"Yeah, me, too." She stood. "Almost a year, wasted."

She walked to the doorway where Bosco stood. "Can I go see her?"

Bosco nodded and motioned to the safe room.

* * *

Sonny waited until she was down the hallway before walking to Antony who still sat on the bottom stairs. He stood over him. "You threw her into the car?"

"Held my gun on her, too." Antony cracked his knuckles.

"You didn't have to do that. I could've got her to come."

"Yeah, right. You've been so convincing over the last year."

Heat filled Sonny's face. "Those were my men. You didn't have to sneak her out or pull a gun on her."

"Your men? But I thought… It doesn't matter. I wasn't taking the chance and if it took a gun, then so be it. Nothing or no one was going to stop me."

Sonny rolled his eyes. His brother always tried to justify his actions as noble. "You told Vic that I found her?"

"Yeah." Antony looked up at him and cocked his head. "Why does that surprise you?"

"It doesn't. I figured you'd use this to win her over."

Antony stood, red flooded his neck and face. "I've given up everything for you. Why do you think I'd stop now?"

"I've never asked you to do anything for me."

Antony sighed. "No, you haven't."

"So, why do you continue to play the martyr? You want to tell Papa the truth about who killed Carlo, tell him. You want Victoria, go for it. She can't stand to look at me anyway, but don't stand here and act like I owe you for the choices you made."

Antony stared at him.

Figured. Part of Sonny thought Antony enjoyed playing the martyr. "I guess I'll leave. Do I need a code or something to get out of the gate?"

Antony motioned with his head to Bosco and said, "Sonny's leaving."

Bosco nodded.

"I guess you'll be staying?" Sonny asked Antony.

"This is my house. Keep your headlights off until you're down the street."

"Sure thing."

* * *

Antony watched them disappear in the darkness. Three steps and he was at the pool table where Martin stood.

"How'd you get access to this house?" Martin asked.

"By buying it." Antony pushed his hands deep in his pocket. "Susanne wants to see Zoë. Will you bring her by tomorrow?"

"Yes. What's the next move?"

"We need to find out what Susanne knows. Go over the files. Might help us figure out how to fix this."

"Pete could help. After he dodges the feds."

"Okay. Let's regroup in the morning. Bring Zoë by." He rubbed his hands together. "Pete will have fun working with his brother."

"His brother?"

"You didn't know? Bosco is Pete's brother. Doc is their cousin, just got back from Afghanistan."

"I didn't know." Martin laughed. "That's why Pete is so loyal to you."

"And I saved his life."

"He told me about that. Well, I'd better get going. I'll bring Zoë by tomorrow. I'll text you when we're on our way."

Antony nodded.

* * *

Victoria was in awe of the safe room. It was a mini apartment hidden behind a wall in the rear of the wet bar. There was a kitchen, living room, bathroom, and one small bedroom.

Victoria softly tapped on the door to the bedroom then walked in. Her mother sat on the bed.

"I thought you'd never get in here." Susanne patted the spot next to her.

Victoria sat and grabbed her hand. "I can't believe you're here. After all this time."

"I know."

"Why?" Victoria fought the shudder in her chest. "Why'd you leave us? Leave Daddy?"

"I did what I thought was best under the circumstances."

"What circumstances?"

"I can't tell you everything. Not yet, anyway." She tucked Victoria's hair behind her ears. "I'm just glad Antony had the guts to make me leave."

Victoria laughed. "He said he pulled his gun out."

"Yeah. That surprised me. Where's Sonny?"

"I don't know. I think he left."

"Why?"

"I can't be around him, Mom. He's lied to me for a year."

Susanne gently touched her face. "I made him, dear. He wanted to tell you the minute he found me, but I wouldn't let him."

"It didn't stop Antony and I've known him for only a few months. No, Mother. I can't forgive that." She fought the tears. "I asked him to find you. To help me. He wouldn't, and the whole time he was lying."

"Because I made him."

Victoria shook her head. "Don't. I don't want to talk about Sonny. Tell me, what have you been doing? It's been over a year. Did you just sit around?"

"Kinda." Susanne stood and paced the small room. "The guys would take me some places, in other cities, other states, but when we came back here I stayed in the house."

"Sounds horrible."

"Better than the alternative, and I couldn't take the chance of you or Zoë getting hurt."

Victoria nodded.

"I want to see Zoë. Will she come by tomorrow?"

"Of course. I'm sure Martin will tell her."

"Tell me about Martin."

Victoria smiled. "I really don't know that much. Comes from a long line of cops. He seems nice. She's kept him to herself. He's her partner."

"They could get in trouble." Susanne leaned against the headboard.

"That's probably why I don't know him better."

Susanne yawned.

Victoria grabbed a blanket from the chair and covered her mom up. "You tired?"

"Yeah, but I love talking."

Victoria took her hand. "It's pretty late. You sleep. We have the rest of our lives."

Susanne nodded as her eyelids closed. Victoria sat and stared at her. She was thinner than she remembered. Still as beautiful.

She thought about her dad and how heartbroken he was when Mom disappeared. She wished... *No.* She shook her head. *It doesn't matter.*

Her mother's breathing deepened. Victoria released her hand, shut the light off, and found Bosco in the front room. "She's asleep. Where is everyone?"

"Sonny and Martin left. Antony is upstairs, probably on the back porch. No lights."

Victoria nodded. "Thanks."

She walked up the stairs into the great room. One wall was covered in windows and French doors. The moonlight shot into the room, lighting it up. She was drawn to a figure sitting out on the porch.

Antony looked up at her and smiled. "Come sit." He patted the cushion on the wicker couch. "It's not very comfortable. This will be the first to go."

She snuggled next to him on the loveseat. "The house came furnished?"

"Comes with what you see. I guess that's hard to do in the dark. They left some things, the safe room and basement furnished and this outdoor stuff."

She nodded. "Sonny left?"

"Yeah, he looked upset. I'm sure he did what he thought he had to."

"Stop it."

Antony laughed and patted her leg. "Okay."

"I can't thank you enough. If you hadn't…" She cried. "I might have never seen her again."

Antony put his arm around her. "Sonny would've eventually told you."

She stared up at him. "He lied to me for almost a year. How do I forgive that?"

"I don't know. I couldn't. Loyalty, that's all I ask. But he did have his reasons."

"Why are you, of all people, defending him?"

"He is my brother."

"He lied. Not just a little lie either, this was big. He stood by me as I drained my savings hiring PI's, and all the while he knew exactly where she was." She shook her head. "It makes me so angry."

"But your mom…"

She raised her voice. "Stop defending him."

Antony lifted an eyebrow. "Okay." He pulled her close and they sat in silence for a long time.

Finally, he squeezed her shoulder. "You need to get some rest. I figured you'd stay here?"

"I'd like to. If that's okay."

"Of course. You don't ever have to leave."

She laughed. "You'd like that, wouldn't you?"

"Yeah." He grinned. "I'd like that."

"It'd break Lauren's heart."

"She's only after my money," Antony stated.

"Lauren can smell dollar signs a mile away."

"Come on." He stood and reached out his hand.

She looked up at him.

A mischievous grin spread across his face. "Don't you trust me?"

She grabbed his hand. "I trust you."

He led her through the house, up the stairs, down the hallway, motioning into a bedroom. The shades were up and moonlight filled the room. On the floor was a blowup mattress, a pillow and a blanket.

"It's not the Hilton, but it's all Doc could find on short notice. I'll get you a bed tomorrow."

"Thanks."

"The bathroom is through that door, you should find a towel, hairbrush, toothbrush and toothpaste. You can bring other stuff over tomorrow, too. I'll fix up another bedroom for Zoë, just in case she wants to stay, too."

"Where will you be?"

"Where do you want me to be?" He grinned. "In the room across the hall for tonight. Tomorrow, I'll get the security system up and running then move down to the master."

She nodded. "Antony?"

"Yeah."

"Thank you." She looked at him and found herself wanting to kiss him. She was sure he felt the same way, so she waited.

He took her in his arms. "You're welcome." He ran his fingers down her cheek, smoothed her hair away from her face, then pulled her close. "Let me know if you need anything."

She slowly let out her breath and laughed.

"What?" He grinned.

"You don't want to kiss me?"

"Oh, yeah." His arms tightened around her. He pulled her to him and kissed her gently. "But you have a lot to think about."

"Sonny."

He nodded. "Yes, Sonny."

"What if I said I don't want to think about him tonight?"

Antony's grin deepened. He pulled her to him.

Victoria clasped her hand behind his neck and kissed more passionately. She stumbled into the bedroom with him and fell onto the air mattress. It jostled them around like an old waterbed, almost throwing them to the floor. They both laughed.

He leaned on one elbow as she lay on her back. "You're crazy, you know that?"

She looked up at him. "I think you're crazier than me."

He leaned over and kissed her. "You know, tomorrow…"

Victoria pulled him back to her and kissed him. She didn't want to think about tomorrow or her feelings for Sonny. There was nothing she cared about at that moment but him.

He backed away. "Okay, seriously," he said, his face firm.

She momentarily forced the smile away then laughed. It wasn't so much at him, although she could tell he was trying to be honorable, but it just wasn't natural.

His eyes narrowed. "What?"

"You're so cute when you're trying to do the right thing." She kissed him.

"He is my brother."

"I know."

He ran his fingers through her hair. "At some point, you'll have to choose."

"Not tonight."

"No." His arm tightened around her.

She laid her head on his chest and closed her eyes. Right now, she couldn't stand Sonny for lying to her, but she also couldn't help but wonder if her momentary choice of Antony was because he found her mother. She'd examine that one later.

"Do you know why my mother was hiding?" she asked.

"No."

She leaned up on her elbows. "Are you going to find out?"

"Yes."

"You'll protect her?"

"And you." He kissed her.

"I don't know if I can ever repay you."

"I'm not worried about money, really. I got plenty of it." He wrapped his hand on the back of her neck and pulled her into him. "You'll all be safe. I promise."

They kissed.

"Ahem."

Victoria's heart pounded. For a split second she feared it might be Sonny.

They turned to see Doc in the doorway.

Antony sat up, setting the bed into a motion that almost made her roll off. She laughed as he grabbed her around the back and held her on. "What do you want?" Antony's voice was hard.

"I wondered if I could talk to you," Doc said.

"Can it wait until morning?"

Victoria grabbed his arm and pulled herself up. "Go ahead, if you need to."

He turned to her and gave her a quick kiss. "Be right back."

* * *

Antony stood, brushed his fingers through his hair and followed Doc into the hallway. "What the heck do you want? Don't you have a shift to stand guard?"

Doc stood tall. "Yes, but I'm wondering if Victoria needs some protection, too."

"You can't be serious?" Heat crept up Antony's neck at Doc's absurd comment. "I said protect Vic's mom, now get out of my face if you want to keep your job."

"I don't mean to be in your face, but I think you should back off and give her some space. She thought her mom was dead, and you're the hero. She's not thinking about Sonny."

"Who exactly do you work for?" Antony asked.

"You."

"Then I suggest you shut your mouth and go to work." He glared at Doc's back as he walked away. He must be the leak. Crap.

Sonny must've gotten to him. He was the only guy new enough to double cross him. He'd deal with the traitor in the morning.

Back in the room, Victoria stood by the window. The moonlight glistened on her hair. Antony stared at her and grinned. He would have her, and Sonny would just have to get over it.

She turned to him. "Everything okay?"

"Yes." He took her in his arms and kissed her. "Doc trying to be my conscience."

She nodded. Her arms were around him, but something had changed, he could feel it. He looked down at her. "You need to get some sleep. It's going to be a busy day tomorrow."

Victoria pulled away from him.

He cupped her cheeks. "I'll be in the other room if you need anything."

She reached up and held his arms, her eyes filling with tears. "Okay."

Antony kissed her one last time and went to his room.

* * *

Victoria lay on the air mattress. Why was Antony so tempting? Had she really come close to throwing away her faith for a few passionate moments with him? Were her moral convictions and belief in God so shallow she'd toss them aside for fleeting pleasure?

Sonny had lied and ruined everything. Tears flooded her eyes. As hard as she tried to push away the thoughts of him and what they once had away, she couldn't. She loved Sonny. But she thought she loved Antony, too.

Victoria wiped away her tears and sighed. How could she possibly love two men? She wasn't even sure if what she felt for Antony was real love. But if it wasn't, why did it feel right, too?

EIGHTEEN

ANTONY TOSSED A folder on a table in the safe room where Susanne sat. "This is some good reading."

"Glad you enjoyed it." Susanne scooted the folder back to him.

"That's all you're going to say about it?"

Doc brought in a bag of bagels and box of coffee.

"Leave it." Antony glared. He still wanted to beat the crap out of Doc for interrupting him and Victoria the night before. He'd decided Victoria would be his. The heck with what his brother thought or felt. He'd given up Elisa, his family, everything that was rightfully his. No way was he giving up Victoria.

Sullen-faced, Doc dropped the things on the counter and left.

* * *

Victoria woke up with the sun shining in her face. She rubbed her eyes. "What time is it?" she whispered then reached for her phone. It was after nine. "Oh, crap." She dialed Fran at the store, tried to roll but fell off the mattress instead, then stood up.

She combed through her hair with her fingers. "Hey, Fran, it's Victoria."

Fran's voice was pleasant. "How is everything going there?"

"Um, fine." She said, totally confused.

"Antony, Sonny's brother, called and said a family emergency came up. He was so nice and concerned for you. I told him to tell you to take all the time you needed."

"Oh." She smiled. "Thanks. I should be in tomorrow."

"If you need another day or two, just let me know."

"Thanks, again." In the bathroom, Victoria opened a toothbrush and toothpaste, and brushed her teeth.

She ran a Kleenex under her eyes to catch the stray mascara, stood back and looked at herself in the mirror. It would have to do.

On the main floor, the house looked nothing like it had in the dark of the night. It was exquisite. She could barely take it all in. "Wow."

A large wooden arch framed the great room. The walls were painted cream with dark wood floors. Another archway led into the kitchen and down to the basement.

In the basement, Doc pushed himself up from the couch. "You need anything?"

"No, thanks. Are they in there?" She pointed to the door to the safe room.

"Yes. You may want to knock."

She nodded, leaned into the cracked door and listened.

* * *

"Reads like a puzzle." Antony rested against the counter, his arms crossed.

Susanne looked up at him. "Can I explain?"

"Please do." He pursed his lips. "Only if you can be honest. I don't want to hear any lies."

"I don't want Vic to know."

"I won't promise you that. But I need to know everything."

"My husband, Phillip, had put me in a position where Tabor had to come after me so that Philip could kill him, but I was kidnapped. I thought after Phillip was dead they'd let me go, but they didn't. I was held prisoner in that house until Sonny found me."

Antony did a quick pace of the room, rubbing the back of his neck. "I'm trying to be nice, but I hate liars and you're lying."

He took a cup of the coffee and set it in front of her. "Now, I want the truth."

"I told you."

Antony slammed a fist on the table, splashing coffee out of the cup. "I'm not stupid. This says you were in witness protection. You were going to testify against Tabor. A Judge. If Sonny got you out it was from witness protection. Tabor is still sitting on the bench so you're either hiding from Tabor or the Feds. Maybe both."

She sipped her coffee, her face indifferent.

In any other interrogation he'd have already used physical force to get the truth, but that was not an option with her. "I will find out the truth. It'd be easier if you just told me. I can't help if I don't know what's going on."

Susanne shot him a severe look. "Who asked you to help me? I was doing just fine. I didn't need your help. If you would've listened to Sonny…" She shook her head. "I wish you'd have just stayed out of it."

"Because making everyone believe you're dead is much better? You'd rather your two daughters go through life without you than to deal with this? Really?"

She stood, her face hard. "Yes, I'd rather them think I was dead."

"You're heartless."

"You don't know anything about me." She walked down the hallway and slammed the bedroom door.

* * *

Victoria pushed the door open. Her heart pounded and tears filled her eyes. "Did she really just say that?"

Antony pulled her into a hug. "She didn't mean it." He grabbed her hand. "Come on." He led her up the stairs, outside to the wicker loveseat and pulled her down beside him.

"You okay?"

She forced a smile. "I can't believe she'd say that. After all this time."

"She's mad at me." Antony squeezed her hand. "But she's glad she's here."

Victoria shook her head. "I don't know. Hidden for over a year and Sonny knew. She never wanted him to tell us. Maybe it would've been better if we didn't know."

The left side of his mouth turned up into a grin. "Self-pity is not very becoming on you. You can't go back, only forward. Susanne said all that crap because she doesn't want to tell me what's going on. I can't protect her if she doesn't tell me everything.

"This has only started. I'm going to have to ride her, yell, make her mad. I'll do whatever it takes to get the information out of her. It's the only way I can protect your mother. The only way I can protect you."

Victoria wondered what his definition of *do whatever* was, but she shook the thoughts of it out of her mind. He was a survivor. He lived on the streets and she knew his ways of dealing with things was different. Maybe that's what attracted her to him.

"Thank you for calling the store," Victoria said, smiling.

"No problem. Figured you'd want the day off."

"And if Fran had said no?" she asked.

"I would've bought the place and fired her." He chuckled.

Her smile deepened. "You hear from Sonny?"

"Nope. I called Lorenzo. Told him I'd be in later."

"Was he mad?"

"Doesn't matter." Antony leaned back in the chair. "I'll touch base later."

His phone vibrated. He looked down at it and sighed.

"You need to get that?"

"No, just Lauren."

She nodded.

He nudged her with his shoulder. "Jealous?"

Heat filled her face. "Yes, and I know it's stupid."

"I don't mind."

"Course you don't."

He laughed.

Was he going to push her to make a choice?

She'd overheard his conversation with Doc the night before. It had stopped something she now knew she would've regretted because her feelings were all mixed up.

"Zoë should be here anytime," he looked down as his phone vibrated again. "This one, I gotta take." Antony put the phone to his ear and stood.

"Yeah. Hey. Calm down. Yes, I know where it's at. I'll send a guy. His name is Doc." He paced and his neck reddened. "I can't right now." He looked at her and smiled. "He'll be there in ten minutes and keep you safe. I'll come when I can."

Antony ended the call and texted.

Within seconds, Doc arrived and stood before him.

"Go to this address." He handed him a piece of paper at him. "There's a gal there named Elisa. Take her to a hotel and check her in under an alias. Keep her freakin' husband Enrico away from her. Got it?" His eyes were hard. "Stay there."

"Sure thing." Doc left.

Bosco entered the room and handed Antony a folder. "House is yours. Just closed on it."

"Thanks."

When Bosco left, Victoria looked up at Antony. "Who's Elisa?"

"Old friend from KC who married some freak who's abusive. She calls me every so often, says she's leaving him. I end up paying her hotel until she's healthy enough to go back to him."

"That's nice of you."

"Yeah, I keep thinking this time she'll leave him for good, but it never happens." He reached for her hand. "Ready to go see your mom?"

"Sure." She gave his hand a squeeze then let it go. She still wondered how her mom could really believe it was better if they would've kept thinking she was dead.

Bosco appeared, again. "Zoë and Martin are here."

Antony placed his hand on Victoria's lower back. "Go on down. I need to talk to them first."

* * *

Antony met Martin and Zoë at the front door. Zoë whistled as she walked in. "Wow, this place is great? You buy it?"

"Yep." Antony glanced at Martin. "Got possession this morning."

"Looks like it could use some decorating." Zoë spun around, taking it all in.

"It does. You want a job? Get you out of that uniform. Cops." Antony rolled his eyes teasingly.

She playfully punched him. "I would love to."

Antony looked at Martin, "You haven't told her?"

"No."

Antony motioned with his hand. "Go ahead. Vic's already downstairs." He stared at Martin. "Then we need to talk."

Zoë threw out her palms, face-up, and shrugged. "What's going on? Why are you two so chummy?"

Martin turned to her. "Victoria asked Antony to find your mom, and he found her."

Zoë's eyes widened. "What? She's alive?"

"Yes. She's staying in my safe room. Martin can take you down."

She brushed Martin's hands away. "My mother is alive?" Zoë paced. "Unbelievable. How long have you known?"

Antony slid his hands into his pockets. "I found out where she was yesterday and brought her here to keep her safe. Sonny's known for about a year."

"And he didn't tell anyone?" Zoë was almost yelling, her face twisted in a scowl.

Martin took her hand. "Does any of this matter? She's alive and downstairs. Don't you want to see her?"

"No. I don't ever want to see her. If she didn't want me to know she was alive, then she can just be dead. I don't care. You can take me home now." She stormed out of the house.

Antony raised an eyebrow. "Well, that went well."

"Can we meet later? I need to talk to her," Martin said.

"Sure. Text me when and where. I've got a couple of things I have to take care of."

"Sounds good." Martin left.

Antony poured himself a glass of water. His phone vibrated.

Doc seems nice. Elisa texted.

I'll let you know when I'm heading that way.

Okay.

* * *

Victoria sipped the coffee Antony had gotten for them, still in disbelief that her mother was sitting at the table with her. "Are you going to tell me why you've been hiding? You didn't even get to go to Daddy's funeral."

"I know. I'm sorry."

"You're sorry? I want to know why."

"I can't tell you that."

Heat crept up Victoria's neck. What had she expected? She already overheard her mother say she'd wished she'd never seen her and Zoë again. Did she really think her mother would tell her why?

"Daddy was killed looking for you. I think that deserves an explanation."

"Honey, if I tell you, you'll be in the same danger."

"Really? I'd think we already are."

"And that's why I didn't want to be found." Susanne paced.

"How can you say that? You'd rather Zoë and I go through life without you?"

"If it means you and Zoë are safe, then yes. They will go after you as quickly as they went after your father."

They? Who exactly was her mother talking about? Nevertheless, Victoria's heart pounded as the realization of the danger sank in. But did that still warrant thinking her mother was dead? No. Their father was a cop who collared lots of criminals and had death threats on the family all the time. It was part of their life. Her mother's excuse was weak and selfish.

"Who are they?" Victoria demanded. "I have a right to know."

"Yes," Antony said from behind Victoria. "Who are *they*?"

* * *

Zoë crossed her arms as Martin drove back to her place. Unlike Victoria, she had gotten over all of this months ago. Her mother was dead, and she had made peace with that.

"You're really not going to see your mother?" Martin glanced at her.

"No, I'm not. I couldn't care less. It's her fault my dad was killed. She could've let us know she was alive instead of keeping it a secret."

"Maybe she couldn't tell you."

"If Sonny's known for a year, she could've gotten us word."

Martin pulled in the garage, shut the door, and turned to her. "I think you should see her."

"Do you know why she disappeared to start with? Where she was? Who had her?"

"Kinda. Doesn't make much sense. She was with the feds than ran from them. Not sure why or who had her when Sonny found her. Antony and I are working on that."

Zoë stifled a laugh. "You and Antony are working together? You and a criminal who was implicated in two killings. What? Now you're best friends?"

"I wouldn't call us best friends. I can't stand the guy. Seriously. He was working with Pete and I got dragged into the case. I want the collar for whoever is involved in this. Just might help me make detective. If I take Antony down too, wouldn't bother me a bit."

"I see. So you're in this for your own benefit?"

Martin grabbed her hand. "I'm in this because this is your mother. The only way for her to walk free with no worries is to get whoever is after her, the same person who killed your father. If I can do that for her…for you, then I will. If that helps me make detective, even better."

She squeezed his hand. "Guess I can't begrudge you of that. I'll see you at the office later."

"You're not going back to see your mom?"

"No." She leaned in and kissed him. "See you later."

Zoë climbed out of the car, waited until Martin left then walked out the back door, down the stairs and onto the beach. When she reached her favorite spot, she fell onto the sand.

Her mother was alive. Part of her was happy but the anger was overwhelming. Not just about her dad getting killed, but how her Mom had hidden away for so long without a word to her or Victoria. Didn't she love them? Apparently not. If her mom didn't want to see them, there was no way Zoë was going to see her.

NINETEEN

ANTONY KNEW HE'D never get a straight answer from Susanne as long as Victoria was in the room. He rested his hand on Victoria's shoulder, making her turn toward him. "I need to check on Elisa and then stop by Renato's. Bosco will be here. I've also got a few more guys coming."

"Are you worried?" Victoria stood.

"No. I just want you to know the precautions I've taken. If something seems strange or out of the ordinary, lock yourself here in the safe room. Once that door closes, no one even knows it's there from the outside."

"Okay. Thank you. Will you text me when you're on your way back?"

"Yes."

Antony met Bosco upstairs. "I've got a few things to take care of. You have any problems, let me know."

"You okay with Sonny coming by?"

"Not sure if he will, but yes."

"Boss?"

"Yeah," Antony said.

"I think Doc told Sonny we were on to her. He's the only one that could've. You want me to talk to him when he gets back?"

"I'll handle Doc."

"I never would've guessed him to do that. I'm sorry I brought him on board."

"Don't be. Money can get you just about anything. My brother's not stupid. He knew Doc was the weakest link. I'd have done the same. Doesn't make me any less ticked about it. Only good thing is that I needed to find her fast and

Sonny knowing may have helped. Don't tell Doc that." Antony grinned.

"Still, I put my butt on the line for him, and he's disappointed me. If you gotta let him go, do it. Maybe he'll learn a lesson from it."

"And this is why you're the best." Antony gave him a nod. "Appreciate all you do for me."

Antony drove to the hotel, rode the elevator to the fourth floor, went to room 402 and tapped on the door.

Elisa opened it and flew into his arms. "Thank you."

He hugged her then pushed away, cupping her face. The bruising on her chin made his blood boil. "What'd he do to you?"

"It doesn't matter. I'm never going back."

He'd heard that before, so it wasn't anything he was getting excited about. "Do you need a doctor? Have you been putting ice on it?"

"No doctor and yes, I've been putting ice on it and took a nap. I ate some food, and charged it to the room. Hope you don't mind."

"No problem." He walked further inside. A tray of food was almost completely eaten. That was a good sign. "You left him for good." He spun around and stared into her eyes.

"Yes, only…" She turned away from him.

He sighed. That usually meant he'd mend her up and she'd go back to that low-life punk Enrico. "You know he can't hurt me."

She stepped closer. "He's sworn he would avenge his brother if I leave him."

Dead guy in the dumpster. It should be Dimitri that Enrico should be after, but everyone on the streets thought Antony did it. It didn't matter. He could handle Enrico, but that fact didn't detour Elisa from leaving her husband for good.

"Do you remember—"

"Sorry. Not in the mood to walk down memory lane." In fact, he never was. He'd given his heart to her years ago only to have her trample it. It wasn't something Antony had given to any other woman until he met Victoria. His fear was that Victoria would trample it too. Women.

Elisa nodded and sat on the couch, pulling her legs up under her. "Can I stay a few days until I decide what to do?"

"Yes. If you're serious about leaving him, you can stay at my house until you get a place of your own."

"Thanks. I just need to think."

Which meant time to heal before getting the courage to go back. It was a never-ending ride that he was tired of being on.

He'd confronted Enrico a couple of times, but he always took it out on Elisa so he'd given up. Elisa would have to realize she was worth more than being some guy's punching bag. Convincing her to come to that conclusion was something he wasn't about to give up on.

He took her in his arms. "You can't go back to him. Please. Can't you see what he's doing to you? How he's hurting you? I can protect you."

She looked up at him, her eyes moist. "I just don't know."

"Did you call that number I gave you? They can help you if you don't want me to. Or maybe just talk to them."

"I still have it, but haven't called."

Sorrow filled his heart. She was blind to what Enrico was doing to her. The only thing he knew to do was to always be there for her. He kissed the top of her head. "Stay here as long as you want. Forever if it'll get you away from him."

He stood. "Max will be here if you need anything else. Doc is coming with me."

She nodded and stared out the window.

Antony went into the hallway where Doc and Max waited. "You've got that connecting room next to hers?"

Max raised the plastic key card. "Yes."

"Keep her safe, but if she insists on going back we can't stop her."

Max nodded.

Antony pointed to Doc. "You, with me."

At the end of the hallway, Antony grabbed Doc and threw him against the wall, his hand clutching his neck. "You told my brother I was looking for Susanne?"

"I was trying to keep Victoria safe."

"By being a stooge for Sonny?" He shoved him harder against the wall. "You're done. Get your stuff and get out."

Antony released him, hit the down arrow on the elevator, pulled out his phone and texted Victoria. *On my way back.*

* * *

Sonny paced his office at Renato's. How could he have been so stupid? He knew this could blow up in his face and it had. Antony had been in town for a couple of months and had already turned his life upside down.

Two knocks on the door and Clay walked in. "Here's that prospectus." He slid the papers onto Sonny's desk. "I've got Doc waiting for you."

"Doc? Bring him in."

Clay motioned to Doc.

"Sit." Sonny waved Doc toward the couch and grabbed a chair while Clay stood. "What's going on?"

"Antony knew it was me and now I'm out of a job. You said you had my back."

"I'll take care of you." Sonny stood, slid his hand in his pocket and clutched the rosary he carried. It was his mother's. It didn't hold the same meaning as it had for her, but he loved it just the same.

"I bought a new house here in town. There's a second house on the property where you can live. We close in thirty days. I can set you up at an extended stay hotel until then."

"Thanks."

"How did things go last night? With Victoria and Antony, I mean."

"He tried to move in, but I interrupted his plan. There's something going on with them that's hard to explain, but I know she's torn. She still loves you. She asked Antony if he'd heard from you this morning. I wouldn't stay away if I were you."

Was a hired thug really giving him advice on his love life? "Clay will show you around and explain how I work." Sonny stood and reached out his hand. "You can wait outside."

Doc shook it. "Thanks."

Sonny waited until Doc left the room. "I'm going to head over to Antony's."

"You want me to come along?"

"No. Get Doc settled."

*   *   *

Zoë slid into the booth across from Pete. "I know you worked with Antony, so I'm hoping I can talk freely and you'll keep it to yourself."

"Yes," Pete said.

"We found my mom."

"Antony told me."

"I need to know what you know."

Pete tapped on the table. "I don't know much. I just got the folder and glanced through it before giving it to

Martin. The feds are breathing down my neck. Want to know where your mom is?"

"What do you think happened?"

"She was in witness protection but left it. The file said she'd changed her mind and didn't want to testify."

"So if she's not testifying against Tabor, she's hiding from who? The feds? Tabor?"

"Maybe both. My advice is to ask her."

Zoë slammed her hand on the table. "Ask her? She makes me sick. My dad was killed because of her."

"Cop mode, Zoë. You want answers, go to the source. No file will tell you what you want to know. Look her in the eyes. You'll know if she's lying or if she's telling you the truth. You owe your dad that much." Pete swallowed the last of his drink. "I gotta go."

Zoë walked to the counter of the deli. "I need a Coke to go."

She tapped her fingers as she waited. Pete was right. Her mom was the only one with answers.

* * *

Sonny followed Bosco to the basement safe room. "They're in there." He motioned toward the door.

Victoria and Susanne were playing a game of cards, laughing and talking like old times.

He smiled. "This is nice."

Victoria turned with a grin and patted the seat next to her.

Sonny took it as a good sign. "Zoë been by yet?"

"No." Victoria rearranged some cards. "Gin." She laid her hand down.

Susanne laughed. "Again? I can't win with you. Never could."

"Daddy taught me well. Cut throat games of cards every Monday night. Leave no prisoners. Remember?"

"Yes. He'd help you until Zoë was crying then help Zoë until you were crying. You all were ruthless." Susanne picked up the cards and glanced at Sonny. "By the seriousness on your face, you didn't come to play cards."

"No. I need to know how we're going to play this." Sonny drummed his fingers on the table.

"We'd like to know that, too." Antony's stern voice came from the doorway. Martin and Zoë stood next to him.

"I'm not saying a thing," Susanne said.

Sonny shook his head. Susanne acted like the whole situation was an inconvenience. Didn't she realize that if they didn't know the truth her daughter's lives would be in danger?

"Can I talk to you?" Sonny grabbed Susanne's arm and pushed her into one of the bedrooms. "You have to tell them."

"If only you had left me alone—"

"If you hadn't made me lie to the woman I love, we wouldn't be standing here right now in this situation." Sonny's face felt like fire. "You're going to walk out there and tell them the truth. All of it. Then you guys can decide, as a family, how this will play out. It's their lives on the line too."

He watched her pace and wondered what else to say. "Please?"

Stopping in front of him, she placed one hand on the side of his face. "I'm sorry this has hurt your and Victoria's relationship. Really, I am. I know how much you love her."

His anger subsided. "Then tell them so I can try to make it up to her before I lose her."

"Okay." She took his hand and walked them into the kitchen.

"If everyone would like to sit down I will try and explain why I've been in hiding."

Susanne poured herself another cup of coffee from the Starbucks box and took a seat between Sonny and Antony. The girls and Martin sat across from them.

"You know, I was a court reporter to Judge Tabor. I always thought things weren't right, but I overlooked a lot, thinking no one would believe me. The last case your father was working on happened to have Tabor presiding over it. I'd seen other detective's reputations ruined because of Tabor and I couldn't stand by and watch him destroy your dad's. He was a good cop just trying to keep the streets safe."

Susanne sipped her coffee. "I found some evidence of corruption and threated Tabor. I told him I'd tell the authorities everything and testify against him if he didn't let them prosecute your father's case like they should. Tabor explained that if I said anything it would endanger all our lives because he'd made deals with a lot of criminals.

"I ignored his threat and went to the authorities anyway. Because Tabor knew some powerful people, I went into witness protection thinking that would keep you guys safe. When your dad was killed I contacted Tabor and said I wouldn't testify, but if he hurt any of you girls, I would tell them everything.

"I continued to let the government think I'd testify for protection until I could get away from them, but then Sonny found me. He's been helping by hiding me from Tabor and the Feds ever since."

"The men protecting her," Sonny glared at Antony, "the ones you were so afraid wouldn't let you take her, were my men."

Antony stood. "Why didn't you say something that night?"

"You never gave me the chance," Sonny said.

"So why are we in danger now?" Victoria rubbed her forehead. "How would the Feds or Tabor even know you're not still in hiding?"

"That'd be Antony's fault," Martin scoffed.

"Excuse me?" Antony's brows furrowed.

"When you asked Pete to get into the file, it alerted the Feds that someone was poking around which would have gotten back to Tabor."

"Feds only know someone opened the file. They don't know we've moved her. Tabor doesn't either." Antony leaned back in the chair. "Besides, the file said they were close to finding her. If I hadn't found her," Antony turned to Susanne, "You could be in their custody now. Or worse, in Tabor's."

"Then I guess I should thank you."

"But the trial is on hold. You can still testify," Zoë said.

"And risk your lives?" Susanne shook her head. "No."

"And you think hiding from Tabor will keep any of us safe?" Zoë stood and paced, her cop face on.

"No one's been hurt since I ran. You've been safe."

"Mom," Zoë put her hands on her hips. "I know criminals. They won't just walk away. They're waiting, and when you come out of hiding, they're going to clean up the mess." When Susanne looked questionably at her, Zoë's brows furrowed. "They'll eliminate the threat. You. That way they're guaranteed you'll never testify. You'll never be safe until you put Tabor behind bars."

"Then they overturn how many cases?" Susanne asked. "Threaten to arrest how many criminals that had gotten off? The threat will only heighten. They've already killed your father. I can't take that chance."

"Staying in hiding is a better option?" Zoë yelled.

"You need to calm down," Sonny said.

"Calm down?" Zoë turned to him, red creeping up her neck. "My dad was killed and this woman won't do anything to help bring his killer to justice." She turned to her mom. "I hate you." She stormed out.

Antony stood but Susanne grabbed his arm. "Let her go. She needs some time."

Antony nodded and sat back down.

"Zoë's right, Mom. You need to testify."

"And who will keep you safe?" Susanne asked.

"I will." Antony and Sonny said in unison.

Sonny's lips pursed. "I've kept you safe all this time. Why would you think I couldn't keep your daughters safe? We have bodyguards that will protect them and you. You can all live normal lives."

"Normal? You mean always looking over our shoulders. Someone is always out to get us?" Susanne chewed on the inside of her cheek.

"We're Luciano's." Antony laughed. "That *is* normal."

TWENTY

SONNY TAPPED HIS fingers on the kitchen table in the safe room. Susanne's reasons for hiding were finally out in the open. Martin had convinced Zoë to come back, but she still didn't appear interested. At the first lull in the conversation, she and Martin had made a beeline out the door. They claimed work was calling, but judging by the hardness on Zoë's face, it had been more anger than anything.

With only Antony left, now was as good a time as any to try and explain things to Victoria. Sonny leaned over to Victoria and whispered, "Can I talk to you privately?"

Victoria nodded. "I'll be right back."

Susanne grabbed Victoria's hand. "Listen to him."

Victoria turned back to Sonny. "We can go upstairs."

"Thank you."

Antony stood.

Sonny blocked his brother from tagging along. "Give me five minutes to talk to her."

"Take as much time as you need. Not sure it'll change much." Antony chuckled.

If Antony's intentions were to sabotage his confidence, it wasn't going to work. He would do everything he could to fight for the woman he loved, regardless of his brother's affection toward her.

Sonny followed Victoria out to the back patio where she sat. He clung to the cross that was part of the rosary in his pocket, knowing this conversation would give him insight into his future. He prayed it included Victoria.

He grabbed a chair, scooted it closer to her, and sat. "I'm sorry I had to lie to you."

"Lie to me?" Victoria's voice raised an octave. "It's not just the fact that you lied for a year about it. You watched me drain my savings hiring PIs. My dad's life insurance money. That was going to help me start my clothing business. All gone while you stood by, not just knowing where she was, but paying people to protect her."

"You don't need any money." Sonny grabbed her hand and held tight. "I've got enough money to last us the rest of our lives and then some. I love you, Victoria. I knew the chance I was taking by keeping her a secret, but my desire was to keep you safe. And if you knew about it, the people that killed your dad might come after you. I couldn't take that chance."

"Antony knew me for a week, and he helped me. You stood by, claiming to love me yet wouldn't do this one thing for me. You made me believe—"

Sonny stood and paced. Antony, the hero. Sheesh, he had to get her to see the truth. "Don't give my brother so much credit. The only reason Antony found her was because I already had. He tricked me into taking him to her."

"And if he hadn't, I'd still be believing she was dead." Her eyes filled with tears.

"Maybe, but I did it to protect you. Tabor killed your father, and he's after your mother. Do you understand what that means?" He didn't want to scare her, but she needed to understand the consequences of Susanne coming out of hiding. "Once he finds out, he'll be after you and Zoë. The same guy who killed your father."

Tears filled Victoria's eyes, and Sonny was sorry the truth hurt her. He knelt down and took both of her hands. "I won't let anything happen to you. I promise. I want you safe. I love you more than life itself. Don't you understand that?"

Pulling her hand from his, she brushed the tears from her cheeks. "When did you find her?"

"I started looking for her after your dad was killed. I saw how badly you wanted to know. I knew I could find out. When my men found her, she convinced me it was better if I hid her to keep you and Zoë safe. I'd beg her to let me tell you, but she kept reminding me that he killed your father. Is it so wrong for me to want to protect you?"

"No." She squeezed his hands. "I understand that, but a year? How long would you have hidden her from me? Forever?"

"I don't know. Every time you asked me to help you find her, it made me doubt my decision. I saw how I was hurting you."

"And Antony had no problem helping me."

Sonny rolled his eyes and stood, exasperated again with the sainthood of his older brother thrown at him. "You don't even know Antony."

"I can see his heart."

"You see only what he wants you to see. Clay's been investigating his past. He's not a saint."

She paced. "I never thought he was. I know he killed Carlo, and your dad blames him for the death of your mother. And I'm sure he's done things in his past he's not proud of."

"He's killed more than Carlo. He was arrested for killing—"

"That was never proven," Antony said matter-of-factly as he strutted out on the deck. "They couldn't even take it to trial. You want to reveal my past to Victoria maybe we should dig into yours too."

Sonny stood tall. He wasn't about to let his brother make him feel guilty for accidently killing Carlo even though Antony took the blame. "I'm not revealing any *secrets,* but I'm making sure Victoria knows the facts."

"Sure you were." Antony turned to Victoria. "You want to know my past? I'll tell you anything you want to know."

Victoria grabbed Antony's arm and pushed him toward the door. "Would you please let me talk to Sonny?"

He grinned his killer grin and cupped her cheek. "You know I'd do anything for you. Even if it's letting you talk to my brother."

Victoria waited until he was inside then walked back and sat in front of Sonny. "Where were we?"

Sonny shook his head, grunted a laugh, and sat. The damage was done. Antony had already stolen her heart and he didn't think he could get it back. It wasn't anything that surprised him, but it hurt just the same. "My brother… Like I said, he always gets what he wants."

Victoria reached for his hands. "You brother doesn't have me. We do have a connection that I can't even begin to explain. I do love you. I'm just not sure if I can get past this."

"I don't blame you. I knew this might happen."

"And you were still willing to take the chance of losing me anyway?"

"To keep you safe. Yes. I love you that much." Sonny knew if he still had a chance, he'd have to let her go to make her own decision. "Promise me something. While this thing with your mom is going on, listen to Antony and his men. He will protect you but you have to do what he says. There's a killer out there, and Antony will know how to deal with him."

"What about you? Would you keep me just as safe?"

He leaned in, reached for the back of her neck, and entangled his fingers in her hair. "You know I would. But you have to decide. You know, I'd marry you tomorrow."

"Even after I've told you I have feelings for him?" Victoria's eyes filled with tears. "You still want me?"

"Of course." Sonny grinned. There was hope. "I put a contract on the ranch house yesterday here in Ventura. I close on it the end of the month."

"That isn't a house. It's a mansion."

"Could be ours. I'm moving in as soon as I get the keys."

"What's Lorenzo think about that?"

Sonny shrugged. "He didn't say much. I think he knows it's time." He kissed her hands. "You need to stay here with Antony, until they catch whoever is out there. It's not safe to stay at your apartment."

Victoria's head cocked. "You want me to stay here, with him?"

"Yes. Antony and his men will keep you safe. If in a month, you'd rather stay at the ranch, you're more than welcome, but you can't stay at your place. In fact, I wish Zoë would move here too, but with Martin, I don't think that will happen." He stood. "I need to go."

She pulled him back down.

He laughed. It was a good sign. "Was there something else?"

She scooted closer to him.

Sonny's heart pounded. She did still love him. What the heck, he'd take a chance. He cupped the back of her neck and kissed her. "I love you very much. If you ever need anything, let me know."

She smiled, and a tear rolled down her cheek. "I never deserved you."

"Antony's my brother and I love him. Nothing will change that or come between us. Not even you if you choose him. Family is all there is. Just see him for who he really is before you decide. And if you pick him, I'll wish you all the best." Sonny almost choked on the words but knew the only way to have her was to let her go.

He stood and started to walk toward the door.

"Sonny?"

He turned back. "Yeah?"

"Can I call you later?"

He grinned. The glimmer of hope was all he needed. "I'd like that."

* * *

Antony stood at the kitchen window, watching and listening. Sonny always did the right thing. And unfortunately, it wasn't an act. That was just how big his brother's heart was. So how could he steal Victoria from him when Sonny was so willing to give her up?

Sonny came into the kitchen, rounded the island and stood chest to chest with Antony. "She's all yours. You'd better protect her at all costs. You hear me? It's because of you her life is now in danger. If anything happens to her, I'll hold you responsible."

"You'd just walk away?" Antony's eyes narrowed. "Really? Give her up just like that?"

"Listen to yourself? This isn't a competition between you and me. Victoria's a special, beautiful person inside and out. I know you can be devoted and truly love someone. I've seen that with Elisa. But Vic's not some woman you can ditch in a few weeks when you get tired of her."

"You think that's what I'd do?" Antony stepped back, leaned against the countertop, and crossed his arms.

"I don't know what you'd do. I'm hoping you'd give her all the happiness she deserves. But let her decide. And keep her safe."

"Yes, sir." Antony playfully saluted him.

"I hired Doc."

"Figured he'd go running back to you."

"I did promise him a job if you found out."

"Found out about what?" Victoria asked as she took a seat at the breakfast bar. "Doc works for you now?" she asked Sonny.

"Sonny talked Doc into spying on me so I canned him." Antony lifted his cup of coffee and took a sip.

Sonny turned toward Victoria. "I paid him to protect you at any cost and to feed me information so I'd know what was going on."

"And he was so easily bought." Antony said. "He's better off working for you."

"He wasn't that easy, and he did cost me a bundle, but he did his job."

"Then maybe he should come back." Victoria smiled at Sonny then looked up at Antony.

Antony wanted to smack the smug grin off his brother's face. If Doc came back, it'd be to spy. But the double-crosser was ex-special forces, and he could use a guy like that.

"I'd feel safer," Victoria added, "if he was around."

"I'll pay his salary," Sonny added.

"Sure, that sounds perfect." Antony's voice dripped with sarcasm. "Send him back and I'll put him to work. Bosco can continue to train him."

"Thank you," Victoria said. "I'm going back down to see my mom."

Sonny waited until Victoria left, then looked back over at Antony. "I close on the ranch at the end of the month. It's got a second house where I plan on housing the bodyguards."

"Does it have a safe room?"

"No. I told Victoria to stay with you until this is over. I'm trusting you to keep her safe."

"You know I will."

"Do me one more favor."

Antony smiled. He could never deny his brother's requests. "What's that?"

"No pressure. Let her decide."

"What?" Antony grinned. "You think I'd try to sway her my direction just because she's living with me, and I'll see her a whole lot more than you?"

"Yeah, hardly a fair playing field."

"Didn't you just say this wasn't a game?"

Sonny laughed. "I did and it's not. Just give her some space."

"Will do, Brother. No pressure from me. Promise."

"She's going to have to go back to work. Maybe send Doc with her."

"No." Antony sipped on the coffee. "Doc's too fresh. Bosco knows what's expected. I've trusted him with my life. I'd trust him with hers."

"Sounds good. I'm headed into the office. Don't forget you do have a job at Renato's regardless of what's going on."

"Lorenzo won't let me forget it. In fact, I have a meeting in an hour so I'll see you there later."

Sonny held out his hand.

Antony took it and pulled his brother into a hug. "Love you, man, no matter what."

Sonny nodded. "Love you, too. Family is all there is."

TWENTY-ONE

SUSANNE SIPPED coffee at the kitchen table at Antony's estate, thankful that after a couple weeks, she had been moved into a normal room and could roam around the house freely.

The number of men who worked for Antony made her wonder what else he had going on besides helping her and working for Renato's. He never called them bodyguards because he'd claimed on numerous occasions he didn't need any, but they all carried and looked like ex-military or ex-cons.

Trying to make a decision about what to do was weighing on her. Zoë was insistent she testify. Victoria seemed content with playing house and pretending everything was going to be okay.

Victoria strolled in, grabbed a tumbler and lid, filled it with coffee, and stood by the table. "How are you today?"

"Pretty good. You look beautiful as always. Going into work?"

"Yep. We have a new line from Dior arriving today. Can't wait to see it. You heard from Zoë at all?"

"No."

"I would've thought she'd gotten over this by now." She reached out and squeezed Susanne's hand. "I'm sorry."

"It's okay."

Victoria turned. "I've got to get going. See you later this afternoon. Maybe we could go to the beach."

"Sounds wonderful."

"I'll talk to Antony about it. Have him arrange something. Love you, Mom."

*   *   *

Zoë sat across from Martin at the restaurant both decked out in their blues. The waitress set their breakfast on the table. Eggs, hash browns, and English muffins. Better than anything she could make at her place. Course, she'd actually need to buy food if she wanted to cook.

Martin sprinkled salt and pepper on his eggs. "You talk to your mom?"

"Nope."

"You going to?"

"Not sure, but I have an idea." She readjusted the gun on the side of her belt that was rubbing against the booth and bugging her. She'd be so glad to finally make detective, get off the streets, and out of the uniform.

"It's going to endanger our lives." She refilled her coffee cup from the carafe left on the table. "But should get us closer to being detectives."

"So we'll get the bad guy?" Martin smiled then shoved another bite of egg into his mouth and made a quick brush of the napkin across his mouth.

"Definitely." Zoë blew her coffee to help cool it and took a sip.

"What's your brilliant idea?"

Zoë leaned into him and lowered her voice. "We leak to Tabor that my mom has changed her mind and is going to testify against him. He killed my dad to stop her. He won't be able to find mom, so he'll have to come after me or Victoria. When he does, we catch him."

"Why not just get your mom to really testify?"

"You heard her. She won't. But once Tabor thinks she is, he'll make a move. Then we catch him."

Martin gulped his milk. "I'm not worried about you, but what about Victoria? Do you want to take a chance that Tabor might succeed if he goes after her?"

"With Sonny and Antony's watchdogs keeping an eye on her? He'd never get close."

"Could work. How do you suppose we inform Tabor that your mom's willing to testify?"

"Leak it to the press. I can easily get one of them to run it. She is my mom."

Martin swiped his toast through the egg yolk on his plate and shoved the last bite in his mouth. "I think it will work."

Zoë pushed her empty plate to the center of the table and looked at her watch. "I'll call my gal at the paper this afternoon."

"Sounds good."

*　　*　　*

Sonny rested his foot on the wood slat of the gate and watched the jet-black Friesian horse high step around the corral. "She's beautiful. You think Vic will like her?"

"I'm sure she will." Clay paced around him.

"Relax."

"Not happening, boss. There's a killer out there whether you like to think about it or not."

"There'd be no reason he'd come after me. So stop," Sonny grabbed his arm, "and look at this horse with me. I want to surprise Victoria with it when I take her to the house next week."

Clay sighed and turned. "She really is beautiful. Victoria will love her. You know you'll need to hire a farm hand."

"Yes. You should get on that. I also need another couple of guys. Pull who we can from Lorenzo, see if Doc knows anyone. We'll open the house up to them. I'd like at least six. They can rotate in and out."

The owner of the horse approached them and reached out his hand.

Sonny shook it, smiling.

"What do you think? You like her?" the owner asked. "I think I told you her name is Onyx and she's won numerous ribbons at shows."

"She's prettier than the pictures you texted. How long have you had her?"

"About two years. My daughter's been showing her, but she's off to college and said I could sell her."

"She's not attached to this one?"

"Nah. She's got other horses. I have the most money invested in this one."

Sonny turned back to Onyx. The horse had long graceful legs that moved effortlessly and made a floating motion when she moved. Her beautifully sculpted head and shiny coat glistened in the sunlight as she came closer to where they stood.

"I love her. I think Victoria will, too. You still at 20K."

"Yes. She's gentle and well trained. I'll throw in the tack and saddle."

Sonny turned toward the horse as the rider brought her to the gate and jumped off.

"May I?" Sonny asked.

"Of course."

Sonny went into the corral and mounted the horse. He galloped around, slowed down and rubbed the side of her neck.

Trotting the horse back to the rider, Sonny dismounted and passed off the reins, giving her neck another pat Onyx bobbed her head, and her long flowing mane blew in the breeze.

Back on the other side of the gate, Sonny reached out his hand. "I'll take her. I get possession of my place today. When can I get her?"

"We can deliver her tomorrow. Nice to do business with you Mr. Luciano."

"Keep me in mind. I'll probably be looking for another couple of horses in the near future. I'll send you a certified check by the end of the day."

"Thank you."

Sonny and Clay walked toward the car. "Can't wait for Victoria to see it."

"I hate to even mention this, but what if Victoria picks Antony?"

The mere mention of the possibility made Sonny's blood boil. It was something he didn't think about. "You think she will?"

"I hope not, but she is living there, and we both know how Antony operates."

"Doc said he's been keeping his distance, trying to let her decide." Sonny put his sunglasses on. "And if she does? I guess Lauren will be available."

Clay laughed.

* * *

A tap echoed on the office door. "Yes?" Victoria looked up from her paperwork.

Sonny entered and held out a cup of Starbucks.

"For you." He set the hot coffee on the table. "I just wanted to check and make sure we're still on for Friday."

Victoria rounded the desk and gave Sonny a hug. "Yes. I'm looking forward to it. Thanks for the coffee."

His strong arms continued to hold her. Something she had missed. The forgiveness part was hard to get past although her anger was subsiding.

"Your mom make any decisions?" Sonny released her.

She motioned to the couch and they both sat. "No and I'm kinda tired of pushing her, but I do know something needs to be decided. If she's not going to testify, then we need to find another house for us to stay in."

"Not enjoying Antony's?"

Victoria sipped the mocha. "It's not that. He's been very generous, but we can't live there forever. And I don't have the kind of money to set her up in something that safe."

"I can—"

"I know you'll help." Anger rose. If her bank account wasn't drained, she wouldn't have to depend on anyone. "If I had… Nothing."

"Go ahead and say it. If you had all the money back that you spent on searching for your mom. How much was your share of your father's life insurance policy? Twenty-five thousand? Here." Sonny pulled out his checkbook, scribbled on it and ripped the check out. He handed it to her. "Now, you're not dependent on anyone.

"That's not what I meant." She chewed her bottom lip. "It's just—"

"You're right. I let you waste your money. I want you to have it back." He took her hand and kissed it. "I don't ever want you to feel trapped into staying with Antony or with me. You need to do what's right for you and your mother."

Victoria looked at the check. Could she take it? It's not like he'd miss it with all the money he had, and it was his fault she'd lost hers. But would it obligate her to him?

As if sensing her inner turmoil, he smiled. "Take it, please."

"It will help us try and decide what to do."

"I don't want you leaving the protection we can give you, but I do understand the limbo you're in."

"And what about you? You're in limbo, too."

Sonny leaned over, rested his elbows on his thighs, and rubbed his hands together. "I hate it, but I love you and I'm willing to wait."

For how long? She wasn't sure. Maybe spending some time with him on Friday night would help her decide.

* * *

Antony sat in the deli. It wasn't ideal and he didn't like the crowd, but Pete had picked it. Whatever he needed to talk to Antony about had to be important since they'd sworn off seeing each other until the case was closed or the feds were off Pete's back.

The teenage waitress approached him again. "Sure I can't bring you something while you wait."

Antony handed her a ten. "We won't be eating. The two waters are enough and we won't need you to check on us."

She shrugged, slid the money in her pocket and walked to the next table.

Antony stood as Pete walked to the table.

Pete shook his hand. "How'd you lose the feds?"

"They ain't that smart."

They both laughed.

Pete pushed him a paper. "Here's the list of clients that got off when Tabor was presiding over their cases. It's not pretty."

Antony glanced it over. "I'd say not. Any one of these would take out Susanne."

"Or use Zoë or Victoria to get to her."

Antony rubbed his forehead. They'd have to think of another way. "She can't testify or this will never end." Antony folded the paper and slid it into his pocket.

"So what are you thinking?"

"You may not want to know." Antony laughed sardonically.

"Eliminate Tabor?"

Antony raised his brows. "A judge? You can't be serious."

"Just saying what you're thinking."

"We could find another stooge. Surely someone else knew what kind of racket Tabor had going on."

Pete nodded. "Let me do some more poking around."

"Thanks." Antony pulled out an envelope full of cash and handed it to Pete.

Pete hesitated. "You don't have to pay me every time. I could just get you information because we're friends."

Friends? Antony didn't have many and didn't think that should change. Friendship went both ways and Antony wasn't sure he wanted to be obligated to anyone. He pushed the money back toward Pete. "Take it. I'll feel better."

Pete tucked the envelope in his pocket. "Okay, but seriously, you don't have to give me anymore. I heard you fired Doc."

"Yeah, he was spying on me for my brother. Sonny hired him, and now he's back with me temporarily. I'm trying to train him right so when he does go back to Sonny's he knows what he's doing."

"I appreciate that."

"I know you and Bosco haven't gotten to hang-out much but as soon as we get over this Tabor thing, life should calm down."

"Sounds good." Pete held out his hand.

Antony shook it.

TWENTY-TWO

ANTONY SLAMMED THE newspaper on the table in front of Susanne. "What the heck is this?"

Susanne picked it up and read the headlines. Her eyes widened and she dropped it on the table. "I have no idea. I haven't spoke to a reporter or anyone else for that matter."

"Really?" Susanne had lied to him on more than one occasions. This might be no different.

"I haven't talked to anyone outside of this family."

Victoria came into the room. "What's going on? I could hear you guys all the way upstairs."

Antony handed the paper to her. "Take a look at that. Says your mom is testifying against Tabor. The trial is back on."

Victoria read it over then set it on the table. "Mom, did you decide to do this without telling any of us?"

"No. They didn't hear this from me."

Antony picked it up and read it aloud. "Also says you're out of hiding. And Victoria is dating one of the Luciano brothers." He glared at her. "Did you give them this address?"

Susanne stood and placed her hands on her hips. "This didn't come from me. I swear. Remember I told you I'd never testify because I refuse to put my girls in danger."

"Then who would do this?" Victoria asked.

"Only one other person I can think of." Antony rubbed his forehead then brushed his hand over his face. Martin, he suspected. "I'll let you know when I find out."

"Am I okay going to work?"

Victoria's frightened face made his heart break, but he couldn't let her live her life scared or locked in a room. If she were going to become a Luciano, whether with Sonny or with him, she'd have to learn how to live like one.

He put his arm around her shoulders and walked her toward the front door. "You'll be fine. You've got Bosco. He'd never let anything happen to you."

"Okay." She looked up into his eyes. "If you're sure?"

"I'm sure." He brushed his knuckles across her cheek. "Have a great day."

"Okay, thanks."

Antony walked back into the kitchen, picked up the paper and looked at the article again.

"Who would do this?" Susanne asked.

"I'm not a hundred percent, but I'll find out." He pulled his phone out and sent a text. *Meet me now.*

* * *

Martin slid his phone in his pocket. "Gotta meet Antony. He must've seen the morning paper."

Zoë stood. "I'm coming."

"I can handle him. Let him blame me not you."

"I don't care if he knows it was my idea, but I'd just rather not receive his wrath today. I'm already sick of getting it from Victoria for not speaking to my mom."

"Why don't you go see her?" Martin leaned in and gave her a kiss.

"Don't *you* start."

He grinned. They'd been down this road many times in the past few weeks and she wouldn't budge until she was ready. He'd learned she was the most stubborn person he'd ever met.

* * *

Antony drummed his fingers on the table at Mikey's. He was beginning to like the place and thought about investing in it. The silence and service of the owner would be worth every penny he'd spend.

Martin slid into the booth. "Guess you read the morning headlines?"

"What the heck were you thinking?" Antony snapped.

"Not my idea. It was Zoë's. It's to flush Tabor out. We're not sitting around letting Susanne do nothing, and if this is how we have to do it, then so be it."

"And you didn't stop her?"

"Why would I? She's a big girl."

"Who now has a target on her back. You're some piece of work."

"Zoë's a cop. She's not helpless."

Antony clicked his tongue against his perfectly white teeth that had cost him a small fortune. "So was her dad and he had a heck of lot more experience than she does. Or you for that matter."

"This was her decision and her doing."

"You could've stopped it."

"I didn't want to. I'm with her. Flush him out and let's end it."

"And you get a nice collar no matter what the cost? You're an idiot." Antony slid out of the booth and stood.

"Don't ever ask me for help again," Martin snapped.

"I don't think I asked for it to start with." Antony spun around on his heel, dropped a twenty on the bar and left.

* * *

Martin knocked on the door of Antony's estate, his jaws tight and fists clenched. Who did Antony think he was, calling all the shots and acting like a mob boss? *What a jerk. I'm a cop. And what was Antony? Nothing but a two-bit criminal.*

He knocked harder, sighed and tapped Antony's number in his phone contacts.

"What now?" Antony shouted.

"I need to see Susanne. It's for Zoë. Tell your goons to let me in."

"I just left you. Why didn't you mention you were stopping by then?"

"Because you stormed out like a two-year-old," Martin yelled.

"You know, when you're asking someone for a favor, insulting them isn't the smartest thing to do."

"Just tell them to let me in."

Antony hung up.

Martin looked at the phone, shook his head, slid it in his pocket and gave the door another pound. Nothing. As he took a step away, the door opened.

"You can come in," Max said.

"Your boss call?"

"Yes."

"I need to see Susanne." He pushed his way into the foyer.

"She's in the kitchen."

Martin found Susanne sitting at the table, a cup of coffee in one hand and the newspaper in front of her. "I see you've read the headlines."

"Yes. I'm trying to figure out who would do this?"

"Zoë did."

Susanne's eyes widened. "Why would Zoë do this?"

"Because we can't live like this. You can't stay in hiding the rest of your life. Let's get Tabor while we can."

"It won't stop with Tabor. If his cases are overturned, I'll have even more people after me."

"No. We'll just flush Tabor out."

"What's to flush? He walks into that courtroom every day. He's not in hiding."

"What I mean is, it'll get him to try and locate you." He slid her a cell phone. "The number to this phone has been placed strategically on Zoë's desk. Somebody is helping Tabor and they'll check her things to see if they can find out where you are. They'll find the number, give it to Tabor and he'll call you. That's when we can get him."

"How exactly will we do that?" Susanne asked.

"He'll want to meet with you, talk things through. Try to convince you not to testify."

Susanne refilled her coffee, blew on it and took a sip. "The convincing is what I'm worried about."

"We won't let him hurt you. You confront him about killing your husband. If we can get him to talk, confess to it, we can get him without you even testifying. We'll get him on murder."

Martin didn't mention that the Feds and DA's office would still pressure her to testify. Getting Tabor and making detective was all that mattered to him.

"I won't wear a wire," Susanne said.

"Either you wear one or we can plant it at the place you meet. Just pick it-up if this phone rings. Also, it's our way of communicating without me having to get permission from Antony."

She nodded. "Can I reach Zoë on this?"

"Yes. Our numbers are programed in. I also put Antony's and Sonny's."

"I guess with this story leaked, I have no choice, do I?"

Martin shook his head. "Nope."

"Antony okay with this?"

"I don't give a rip what Antony thinks."

"Well, you should," Antony's voice came from behind them. "Because she does nothing without our input."

Martin turned. Antony, Sonny, and Zoë walked into the kitchen.

Susanne rounded the table and wrapped her arms around Zoë. "I love you so much. Thank you for finally coming."

"Antony didn't give me much of a choice." Zoë's eyes moist with tears.

Susanne tucked Zoë's hair behind her ear and patted her cheek. "You're so beautiful."

Zoë untucked her hair. "Thanks. I'm the one who talked to the papers. I want this over. If Tabor killed Daddy, I want him behind bars."

Susanne brushed away the tears and nodded. "Okay. I guess I don't have much of a choice. You've been so brave. I guess it's time I do the same."

"Well," Antony clapped his hands together. "Now that *that* is over, Sonny and I would like to know about this brilliant plan you all came up with."

* * *

Sonny listened as Martin and Zoë talked out some sting, wiring Susanne, and getting a confession out of Tabor about killing her husband, but it was Antony he watched.

He knew if there was any chance of endangering them or Victoria, Antony would squash the plan in a second.

"So we just wait?" Sonny asked.

"Yes. Tabor will have to contact Susanne. Nobody knows where she is." Martin said.

"With the morning paper, it won't be too hard to figure out whose place to case." Antony got a soda out of the fridge, popped the top, and took a drink. "Anyone else want anything?"

Heads nodded, so Antony pulled out a few cans and set them in the middle of the table.

"How quickly do you think they'll figure out Susanne's here?" Sonny asked.

Antony spun around. "Not long."

"Maybe she should move out," Zoë said.

When Antony cut his eyes to hers, she grinned. "I'm only saying, Vic and Mom shouldn't be in the same place. Safer that way then there's less chance of both of them getting hurt."

"Victoria could move in to my place." Sonny's heart pounded. He'd love the same opportunity his brother had to play house with her and try to sway her feelings.

"You don't even have a safe room," Antony stated.

"I've got a top-notch security system, just as many bodyguards as you, and a wall surrounding the property."

Zoë brought up her hands. "Man, I'm sorry I brought *that* up. Boys, lower the testosterone. Why don't we let Victoria decide?"

Sonny wasn't sure he could take the blow if she chose to stay at Antony's, even if it was just because she felt safer.

Antony crushed the empty can in his hand and tossed it in the trash. "She stays here unless we see a threat. I think with the safe room, its better. If they find her here, we'll take her to Lorenzo's."

Sonny reluctantly nodded. The safe room was a better option if someone came after them, but he wasn't too keen on the idea of Victoria staying with Antony any longer than she needed to.

Zoë hit Martin's arm and stood. "I think we need to get to work." She looked at Susanne. "Let us know as soon as Tabor contacts you."

Susanne nodded. "Please be careful." She squeezed Martin's arm. "Take good care of her."

After Zoë and Martin left, Susanne picked up the half-filled cans of sodas, dumped them out and tossed the cans in the trash.

"You okay with this?" Sonny asked her.

"I don't really have a choice since the paper ran that story, but I'm sure it'll work out," Susanne said.

Antony sat and crossed his leg. "That's true."

"I'm going upstairs for a bit." Susanne left.

"What about you?" Sonny asked Antony.

"I guess this is as good a plan as any." He pulled a piece of paper from his pocket, unfolded it and handed it to Sonny. "I got this list from my guy at the department. It's the possible cases that could be retried if she testifies. That's a lot of bad guys that might go to jail."

Sonny looked it over and shook his head. "We can't let her testify. I'd rather have just Tabor after her than any one of these."

"My thought exactly. The problem is Martin."

"What about him?"

"He wants to nail Tabor any way he can and he doesn't care who it puts in danger. I'm not sure what he'll do behind our backs."

Sonny gave the list back to Antony. He could see the ambition in Martin's eyes. It appeared he didn't even care how it affected Zoë as long as he got the bad guy.

"You might want to move that gun up to your waist."

Sonny laughed. "You don't think I could pull it fast enough around my ankle? I do move it up when I feel threatened, you know."

Antony stood. "I think I'd feel better if it was on your waist all the time."

"Got it. Move my gun to my waist."

Antony's phone pinged. He looked at a text then slid the phone in his pocket.

"About the case?" Sonny asked.

"No. Lauren."

"Lauren? Didn't know you were seeing her."

"Can't sit at home all the time."

"Lauren looked good in her latest spread in Elle."

"You actually saw that?" Antony laughed. "I mean, I had to because she showed it to me. How'd you see it?"

"I didn't go buy the magazine if that's what you're asking. Victoria showed it to me. It had some new up-and-coming designers in it that were at the store the other day. Didn't Lauren tell you?"

Antony's face flushed. "Lauren's not much of a talker. But she looks mighty fine on my arm."

Sonny walked toward the door. "We'd better get back before Papa sends Vince to find us."

Good. Antony was biding his time with Lauren. That might give Sonny the chance to show Victoria just how much he loved her.

TWENTY-THREE

VICTORIA PLACED THE purse strap over her shoulder and turned to Bosco. "You ready?"

"Yes, ma'am. I'll get the car."

Antony came down the stairs. "Have a nice day at the office, dear."

Victoria laughed. He'd been acting strange for the last few weeks. She assumed it was his way of backing off and letting her decide who she wanted to be with. "Thanks."

"Will you be home for dinner? I can grill."

"I'm sorry, but, I've got plans."

"Sonny?" he asked.

"Maybe."

Antony gave her a devilish grin, his dimples deep. He stepped closer, and stared down into her eyes. "Hmm, like a date? Because if it's a date then to make it fair, we get to go out on one too."

"Yeah, but I see you all the time."

He moved even closer.

Her heart pounded, and she swore he was going to kiss her.

"And yet, I feel like we're never alone," he said.

"We're not," she whispered. "Doc always seems to be lurking somewhere."

"I don't lurk," Doc said.

Antony's raised a brow, eyes still staring into hers, searching her soul. "He lurks," he said to her then yelled, "Get lost."

"Yes, sir."

"He does have the worst timing." Victoria grinned.

"You know why?" Antony asked.

"Sonny."

"Yep." He kissed her forehead. "Have a great day." With a wink, he spun around and left her wanting more.

She walked to the front porch where Doc stood. "You should keep your nose out of my business."

"I'm sorry, but I just don't think Antony knows his boundaries."

"You think I can't handle Antony? I can so butt out."

Doc nodded. "Yes, ma'am."

She readjusted her purse, went down the stairs and climbed into the car. Bosco took off toward Francesca's.

* * *

Victoria glanced up from her phone as Bosco pulled into a gas station. "What are we doing?" It wasn't like Bosco to stop anywhere unless she had asked.

"Boss," Bosco had his phone to his ear. "He's followed us from the estate. Silver Chevy, four-door. On the side of the gas station. Fifth and Walnut."

Bosco glanced at all his mirrors then around the car. He took the gun out and clicked the safety off. "Antony's on his way. Lock the doors and stay in the car." Bosco slid out of the car, shut the door, and looked around.

Victoria's heart pounded and palms sweated. She touched Sonny's number on her phone. "Something's going on and I'm not sure what to do. Bosco has his gun out. Can you come?"

"Where are you?"

"At the gas station on Fifth and Walnut. Please hurry."

"I'm on my way. Trust Bosco. He knows how to do his job."

"Okay." She clutched the phone in her hand and watched.

Bosco rounded the back as if he was coming around to open her door.

Antony's black BMW flew into the lot then skidded to a stop, barely missing the silver car. He jumped out, bolted toward the Chevy, threw the door open and yanked a man out. In one motion, he swung him around and threw him face down on the hood of the car. Antony's gun pressed against the man's cheek.

Victoria got out. Bosco grabbed her arm and pushed her back to the car. "Get back in until it's secure."

"It looks pretty secure. Antony has his gun in the guy's face." She brushed past Bosco and walked closer to the commotion.

"Who are you?" Antony demanded. When no answer came, Antony flung him around and backhanded him across the face. "I said, who are you?"

"FBI."

"Yeah, right."

"In my front jacket pocket is my ID. I swear."

"Bosco," Antony yelled. "Call the police."

"No, no police," the man said. "Can I get my ID out?"

Sonny's car zoomed into the parking lot. He was climbing out before Clay completely stopped. He ran to Victoria and yelled, "Antony, you good?"

"Says he's FBI." Antony pushed the gun harder into his face. "I hate liars."

Sonny wrapped his arms around Victoria. "You okay?"

"Yes. Is he really FBI?" she asked.

"They'll find out."

Bosco was on the guy helping search pockets. He tossed a pocket-knife on the hood of the car, pulled out a wallet then his driver's license. "Says his name is Charles Stockholm."

A black Cadillac Escalade pulled up behind them and two men climbed out.

"So, Chuck," Antony grabbed his arm. "Dwyer here is going to take you for a ride. I'm sure you'll be very helpful in supplying him with some information. Eddie will follow in your car. As soon as you answer all our questions, you'll be free to go."

Charles's eyes widened as Dwyer grabbed him and threw him into the back seat where Victoria could see another one of Antony's men sitting.

A shudder ran through her and she leaned closer to Sonny.

The black Caddy and silver Chevy disappeared.

Bosco stood on guard beside Sonny and her, combing the parking lot with his eyes, his gun still at his side. Antony joined them.

"Who do you think he was?" she asked him.

"Not sure." Antony smiled. "I wouldn't worry too much. He wasn't carrying a gun. Looks too puny to be a kidnapper. My guess is he was following you to see your routine, but he answers to someone else. That's the name I want."

"And how will you get that information?" Victoria swallowed hard, unsure if she really wanted to know.

"Any way I can."

Sonny's arm tightened around her. "Let's get you to work."

She stared at Antony's hard eyes, but judging by the grin on his face, he was having fun. He had lived on the streets. Maybe this was normal for him.

Sonny led her to his car. "I'll drive you. Bosco and Clay can follow."

* * *

Sonny helped Victoria into the car, shut the door, and walked around to where Antony stood. "You going to call the cops and turn that guy in?"

Antony laughed. "Oh, sorry… Were you being serious?" He rolled his eyes. "How'd you know to come?"

"Victoria called." Sonny followed Antony to his Beemer.

"Lucky you." Antony climbed into the car. "We're taking him to Lorenzo's."

"I'll be over shortly." He slammed Antony's car door and waited until he left the parking lot before returning to the others. "Follow us," he said to Clay and Bosco.

Sonny climbed in the car with Victoria and pulled out. "You sure you're okay?"

"I didn't even notice the car."

"Bosco is trained to see things like that."

"You mean he's not just my chauffer?" She tried to joke, but knew it sounded weak. Her hands started shaking again.

Sonny pulled into the parking lot of Francesca's and killed the engine. "Come here." He pulled her into a hug. "You sure you're okay?"

"That really scared me."

He cupped the back of her neck. "I know, but he was just following you. He didn't have a gun."

"But the next guy could, couldn't he?"

Sonny pulled her closer. "No one will ever get that close to you. That's why you have Bosco."

"Thank you for coming."

"I'm glad you called."

She laid her head on his chest. He savored the moment, knowing it would end too soon. His arms tightened around her.

"I've missed this," she said.

"Can I ask you something?"

"Sure."

"Why'd you call me? Antony had it under control."

She looked up at him. "I wanted you there."

"I'm glad."

"Me too." She reached up, grabbed the back of his neck and pulled him into a kiss.

His heart raced. Had his backing away helped her realize how much she still loved him? "And what was that for?" he asked.

"For loving me."

"We still on for tonight?"

"Yes. And you won't tell me what we're doing?"

"Nope. It's a surprise." Sonny got out of the car, jogged around to the other side and helped her out. He put his arm around her as they walked toward the entrance.

Bosco and Clay followed close behind.

Once inside, Victoria turned toward him. "See you tonight."

"I can't wait."

Sonny jogged back to the car where Clay waited for him, pulled out his phone, and called Antony. "You find anything out from the guy?"

"Not yet. Where are you?"

"I just dropped Victoria off at the store. She's pretty shook up. I'm headed your way." He hoped the incident that morning would help Victoria realize why he had kept her mother hidden. It was to protect her.

* * *

Antony paced in front of Lorenzo's desk. Waiting for his father was wasting time. He wanted to go to the basement and find out what the little punk knew and why he was following Victoria.

Lorenzo wheeled himself into the room. "I see you have a guest."

"Yes. I didn't think you'd mind if I used your basement for a little interrogation. You never carpeted that back room. It'll be easier to clean up any blood."

Lorenzo laughed. "What do you have going on?"

"We found Victoria's mother, and somebody's after her. And Vic and Zoë. This guy was following Victoria today, and I need to know who he's working for. Sonny doesn't have the stomach to do what needs to be done, so I stepped in."

"You got that right," Lorenzo said.

"I didn't have anywhere else to work, so I hoped you wouldn't mind."

"Just clean up your mess."

Antony turned. Sonny stood in the doorway. "Brother." He walked past him. "Come on."

Sonny followed. "Did I just hear that right? Papa likes the fact that you brought that guy here?"

"I think if I had offered, he would've let me carry him down the stairs so he could watch." Antony stopped at the top of the stairs. "Now, if you're going to try and interfere, stay here. I'm not sure what my guys have done to this punk, but they said they got some info."

"Okay. You call the police yet? Martin or Zoë?"

"Why would I call any of them?"

The brothers walked down the stairs, through the finished part of the basement into a darkened room with concrete floors, unfinished walls and ceiling.

Charles sat in a chair in the center of the room. Eddie stood in the corner while Dwyer circled like a vulture. Charles looked untouched.

Antony's brows furrowed. "Has Chuck told us everything we need to know?"

Dwyer stopped pacing. "Chuck, here is not a fan of pain. He's been quite helpful and Eddie didn't even have to mess up his manicure."

"Shut up," Eddie yelled.

Antony fought a grin. "What'd Chuck tell you?"

"It's Charles and I said—"

Antony threw up his hand. "Huh uh. Chuck. I need you to stay quiet. I want to know what you've already told them. Then I'll decide how helpful you've actually been."

"But I told them…"

Antony glared at him. "Not another word until I ask. Got it?"

Charles's eyes widened and he nodded frantically.

Antony motioned to Dwyer as Sonny crossed his arms and leaned against a two-by-four in the framed-in wall.

Max hurried in and set two hand-guns on the desk. "Found them in his car."

Antony picked them up one at a time—dropped the full clip, made sure the chamber was clear, then set them down. His neck burned and his blood pumped furiously through his veins. The goon could've used those on Victoria.

He took two steps and backhanded Charles so hard he flew off the chair and hit the floor.

Charles got to his feet and wiped the seeping blood from his mouth.

"Sit," Antony demanded.

Charles cowed back into the chair.

"Now. Let's start again. Dwyer, what information has…Chuck given you."

"Chuck here," Dwyer paced again, "says he works for Tabor."

"What was he doing for Tabor?"

"Suppose to just be checking things out."

"It's true." Charles recoiled, probably ready for Antony to backhand him again.

"And the guns, Chuck. What were they for?" Antony asked.

"Just for protection. They weren't even out. One was in the trunk and the other in the glove box."

Antony turned to Max. "True?"

"Yes."

Antony circled Charles and glanced at Sonny, surprised he'd kept his mouth shut.

"I'm in a good mood, Chuck, so I'm going to let you go, but tell your boss I want to meet with him."

"How will he get a hold of you?"

Antony pulled a business card out and jammed it in Charles's shirt pocket, then patted him on the cheek. "Thanks." He motioned with his head and Dwyer grabbed Charles's arm and pulled him up.

"What about my guns?" Charles asked.

"What guns?" Antony grinned. "Get him outta here."

Eddie scooped the guns up and took them away.

"That went well." Antony rubbed his hands together.

"What are you going to do once you meet up with the honorable Judge?" Sonny asked.

"Give him a chance to turn himself in."

"You think he'll do that?"

"No, but I always like to give people the option." Antony flipped the light off and they walked up the stairs. "So you got a date with Victoria tonight, huh?"

"Yeah."

"Good luck."

Antony went into his office, shut the door, and sat in the chair. Unfinished paperwork littered his desk. A date. Maybe he was wrong to sit back and let her decide. He might need to step it up since it looked like Sonny wasn't waiting any longer.

TWENTY-FOUR

VICTORIA GRINNED as the iron gates creaked open. Bosco drove the car into the drive and stopped. She jumped out and met Sonny coming out the front door. "Is it yours? You closed early?"

Sonny held up the keys. "It's all mine. The second house, down there," he pointed, "is where the bodyguards live. There's a barn and over the hill is a pond. I got the whole thing, all twenty acres.

"I've got a couple of things to show you." He took her hand and led her to the barn where a man held the reins of a large black horse.

Sonny motioned towards the animal. "For you."

"What? The horse?"

"Yes, the horse. You said you always wanted one. Here she is."

Her heart skipped a beat as she walked into the corral and took the reins. "You bought me a horse?"

"Not just any horse. Her name is Onyx. She's a Friesian. Used to be a show horse. Real gentle. I think you'll love her." Sonny grinned.

"I already do." Victoria rubbed the mare's neck. "She's gorgeous. I mean I've never seen a horse so beautiful. She had to cost a fortune."

"You want to ride her?"

"Now? Gosh it's been years since I've ridden."

"Yes, now."

Sonny motioned to the older man. "This is John. He's the stable man."

"Nice to meet you."

John motioned with an opened hand. "Hop up."

Victoria put her foot in the stirrup and pulled herself up on the English saddle. She grabbed the reins and took Onyx around the corral, smiling.

Bringing the horse back to John, she slid off. "I love her, but she's too much, Sonny. You can't just give me a horse."

"I did."

Another man came into the barn. "Sonny."

"Yes."

"It's all set up."

"Wonderful. Victoria, this is Bruno. He works for me, but I'm not sure you've ever met him."

She left Onyx and shook Bruno's hand. "Nice to meet you. What's all set up?"

"I'll show you. Come on."

Sonny motioned toward the golf cart, waited for her to get on, then took his seat behind the wheel.

"It's the best way to get around the place."

She held the bar and allowed the cool breeze to blow through her hair. They drove over the hill, down by a pond then stopped at an open field where a table had been placed with two guns and further down some targets.

"What are we doing here?" she asked.

"I want you to know how to shoot. I bought you this new little Berretta Bobcat. Small enough you can carry it in your purse. You'll need to get your conceal and carry permit. I've got an instructor lined up if you'll do it. I'd feel safer if you carried. At least until this thing with Tabor is over."

"I haven't shot a gun for years. My dad used to take us all the time." She picked it up, pushed a button and dropped the clip. "How do I check the chamber?"

He came around and stood shoulder to shoulder. "Here," he pulled back the slide. "See, no bullets."

The warmth of his body touching hers sent a ripple of desire through her. She breathed deeply, taking in his woodsy cologne, and smiled. "Thanks."

He picked up an over-the-head earmuff and placed it on her head.

She brought her hands up and covered his, getting lost in his eyes.

He grinned. "Ear protection."

She wanted to kiss him so badly, but did that mean she'd made her decision? If Sonny was the one, why was she still attracted to Antony?

Bosco rolled up on a golf cart making her turn. He sent a silent hello with a jerk of his head.

Victoria shook off the momentary lust, reached around Sonny and took the gun. She slid the clip back in, aimed at the target and pulled the trigger.

After the first magazine was empty she looked down at the other gun.

Sonny picked it up. "Smith and Wesson. I wasn't sure if you wanted to shoot something bigger."

"Sure."

"It's loaded and ready to go."

She sighted in the target and emptied the clip. "I like that little one, but I really don't know if I want to carry. I'm not sure I could use it."

"If your life was in danger you would."

"But isn't that why I have Bosco?"

"Yes. And he's great, but you should have one just in case." The lines on his forehead deepened.

"Is there something else?"

Sonny took the Smith and Wesson and set it down. "When we searched the guy's car, the one who was following you today, he did have a couple of guns in it. One was in the trunk and one in the glove box, so it didn't look like he was planning on using them, but we don't know. That's why I'd feel safer if you carried."

Her heart pounded as the morning came rushing back. There was no doubt in her mind that Tabor would use her to get to her mom. But could she aim a gun at someone and shoot them? She wasn't sure.

"I'll think about it."

"I wanted you to know that Antony and I are meeting with Tabor tomorrow."

"You are? Is that safe?"

"Yes. He's not going to do anything to us. Antony insists we talk with him before anything else happens."

"Okay. Be careful."

"I always am."

Clay drove up in a golf cart, climbed out and walked toward them. "Dinner's ready."

* * *

"Great. I'm starving." Sonny tried to hide his disappointment that she didn't want to carry even though it didn't surprise him. "Clay, will you bring the guns?"

"Yes."

"Want to drive?" Sonny asked Victoria.

"No, you go ahead."

They headed up to the front of the house with Bosco following close behind.

"I still can't believe this is yours."

"Could be ours," he raised his eyebrows playfully, silently praying she felt the same way.

Victoria followed him through the great room, out the French doors and onto the patio that overlooked a large pool. "Why Mr. Luciano. Are you trying to buy my love?"

He grinned, pulling her into his arms. "Would it work? If you say yes, I can drop another wad on something."

She giggled, wrapped her arms around him and pulled him closer. "You've always had a very generous heart."

"You know you're killing me. I want to kiss you so bad it's not funny."

She moved closer. Her body trembled. "Then why don't you?"

He slid his hand behind her neck, entangling his fingers in her hair. Their eyes connected and he wanted her more than ever before. He was inches away from her lips when he heard a throat clear.

"Mmm hmm. You guys need anything?" Bosco asked.

They both turned.

Bosco stood with his hands buried in his pockets, his face red.

"We're good. Thanks," Sonny said.

"Well, I'll just wait here…in case you do." Bosco rolled back on his heels and whistled.

Sonny let go of her and backed away. He ran his fingers through his hair. "What's the deal with him? I feel like a schoolboy who just got caught doing something wrong."

She patted Sonny's chest and grinned. "He's just being over protective, I'm sure. There was that guy following me, remember?"

Bosco went inside.

Sonny pulled the lid off a tray of the food. "We should eat." He handed Victoria a plate.

*　　*　　*

Victoria glanced at Bosco who stared at them through the glass of the French doors. Sonny may not understand what he was doing, but she did. Bosco was lurking like Doc always was at Antony's house as if to teach Sonny a lesson.

She set her plate on the patio table and waited for Sonny to sit. "Did Janice do this?"

"Yep." He sat next to her. "She always does a great job."

Victoria twirled the pasta on her fork. "You bought any furniture yet?"

"Just the bedroom stuff so I could move in." He grinned and took her hand. "I was kinda hoping you'd help me with the rest of the house. Would you?"

Victoria set her fork down. How was she supposed to answer that? If she said yes, he'd think she was making a decision. Part of her was ready to commit. Watching Antony, this morning with the guy that followed her was scary. There was something hard and almost criminal about Antony, yet she couldn't deny she was still drawn to him.

Sonny was strong and every bit as protective as Antony, but he did it in a kinder, gentler way.

"Tell me what you're thinking," Sonny said. "We've always been honest…well, except when I lied to you for a year about your mom."

She smiled. "After that guy followed me this morning, I understand why you were afraid for me. It made this whole thing real. I know you were trying to keep me safe. I understand that now."

"But am I forgiven?"

"Yes."

Sonny pulled her to him.

"You finally going to kiss me?" Her heart was about to leap out of her chest.

"Oh, yes." His grin widened.

The French door slammed and they both turned.

Bosco stood awkwardly with his hands on his waist. "Um, I was just going to make a plate."

Victoria raised an eyebrow. "Go right ahead."

Sonny leaned in and whispered, "What's his deal?"

"Let me take care of it." She walked over to Bosco who scooped some Fettuccini Alfredo on his plate. "I don't need a chaperone. You don't have to *watch* us."

"Sorry, I do. Orders."

Victoria nodded and went back to her seat. "Seems Antony is trying to teach you a lesson."

Sonny's forehead wrinkled. "Why? I don't understand."

Bosco went inside, stood at the French doors staring at them, and ate.

She laughed. "Bosco is doing what you asked Doc to do. To watch Antony and me. Interrupt us anytime we appear to be close."

Sonny scooted his empty plate to the center of the table. "I didn't ask Doc to do that. All I said was to protect you at all costs and fill me in on anything I might not be aware of. I can't help it if Doc thinks you need protecting from my brother."

"Well, it does get annoying. Could you tell him to stop?"

"I'll text him later." Sonny leaned in. "So I'm not going to be able to kiss you?"

Her heart pounded and she moved closer and whispered, "Not without being interrupted."

The French doors opened. "Getting seconds," Bosco said.

Sonny cupped her face and grinned. "Help yourself." He pulled her to him and kissed her, gently at first then more passionately.

She brought her hand to the back of his neck and drew him closer.

"'Scuse me, um, you got any refills on the…oh never mind." Bosco went inside.

Her cell phone vibrated. She pulled away from Sonny, grinning. "I think we embarrassed him."

Sonny patted her leg, "You'd better get that."

She pulled her phone out and looked at the text.

I'll cut the night short if I have to. Stop it.

She turned to look at Bosco through the glass of the French doors and held the phone up. "Really?"

Bosco shrugged.

She slid the phone in her pocket.

Sonny leaned back in his chair. "About decorating. No commitment on your part, just helping me pick out furniture."

"I'll help with the living room. You're on your own with the rest of the house. Maybe Janice can help, or Zoë, I know she'd love to."

"Zoë's already going to help Antony, so I'm not sure if she'd have time."

"True."

"What's really holding you back?"

Victoria kicked off her shoes, rolled up her jeans and sat at the side of the pool. She stuck her feet in. "Oh my, that's cold."

"I could've heated it, but didn't figure you'd want to swim tonight." He took off his shoes and socks, rolled his pants up and sat next to her.

"Honestly," she gently moved her feet back and forth in the water. "I still don't know how I feel. I love you both, if that's even possible. Antony scares me I won't deny that. I can see myself with you for the rest of my life, living here with a family, but I just need to be sure."

"I love you and I want you to be sure. But if you choose me, I have to have all of you. I mean, you'll be around Antony all the time. I don't want you regretting anything."

"I understand. I couldn't be with you if I didn't give you my whole heart. Promise." She patted his hand. "I should be going."

They both returned to the chairs, put on theirs socks and shoes, and walked to the car.

Bosco stood with the door open.

"Guess no good-night kiss," Sonny said.

"Not tonight." She leaned into Sonny, "I don't think I could stand to see that look of panic on Bosco's face again."

Sonny laughed. "Love ya, Lady."

"I love you, too." She climbed into the car and they headed back to Antony's.

TWENTY-FIVE

ANTONY GLANCED AT his watch as Lauren babbled on about something. She was the last person he wanted to be with and he was anxious to get home and see how Victoria and Sonny's date went. Once he got a text from Bosco letting him know they were heading out, he'd ditch Lauren and get home shortly after Vic. Maybe she'd have a twinge of jealousy that would help his cause.

Lauren placed her hand on his and squeezed it. "Does that sound all right?"

Now he wished he'd listened. "Let me think about it." It was a generic enough answer that she'd fall for.

His phone vibrated, and he read the message they were on their way home.

"Listen, I gotta go." Antony stood and threw some bills on the table.

Lauren pouted. "But the night is young."

"I know, but I've got an early meeting in the morning."

He led her to the car and drove toward Lauren's apartment.

"Walk me to the door?" Lauren said.

"Sure."

Antony jogged around the car, opened her door and helped her out.

When they got to her apartment, she turned and clutched tightly to his hand. "Call me later?"

"Of course."

He dropped her hand and spun around on his heel.

"No kiss?"

Antony turned back, leaned in and gave her a quick peck on the lips. "Later."

He hurried to the car before she could protest then drove back to his place.

Inside, Bosco met him in the great room.

"So?" Antony said. "Did you do as I asked?"

"Felt like an idiot but, yes. I interrupted them just like Doc does to you."

"You looked very uncomfortable every time." Victoria laughed as she came in and plopped onto the couch.

"Every time? How many times were there?"

"One was too many." Bosco ran a hand through his hair.

Antony squeezed his shoulder. "Yes, but you can take orders. I appreciate it. You can go. Take Doc with you." He looked down at Victoria. "Sonny say anything?"

"He asked what was going on. When I told him, Sonny swore he never asked Doc to do that."

"You believe him?"

"Yes. He said he'd text him and tell him to stop. But you really can't blame Sonny if he doesn't say anything to Doc. I am living here, and you do have more opportunities to sway my feelings in your favor."

"Is that what I'm doing? Because I don't feel like you've given me a chance. But I'm more than happy to start swaying."

"It might be tough. Sonny bought me a house, a horse and a gun."

"A gun? Nothing sexier than a girl packin' a pistol." Antony winked.

"I even got to shoot it."

"Where is this gun?"

She fought a grin.

"You forgot it?"

"Well, I felt bad for Bosco so I thought I'd better get him home."

"So you had to cut your night short? That's even better. Maybe he should get a bonus."

Victoria laughed. "He deserves one."

"Do you think Doc will stay out of my business now?"

She shrugged. "Not sure."

"I know one way to find out." In one quick swoop, he pulled her up, wrapped his arms around her and kissed her so fast she couldn't have resisted even if she'd wanted to.

* * *

Antony's allure was hard to ignore. His scent, his virility, the way he'd gathered her into his arms as if she were already his. If only he hadn't come and muddied up the memories of Sonny that she'd thought were once again set in stone.

Someone cleared his throat, relieving her of an uncomfortable moment.

Antony held her tight. "Ignore it."

"'Scuse me." Doc said.

"Bosco?" Antony yelled.

Bosco came and grabbed Doc's arm. "Give them some privacy." Bosco pulled Doc out of the room.

"Now, where were we?" Antony pulled her closer but she backed away. He got the hint and released her. "How long are you going to string us both along?"

"Are you making me choose? I figured Sonny would push me to pick first."

Antony laughed. "I'd never do that." He sat and pulled her down beside him.

"What'd you do tonight?" she asked.

"Went out with Lauren."

Victoria nodded. How easily he played the field, making sure his nights were filled with someone. Anyone. Despite Antony's claim of devoted love, it didn't appear she was that special to him since he wasn't sitting around waiting on her.

Best if she changed the subject. "Sonny says you're meeting with Tabor tomorrow."

"Yep."

"Not worried about it?"

"No."

That was Antony. Never gave more information than was needed. If he was worried, he wouldn't tell her anyway.

"What happened with that guy that was following me?" she asked.

"Got the information I needed then let him go." Antony crossed his leg. "He wasn't a fan of pain so he was very helpful."

"You mean you beat it out of him?"

"Well, I wouldn't say beat."

Victoria stood. How could he be so cold and uncaring? "Did you call the police?"

"Why would I do that?"

His indifference scared her. He reeked survival at any cost. But she wondered if there was a better way. "Was Sonny around when this interrogation was going on?"

"Yeah, but he didn't participate. He's never liked violence."

"And you do?"

"Only when I have to. I'm not afraid to do what it takes to protect those I love."

"Guess it's a good thing you're around." She forced a smile and rounded the couch. "I'm going to bed."

"You know you owe me."

"What?"

Antony tapped his fingers on his shoes. "You went out with Sonny so you owe me a date."

"I guess that's only fair." His face was devilish handsome but scared her. Afraid he'd take her down a road she didn't want to travel.

"When?" He raised his eyebrows.

"Next week?"

He nodded, but he didn't seem as cocky and confident as before. Almost like he'd sensed her hesitation.

Antony stood, took her hand and pulled her into a hug. "Next week will work."

Her heart pounded. She had to get away from him. From both of them to make a decision. This limbo was driving her crazy.

There was no way Antony would let her go anywhere. She'd have to sneak away.

Pulling away from him, she smiled. "How about Wednesday?"

He cupped her cheeks. The cockiness had returned. "Any day works for me."

"I'm going say good-night to my mom. Is she up in her room?"

"I think I heard the TV on downstairs."

"Okay, thanks."

* * *

Victoria grabbed the remote, turned the volume down, and sat next to Susanne on the couch in the basement. "Hey, Mom."

"Hi sweetie. How'd it go with Sonny?"

"Good. He's so wonderful. He got the house and bought me a horse. She's beautiful."

"He loves you very much."

"I know he does."

"Have you made any decisions yet?"

"No, but I need to talk to Doc. Would you mind going upstairs and asking him to come down."

"And make sure Antony doesn't catch on?"

"Yes. Or Bosco."

"You going to tell me why?"

"I'd rather not." Victoria smiled.

"Okay."

Five minutes later, Doc rounded the staircase and sat in the chair across from her. "Your mom said you wanted to talk to me."

"I need your help."

"Okay."

"I need some time away from Antony and Sonny so I can make a decision. I can't do that here."

"Why are you asking me? You've acted very annoyed whenever I'm around. I figured you hated me."

"I'm asking you because Bosco would tell Antony. I don't think you will. You seem like a sensible man and understand why I need this. Once we're away, I'll let them know that I'm okay and with you."

"And you think they won't look for you?"

"They might. I think I can convince Sonny to give me the time. He'll know you'll keep me safe." She studied him. They weren't the best of friends, but he appeared to be able to do the job he was hired to do. "You'll protect me, right?"

"Of course." Doc paced the small room. "Let's just say I agree to this. Where are you thinking of going?"

"I'm game for ideas. Somewhere they won't find us."

Doc rubbed his forehead. "I've got a buddy I served with in Afghanistan who has a place up the coast. Take us a couple hours to get there. I'll set it up."

"Okay. How do we make sure they don't find us?"

"You text or call Sonny and Antony as soon as we get on the outside of town. Then phones get shut off. That way they can't trace the pings off the towers."

Victoria nodded. "It could work."

"When?" Doc sat and rubbed his hands together.

"Tomorrow afternoon. They're meeting with Tabor so they'll both be preoccupied."

"I wasn't sure you knew about the meeting."

"Sonny told me."

"How do you plan on losing Bosco?" Doc asked.

"That's a tougher one, but still doable. You have the car at the loading dock. It's the easiest place for me to sneak out of."

"You know you can't bring a suitcase."

"I thought about that. I'll throw some essentials in my purse when I leave for work and we can pick up clothes on the road." She chewed her bottom lip. "How will you get out of here?"

"I'll figure something out. We'll change cars with a friend of mine. With Antony's connection at the police department, they could easily trace the plates of the one Sonny gave me."

"Okay. Thank you." She held out her hand and Doc shook it.

* * *

Doc spent most the night trying to decide what to do and came to the conclusion that Sonny needed to know.

The next morning, as soon as Antony left for a meeting, Doc went to Sonny's office. He was taking a chance by being there and telling Sonny, but he owed him the truth. If there were any questions, Sonny could easily send along a few more men.

"How'd you get away from my brother?"

"I told Max you needed to see him."

"What can I do for you?" Sonny leaned back in the chair.

"I wanted you to know that Victoria has asked me to take her away for a couple of days, so she can decide…you know, between you and Antony."

"Oh." Sonny rounded the desk and sat on the corner of it. "So she's close to making a decision."

"I think she would've already chosen you if she didn't live at Antony's place. He confuses her."

"I can understand that, but his place is the safest."

"Besides the safe room, I think she'd be just as safe with you."

"You're kinda paid to say that. I do sign your checks, but thanks anyway."

"I'm being truthful."

Sonny motioned to the couch and chairs. "Let's sit. Then tell me what the plan is."

"So, you'll let her go?"

"If I think it's safe, yes. Vic has every right to live her own life. I've told her that numerous times. I just want her protected."

Doc knew he was being sincere. Sonny's love for Victoria ran that deep. He wouldn't trick her or entice her like he'd seen Antony do.

"I'm picking her up at the store. She thinks she can get away from Bosco. I'll take her up the coast to a friend's house. We'll trade the car I'm driving for a buddy's so Antony can't have anyone at the police department find us."

"Sounds like you've got it covered. You confident you can keep her safe?"

"Yes. With you and Antony meeting with Tabor, I doubt Tabor's got anyone tailing any of us. If someone was following Victoria, Bosco would notice, like he did before."

"True." Sonny leaned over and pulled the baby Glock that was holstered in the strap on his waist. He pushed it toward Doc. "I'd like you to give this to her. Make her carry it. I'd feel safer if she did."

"I can try. Will she recognize it as yours?"

"No. She's never seen mine up close. I bought her one and she shot it a few times but wouldn't take it."

"Thanks," Doc said.

"If you need me to help distract Bosco, I can."

"No. I think we got this. Thanks for understanding. She'll call you once we're on the road."

"Okay. Let me know if you want me to send a couple of guys."

Doc stood. "I will."

* * *

Sonny sent a text, and within seconds, Clay was standing before him. "Doc is taking Victoria away for a couple of days. I need you to get Bruno and Sean to follow them. They'll need two different cars. Doc is good and will be watching for Tabor's men, so tell them not to get caught. No interference, just there if Doc needs them. The plan is to leave when we meet with Tabor so get them over at Francesca's soon. Not sure when it'll all go down."

"You think she can get away from Bosco?"

"I've been thinking about that. Put Sean on the dock. If she needs help, have him stop Bosco."

"Sure thing." Clay said, walking out the door.

Sonny stared out the window as the tide rolled in, calm and soothing like his soul. He knew Victoria would choose him. His confidence was unwavering.

TWENTY-SIX

MICKEY'S WAS about half-filled with customers eating late lunches or starting an early happy hour.

"I can't believe Tabor agreed to meet us." Sonny was still a bit shocked his brother had included him. He'd been certain Antony would do things on his own and use it to win Victoria's heart.

"Not sure it'll do any good." Antony spun the water glass. "Victoria told me she loved the house you bought."

"I bought her a gun, too." Sonny pulled it out and slid it across the table. "Says she doesn't want to carry it because she's not sure she could use it. Maybe you could convince her."

"I don't know." Antony sighed. "She has a mind of her own and pretty much does what she pleases."

Sonny grinned. Antony sounded almost defeated but Sonny wouldn't put his guard down. His brother may have backed off but doubted Antony had really begun to fight for her.

Sonny grabbed the gun and slid it back in his pocket. "Guess I'll try again."

"There he is." Antony motioned with his head.

They stood as Judge Tabor walked to the table. Sonny held out his hand and Tabor shook it. "Sonny Luciano and I think you know my brother, Antony."

"Yes, we spoke on the phone." Tabor shook Antony's hand and sat. "What can I do for you two?"

"We have a little problem." Sonny ignored Antony's piercing eyes. He knew his brother liked to be in charge, but this was Victoria's life and Sonny wasn't about to sit back and let Antony call all the shots.

Tabor waived the waiter over. "Ice tea please." After the waiter was out of earshot, Tabor leaned back in his chair. "What would that be?"

"Victoria Stone is my girlfriend. I will marry her someday. You go after her, her mother, or her sister then you become our problem."

Antony raised an eyebrow and grinned. "And nobody messes with our family."

"You seem squeaky clean," Tabor said to Sonny, then turned to Antony. "You, on the other hand, have quite the rap sheet. Must be why the girlfriend is staying with you. My guess is Susanne's there, too. You can try to protect them all, but my men can get to her." He laughed sardonically.

Sonny flew to his feet and pointed, his neck on fire. "You had better—"

Antony grabbed his arm and pulled him back down.

Sonny took deep breaths. He couldn't believe Tabor has so flippantly made a threat on Victoria's life.

"Listen," Antony clasped his hands together on the table. "I will do anything to protect my family and those I love. *Anything*. Susanne won't testify."

"That's not what the papers said." Tabor flashed hate-filled eyes.

"They got their facts wrong. I'd like your word that no one will touch Susanne, Victoria or Zoë."

"I'd like to talk to Susanne myself. Hear it come from her mouth and see her eyes."

"We could arrange that." Sonny gulped the water. "But I want this to end."

"I want the same thing."

"We'll be in touch." Antony stood.

Tabor left.

Sonny wondered if the judge had walked away believing Susanne would say nothing?

"I'll see if Susanne will meet with Tabor by the end of the week." Antony clicked his fingers at the waiter. "I need a sandwich. The club. Sonny, you want anything?"

"Same. Thanks."

Sonny drummed his fingers on the table. "You think she'll do it and be wired?"

"She'll meet with him, but I doubt she'll be wired."

The waiter set their lunches down.

Sonny swallowed a bite of the sandwich. He'd eat slow to make sure he'd distract Antony so Victoria could put her escape plan into action.

* * *

Victoria stood and stretched, hoping it would slow down her pounding heart. Trying to get away from Bosco shouldn't be such a big deal, but he'd parked himself right outside her office door since this thing began and had followed her like a puppy dog.

Victoria grabbed her purse and opened the door.

Bosco stood. "We going somewhere?"

"To the dock. I've got a shipment coming in and wanted to check them out."

"With your purse?"

Dang. He noticed everything. She thought fast. "Well, I need to stop at the restroom. I'm on my period. I can't just carry maxi pads and tampons around in my hands, you know?"

Bosco's face turned three different shades of red.

They rode the elevator down to the first floor. Inside, the restroom, she looked at her watch and paced. Her phone vibrated. It was Doc.

You coming?

Yes. Bosco is tougher than I thought.

After what she thought would be enough time, she came out and went to the dock. She pushed her purse toward Bosco.

He looked at it. "You gotta be kidding? I'm not here to hold your purse."

She stifled a laugh. "Fine then. Would you ask Jim if the truck came in?"

"Jim?"

"The guy with the clipboard. Over there." She pointed to the far end of the room.

He sighed and walked away.

She hurried to the door on the dock and glanced over her shoulder. Bosco had his back to her. Clutching her purse tightly, she rushed out the back door. The fresh air felt good but didn't stop the sweat from forming on her forehead as she jogged down the stairs.

Bosco grabbed her arm. "What are you doing?"

"Let me go." Yanking her arm was useless. It only caused his grip to tighten.

"Back inside."

A guy grabbed Bosco's arm and jerked him around. She used the opportunity to run to Doc's car and jump in. She turned just in time to see the guy pummel Bosco in the gut.

Bosco punched and shoved him to the ground then ran after them.

"Go. Go. Hurry." Victoria pounded on the dash.

Bosco chased them, then ran to his car as they raced out of the lot.

* * *

Bosco got into the car and turned it over. Nothing. He turned the key again. Nothing.

The guy walked up to the car and knocked on the window.

Bosco stepped out. "Sean?"

Sean laughed and pushed his starter cable toward him.

"What the heck?" Bosco gave him a shove. "She can't just run off like that?"

"She'll be fine. Doc's with her. It's you I'm worried about." Sean smacked his shoulder. "Have fun explaining that one to Antony."

Bosco's right hook hit Sean before he could dodge it. "Put that back in my car."

Sean rubbed his jaw, dropped the cable on the ground and walked away.

Bosco pulled his phone out and dialed Antony's number. His blood pounded furiously through his veins as he paced. This was a first. He'd never let his boss down.

* * *

Antony ran the napkin across his mouth when his phone rang. Bosco's name flashed on the screen. His heart rate increased as he hugged the phone to his ear. "What happened?"

"She's gone. Went with Doc somewhere. They ambushed me."

"They? Who's they?"

"Sean and Bruno."

Antony's eyes met Sonny's. "Sean and Bruno?"

Sonny grinned. "I can explain if you let me."

"Get back to the house," Antony said into the receiver. "I'll be there shortly."

Antony slid the phone into his pocket and pushed the sandwich plate to the middle of the table. "What's going on? Is she safe?"

"Yes. Victoria doesn't even know that Doc told me. She wanted some time away from both of us to make her decision. I think she deserves that."

Antony pounded on the table. "She's vulnerable. Tabor could have people following her."

"Doc has it under control. Bruno's following them and Sean will catch up. She'll be fine."

"You know where she's going?"

"No, but I trust my men." Sonny ate the last of his chips. "Be patient. She'll call me."

* * *

Victoria stared at Doc. "Wasn't that Bruno?"

"Who?" Doc's eyes jumped from the road to the mirrors then back to the road. "We're going to stop at a friend's and change cars."

"Okay." She pulled her phone out and called Sonny.

"Hey, gorgeous. I hear you're on the run." There appeared to be laugher in his voice.

"You've heard? Well, I guess you would since Bruno was there. I can't believe he punched Bosco."

"He punched Bosco?" Sonny asked.

"Yeah. I don't think it did anything to Bosco, but gave me enough time to get away. How'd you know?"

"Doc told me."

"He did?" Victoria punched Doc in the arm. "And you're okay with it?"

"I understand why. I wanted to keep you safe. If you see anyone else you know, it's okay."

She laughed. "Might we see Sean?"

"You might. Both are following. Neither will tell me where you're at. Take your time and let me know when you're heading back."

"How'd it go with Tabor?"

"Unfortunately, there's nothing to tell."

"Antony with you?"

"Yes," Sonny said.

"Will you tell him I'm okay?"

"I'd be happy to."

"Was that sarcasm?" She smiled, staring out the window as the city disappeared from her view.

"Yes, Ma'am. But I'll tell him. Be safe."

* * *

Sonny slid the phone into his pocket.

Antony seethed and drummed his fingers on the table. "You just let her go like that? When there's someone out there that might want to kill her? Or use her to get to her mom?"

"Victoria needs time to think, and she can't do that at your place. Give her a couple days."

"With only Doc protecting her?"

Sonny wanted to smack him. Did Antony think he was stupid? "Bruno is following them and Sean will catch up. That is if Bosco hasn't killed him."

"I would've sent Dwyer and Eddie."

"You wouldn't have let her go."

Antony stood. "You're right, I wouldn't have. Dumbest thing you've ever done." He stormed out.

Sonny gulped his water.

Clay sat. "He looked mad."

"Yeah, but Vic got away and that's all that matters. How's Sean?"

"Thinks he'll have a black eye and said his jaw may be dislocated, but he likes to exaggerate. Bruno's giving him directions. They're heading up the coast."

"Susanne called. Wants to talk to you and Antony."

Sonny stood and threw some cash on the table. "I'll text Antony."

* * *

Antony swerved in out of traffic, his phone on speaker.

"Hello." Victoria's voice filled the car.

"What the heck are you doing?"

"I need some time—"

"I've heard all of that. You wouldn't tell me? Really? Do you think I'm that cold hearted that I wouldn't understand?"

"I didn't think you'd let me go."

A sadness overcame him. "I wish you would've come to me. I would've had Bosco go with you. But Doc? You're trusting your life with him?"

"You trained him. He'll protect me."

Antony slammed on his breaks, honked and waved a fist at the car in front of him. "Put me on speaker."

"Okay…you're on speaker."

"Doc?" Antony bellowed.

"Yeah."

"Anything happens to her, you're dead. You hear me?"

"Nothing will happen to her."

Antony sighed. "Take me off speaker."

"Okay." She hugged the phone back to her ear. "Please don't be angry. I did what I thought I had to."

"Because you think I wouldn't listen. I wouldn't allow it? I'm sorry you think so little of me. Be safe and if you need anything, you can call. If not, take all the time you want."

Antony ended the call, unable to listen to any more excuses. His heart was hard and cold, but when it came to her, he'd felt it had melted. He'd do anything for her. Didn't she know that? Apparently not.

He could tell he scared her, but was he willing to change to be with her? There was no lying to her or himself. He was who he was. If she couldn't live with that, so be it.

* * *

Susanne sat at the table on the back porch with Special Agent Echo. It had taken her and Echo a while to come up with a plan. They only had to get Sonny and Antony to agree to it.

Sonny opened the French doors and came toward her.

She stood and smiled. "Sonny, thanks for coming. Is Antony with you?"

"Should be right behind me."

"I'm here." Antony slammed the glass door, the lines on his forehead deep as he stared at the stranger. "You are?"

Echo stood and held his hand out. "Special Agent Echo."

"The Feds. Really? This day just keeps getting better." Antony sat.

Susanne ignored his hatefulness. "I want to meet with Tabor. I'm done hiding in this house. I have recorded everything I know that could put Tabor away for the rest of his life. I will meet with him and convince him that I won't testify. Then I come out of hiding and everyone will be safe." She handed Sonny a thumb drive. "This recording is my safety net. If he hurts me, you can give it to the feds."

Antony got up and circled them. "If you had planned this, why would you even call the Feds?"

"In case something went wrong. If he won't be reasoned with, then I will testify and go back into witness protection."

"And you don't think we could've done that without the Feds?" Antony yelled. "I don't care what you do." He stormed off. In a few seconds, they heard a car peel out.

Sonny rubbed his forehead and sat. "Sorry. We've got some things going on that's got him worked up. Why did you call the feds?"

"I needed to make sure they'd take me back into witness protection. I did kinda ditch them when you found me."

Sonny nodded. It made sense. "What makes you think that Tabor will listen to you this time as opposed to last time?"

"We're all older. He's got grandkids. I don't know. I'm just hoping, I guess."

"And if something goes wrong? You just disappear like last time? You think that Victoria and Zoë deserve that?"

"No. But they can't live in constant fear. I won't have to hide like I did last time. They can come visit with precautions taken. Right Agent Echo?"

"Yes. We can secure locations where they can meet."

"You're willing to do that?" Sonny asked.

"Yes. We can't be in this limbo anymore. It's driving us all crazy."

"You decide when this meeting will take place?"

"Saturday." Echo stood.

"Okay. Let me know the details when you iron them out."

TWENTY-SEVEN

VICTORIA WAS RELIEVED when Doc finally pulled the car into a garage that was attached to a beach house. "This is nice. Thank your friend for letting us borrow it."

Doc carried in the food they had picked up along the way.

"Can we eat out on the deck? It's such a beautiful night."

"Sure. Let me check it out first. See if Bruno and Sean are here yet. I'll put one of them on the beach."

She waited until Doc waved her outside then sat down and took a long sip of her Diet Coke as he handed her a hamburger and fries. The warm breeze off the ocean felt good.

"So tell me. Why'd you double cross Antony after he hired you and start working for Sonny?" She took a bite of the burger.

"I don't know. Bosco's my cousin and is faithful to Antony. There's something about him that triggers me. I don't like how he operates. Sonny appeared much more concerned with your welfare than Antony."

"You don't think Antony loves me?"

"I think he does, in his own way. But the guy knows nothing about real love and sacrifice."

"You hardly know him."

"I've known him as long you have."

There was no arguing that statement. She ate some fries and washed them down with her drink. "You've known Sonny as long as you've known Antony and you think he's better for me?"

"Yes."

"Why?" Not that she would take the advice from a guy she hardly knew, but he appeared sincere.

"Sonny loves you so much he'd rather give you up than for you to be unhappy. That's gotta count for something. I told him you wanted to get away for a couple of days and he was willing to let you go. Even helped us. Would Antony have done that?"

"No." She had no doubt that Antony loved her, but in a possessive, controlling way. It fit his personality and probably came from years of living on the streets. Even though she understood the reason for his attachment, she didn't like it.

She swallowed the last bite of cheeseburger, crumbled the wrapper and scooted it to the center of the table. "I'm going inside. Which room is mine?"

"I put your stuff in the master, at the end of the hall. I'm going to check the grounds."

"Thanks." Victoria waited until Doc left then stared out at the ocean. The soft rushing of the sea water calmed her. It was the perfect place to decide who she wanted to spend her life with.

Two car doors slammed. Then voices. Arguing.

"Get out of my way!"

"How'd you find us?"

"Where is she?"

"Answer me."

"I don't answer to anyone. Now, where is she? I swear I'll shoot you."

Victoria stood, recognizing Antony's voice.

The front door flew open and he took a few steps inside. Antony's lips pursed, hard lines on his forehead, and a scowl on his face.

Ignoring it seemed the best form of attack. "Doc, Bruno. It's fine. Let him in."

"What were you thinking?" Antony yelled. "Running off like that?"

"You want something to drink?" Victoria waved Doc and Bruno out of the room and went into the kitchen. "We don't have much. Water or coffee." She made a glass of water and handed it to him.

Antony set the water down and rubbed his forehead. "Why'd you run off? You could've been followed and gotten hurt."

"Obviously I was followed or you wouldn't be here right now."

He paced. "I don't understand why you can't just do what I ask. It's to keep you safe."

"I don't take orders. This is my life and I won't live it like a prisoner."

"You'll have to get used to it."

"Are you saying this will be my life if I choose you? Because if that's the case, I can make my choice right now." She wasn't about to live scared or with a domineering man who wanted to know her every movement.

"Unbelievable. You're going to blame this mess on me? I did you a favor by finding your mom. You knew what that might uncover. Now I'm the bad guy?"

"I didn't say that. My dad was killed because of the trouble my mom got herself into. But I won't live like a prisoner. I needed to get away. Sonny understood that. Why couldn't you? You had to follow me. Really?"

"Sonny hasn't seen what I've seen or lived through what I have. One bullet. That's all it takes and everyone's lives are changed." Red filled his neck as he paced. "And you can't tell me Sonny is better than me because he's sitting in his office in Ventura. You think he doesn't know where you are? He had two of his bodyguards follow you. He's a saint and I'm a horrible person because I'm here, willing to protect you?"

"Sonny's not a saint and yes, he sent two bodyguards, but he respected the fact that I need some time to think. Time away from both of you to make a decision." Victoria grabbed his arm to stop his circling of the room. "How did you find me?"

He pulled away, opened the French doors, and went out on the deck.

She followed. "I'd like to know how you found me."

Leaning against the railing, he crossed his arms. "You won't like it."

"With your track record, I doubt it'll surprise me." She tried to sound light hearted hoping it would calm him down. His anger scared her when it flared.

"I put a tracking device in your purse."

"Really?" It sounded like something Antony would do, but Victoria was surprised Doc hadn't thought to look.

"Yeah. Good thing you're not like most women and change your purse out daily."

Antony ran his fingers through his black hair. "I'm sorry if I made you feel like you couldn't talk to me about this. I'd have let you go."

"No you wouldn't."

"Okay. I wouldn't have." He looked around. "Seems like a pretty okay place. Does Doc have Bruno and Sean somewhere?"

"One is below, on the beach. The other one circles the house like a vulture."

"I'd like to leave Bosco here."

"He's still alive?"

Antony laughed. "First time he's let me down. He assures me that will never happen again. I'd also like to keep the tracking device in your purse as a precaution, until this is over."

"Sounds kinda creepy."

"I won't track your every move, but if something happens...I'd feel better if I knew I could find you."

"Okay."

"Bosco—"

"Goes home with you," she insisted. "I have Doc, Bruno and Sean."

"You won't even let the guy redeem himself? I really would feel better if he was here. Doc's still pretty green."

"He's ex-special forces. I think if he needed to, he could pull a trigger." She grinned. "But, if it will make you feel better, Bosco can stay, but tell him to back off just a little. He's here only to help Doc, not be in charge."

* * *

Antony's heart was finally falling into a steady rhythm. "That won't be easy for Bosco. He's a pretty in-charge kind of guy."

"He follows orders, so if you tell him, he'll do it."

Antony nodded. Nothing wrong with letting her believe it. "Okay. You win. Doc's in charge. Bosco is there if needed."

"Deal."

He could tell she wanted him to leave. Sounded like she was close to making a decision and by her earlier words, Sonny was going to win her heart, but he couldn't change who he was, not even for her.

"How long will you be staying away?" he asked.

"A couple of days, maybe."

"Well, I guess I'll head back." He cupped the back of her neck and tried to pull her into a kiss. When she backed away and shook her head, he knew it wasn't a good sign. "I love you."

"Thanks."

They walked through the house then out to his car. "Bosco, you're staying here." Antony stood in front of Doc. "She gets hurt in anyway, I'll hold you responsible and I won't be nice."

Doc gave him a head jerk. "I hope she chooses Sonny."

Antony's right hook clobbered Doc before he could react.

Doc charged, but Bruno and Sean grabbed his arms and held him back. Bosco stood between all of them protecting Antony, like he needed protection from the punk.

Antony turned to Victoria. "I'm always here if you need anything."

"I know. Thanks."

Antony climbed into his car and left. Tears brimmed his eyes, but he hardened his already hard heart.

With a tap on the call button, he shouted, "Call Lauren."

"Hey sexy." Her voice filled the car and even though it wasn't Victoria, it soothed his anger in a strange sort of way.

"You got plans for tonight?"

"Only with you."

Antony laughed. "I'll see you at six." He hung up the phone and sighed. Maybe Lauren could help him forget.

* * *

Victoria put both hands on her hips and turned to Doc who was pacing like a mad dog.

"I can't believe he punched me." Doc ran the back of his hand over his mouth.

"You deserved that." She stormed into the house, grabbed the water glass off the counter, placed it in the sink then turned to Doc and Bosco who had followed her inside. "Seriously, that was just rude."

"If he hadn't punched you, I would've." Bosco flexed every muscle in his chest and arms. "I know you're my cuz and all, but that was a pretty stupid comment to a guy who knows he's going to get dumped."

Victoria glared at them. "Where the heck were you guys? All hiding underneath the deck? Do you know everything we said?"

Bosco shrugged. "We're paid to know what's going on."

"And you think I'm going to pick Sonny?"

"Sounded like it."

She shook her head and laughed. "Why can't I be normal? I have to discuss my love life with a bunch of hired thugs."

"Hey," Bosco pursed his lips. "I take offense to that. We're more than hired thugs."

"Really?"

"It's not all about the money. We care."

She almost laughed at Bosco's seriousness. It wasn't easy for him to appear soft and loving.

"I'm going out for a walk on the beach. Bosco, I'd like you to walk with me."

Bosco's chest filled and he grinned. "Gladly." He strutted to the French doors and waved for her to exit.

She didn't turn back to see Doc's face. It wasn't that she didn't think Doc would protect her, she picked Bosco because she figured he'd talk less. She needed to think.

After kicking her shoes off. The sand felt good between her toes. She found a spot and sat. Bosco stood. The waves were loud and soothing like Sonny's love. They were also strong and vibrant like Antony's love. But she knew she couldn't live the way Antony would expect her to. Bodyguards was one thing, but a tracking device and never going anywhere without tell him? That wasn't an option. Sonny protected her just as much but less invasively.

After sitting for almost an hour, she closed her eyes and prayed as the mist from the ocean sprayed her face. Yes, she knew Sonny was who she'd like to spend the rest of her life with.

She stood and went back to the house. Inside, Doc stood. "You okay?"

"Yes. Why wouldn't I be?"

"Just asking. You need anything?"

"Nope. I'm heading to bed."

Victoria cracked the window, hoping the ocean would soothe her to sleep. Sonny came to mind. She could see him like a movie in her head. Their wedding, a family…a future. Contentment washed over her and she smiled. There was no denying it. She was in love with Sonny.

TWENTY-EIGHT

VICTORIA WOKE up with an overwhelming peace. Despite Antony's attempts to win her heart and her apparent attraction to him, Sonny was part of her soul. A comforting love that ran deep. One she couldn't walk away from.

She reached for her phone, powered it on, and called Sonny.

"Good morning. You okay?" he asked.

Victoria laughed. "I'm sure you know I am."

"Well, yes. Bruno checked in and said all was well. What's up?"

"What're you doing tonight?"

"Nothing. Why?"

"I wondered if you'd meet me."

"Where?"

"I'm sure you know where." Funny thing was, it didn't bother her that he might know.

"I really don't know where you are. I told my guys not to tell me unless there was some kind of trouble. But if you give them the go-ahead to tell me, they will."

She smiled. "I'll have Doc call you. Come hungry. I'll cook something."

"Sounds good. See you around six."

Victoria got dressed and went to the kitchen.

Doc handed her a cup of coffee while Bosco stood at the French doors.

"So, Sonny's coming tonight." Doc said.

"News sure travels fast." She blew on the coffee, took a sip, then grabbed a pen and paper, and jotted down a few things. "He's coming for dinner and I'm cooking. One of you will need to go to the store and get these items."

Doc grabbed the list and slapped it into Bosco's hand. "You heard the lady. Go pick up this stuff for her."

"No way. Send Bruno." Bosco tossed the paper on the counter.

Doc snatched the list and stormed off.

Victoria glanced at Bosco. "You get in much trouble for losing me?"

"First and last time that will happen. I let my guard down because I thought I could trust you."

She laughed. "Sorry. I knew you'd tell Antony and he wouldn't let me go."

"You were right on that. I'll just be around if you need anything."

"Thanks."

Victoria grabbed a bottle of water and went out on the deck. She couldn't wait for Sonny to get there, but she'd keep busy today and make his favorite Italian dishes for dinner.

* * *

Sonny's heart pounded as he pulled the car into the driveway of the beach house. "Looks like this is it."

Clay nodded. "There's Bruno."

Bruno motioned to the side of the house. "Victoria's on the back deck. You can walk around."

"Thanks."

Sonny took the steps two at a time to the top of the deck.

Victoria eyes beamed and a glow on her cheeks made his heart almost leap from his chest. Could she have made her decision? Was he really the one she loved?

Opening her arms, she hugged him. "I'm so glad you're here."

Sonny rubbed her back. "Thanks for inviting me. I'm starved. Didn't take time for lunch."

"I cooked Pasta Gina. It'll be ready in a bit. I'm glad you dressed casual."

He glanced down at his khaki walking shorts. "I figured with a beach house, we'd spend some time on the beach."

"Oh, yes." She grabbed his hand and led him back down the stairs.

They kicked their shoes off and he let the soothing sand surround his feet and toes. When she grabbed his hand, he thought he'd melt.

Stopping, he pulled her to him. The water rushed over their feet. "You better tell me what's going on because you're driving me crazy."

"I missed you."

He wrapped his arms around her. "You did? You've been gone one day."

"It felt like an eternity." She grabbed the back of his neck and pulled him into a kiss. "I love you."

"Really?" He backed away, furrowing his brows. "I saw Bosco outside. I guess Antony was here."

"He came yesterday."

"You invited him?"

"No, it wasn't like that."

He nodded and tried to act annoyed while he reached into his pocket and clutched the three-caret diamond ring.

Turning away from her, he took a couple steps but she grabbed his arm. "Sonny, really, I didn't invite him. He put some tracking device in my purse, and I didn't know."

Sonny looked back at her, the ring in his fisted hand.

"You have to believe me. I've made my decision. It's you I want to be with. I love you, Sonny."

"I'm glad about that." Sonny stepped closer. "Otherwise, this would be very awkward." He opened his hand, exposing the engagement ring. "Because I would love for you to marry me."

Her smile spread from ear to ear. "You what?"

He took her hand and slid the ring on her finger. "Marry me."

"Oh, Sonny." She admired the ring then jumped into his arms. "I'd love to."

He swung her around, bringing her into his entire being. The ocean waves washed over their feet at a fast rate, almost as if they were applauding their love.

Leaning back a little, he cupped her cheeks and planted a firm kiss on her lips.

* * *

The kiss made Victoria weak in the knees, and she never wanted the moment to end. Her pulse raced as she dug her fingers into the back of his neck and kissed him more passionately. He was hers and she was his. Forever.

He pulled away, laughing. "We'd better stop or we might be on the next plane to Vegas."

"That would be horrible." She giggled.

"So you get to plan the wedding of your dreams. Anything you want. Sky's the limit."

Taking his hand, she kissed it and pulled him along the beach. "Thank you. Maybe around Christmas?"

"That'd be the best Christmas present ever."

They walked up to the beach house and sat on the couch in the great room.

"What'd you tell Antony when he was here?"

She snuggled closer, entangling her fingers in his. "To leave. I think he knew I wanted to spend my life with you." She kissed him. "He took his frustration out on Doc as he left."

"He punched Doc?" Sonny chuckled. "Why?"

"Some rude comment he made. One thing I'll say about Doc, he's faithful to you. Doesn't care for Antony one bit." She grinned. "Isn't that right, Doc?"

"You know it," Doc yelled from another room.

"Will I get used to them always listening?" Victoria asked.

"Yes." Sonny held her hand up and admired the ring on her finger. "You'll forget they're around."

"Did you talk to Antony today? I thought he might've said something."

"A little at work, but he was in an *I hate the world attitude,* so I didn't say much."

The buzzer on the oven went off. "Well, Mr. Luciano. Sounds like dinner is ready."

"Yes, soon to be Mrs. Luciano. Let's eat." He kissed her.

* * *

Sonny tightened his arm around Victoria and she nestled into his side as he drove. "I'm glad you decided to come home tonight."

"Me too. I know I was only gone a day but seems longer than that." She kissed his hand. "I think I'd like to move out of Antony's, but I'm not sure your place is where Mom and I should go."

"Why? I've got a top-notch security system and Bosco could come with you."

"It's not the security that worries me." She turned to him with raised eyebrows and kissed his cheek.

"I am irresistible. I understand. Stay at Antony's."

"You don't think it'll be awkward?"

"We're getting married. He'll need to accept that. Better to get it over with now than later."

She snuggled back into his side. It felt good and right. She closed her eyes and savored the two-hour drive.

Sonny pulled the car into Antony's estate, parked and carried in her suitcase.

Susanne came around the corner. "You're home?"

Victoria grabbed Sonny's hand. "We have some news." She held out her left hand and wiggled her ring finger. The diamond glistened in the light.

Susanne's mouth dropped open. "It's beautiful. You mean, you two are getting married?"

"Yes." They said in unison.

"Around Christmas." Victoria kissed Sonny. "I can hardly wait."

"I offered a Vegas trip, but she declined. It's going to be a big affair, I hope." Sonny wrapped his arms around her.

"Small, but big in its own way." Victoria grinned.

"I need to go. You can break the news to Antony, or I can tell him tomorrow."

"He's not here." Susanne sat back on the couch. "Seemed very angry when he left."

Victoria nodded. "If I see him I'll tell him."

"He probably has already guessed or Bosco told him." Sonny led her back to the front door.

"I'll see you tomorrow?"

"Of course. Love you."

He cupped the back of her neck and pulled her into a passionate kiss.

She was positive she'd made the right decision.

Back in the living room Victoria fell onto the couch next to her mother.

Susanne grabbed her hand. "Let me see this rock again. Wow. How big is it?"

"Not sure. I'd guess two to three carats. Isn't it beautiful?"

"So, tell me how he asked."

"I wasn't even expecting it. I'd asked him to the beach house because I'd made my decision, that he was the one. Antony had come up earlier. Sonny acted like he was mad about his brother showing up, only he was pretending so I'd be surprised. It was so sweet."

"You content? Happy with your decision? No second guessing?"

"Yes. I know he's the right one. I won't deny that there's something between me and Antony, but it's Sonny I want to spend my life with." Victoria wiggled her fingers admiring the ring, again.

"I'm glad you came home. I'm meeting with Tabor Saturday."

Victoria's eyes widened. "Is that safe?"

"I can't be in this limbo anymore. I called the meeting. If Tabor won't drop it then I will testify and go back into witness protection."

"Mother, no. Not with my wedding coming up."

"Sweetie, I have to do what is safest for you and Zoë. If that is going into hiding again until the trial, then so be it. But it'll be different this time. I'll write letters, even meet up with you girls. We can find a secure place, so it won't be as bad."

"And I'll know you're alive." Victoria did want the hiding and worrying to end. "I guess I can't complain about that. But I want you to help with wedding plans."

"I want to, also, but that might not be in the cards for us."

"Did I hear you say wedding plans?" Antony's voice didn't sound angry even though his neck was red.

Victoria smiled. "Yes. Sonny asked me to marry him and I said yes."

*   *   *

"Congratulations." Antony made himself a drink. He wasn't one to give up but with that rock on her hand it was going to be kinda hard to talk her out of it.

Susanne patted her leg. "I'll let you two talk."

"Thanks." Victoria waited until Susanne was gone before standing. "We're planning to get married around Christmas."

Antony nodded and set his glass down. "Did you ever love me or was that all an act?"

"I still love you. There's no way to explain how I can love you both. But my life is with Sonny."

Something small and tight turned over in his stomach. He searched her eyes. "I'll do anything for you. Give us a chance."

She grabbed his hands and blinked away the tears. "I'm going to marry Sonny."

Defeat. He'd never get used to it. Why could he win every battle he'd ever fought except in love? Elisa broke his heart years ago. Now Victoria had done the same. Women.

Last thing he'd do was let her see his pain. He leaned in and kissed her cheek. "I know my brother will make you very happy. Remember our deal."

"Our deal?"

"You said if you chose Sonny I could still flirt with you and tell you how much I love you."

The laughter forced the tears out of her eyes. She brushed them away. "Ah, yes. You think Sonny will mind?"

"Of course. That's what'll make it even better." He pulled her into a hug. "Man, I'm going to miss what we could've had."

* * *

Relief overcame Victoria. "So you don't hate me?"

Antony grinned and sat down on the couch. "I could never hate you. I'm a bit angry that you never even gave us a chance, but whatever."

Victoria figured his apparent indifference was his way of getting over it or hiding his feelings. She sat next to him. "Mom said she was meeting with Tabor. Is that safe?"

"She's like you. Does her own thing, regardless. We'll try it her way. Like she said, if she needs to go into hiding, she will. At least you'll know she's alive."

She must have read too much into his so called undying love for her. He acted like he couldn't care less that she was marrying his brother. Maybe that was for the best.

"So, let me really look at this rock."

Victoria held out her hand to show him the ring.

Antony raised his brows. "Wow. He must've spent a fortune on that."

"I thought that, too."

"Guess you're worth it."

She playfully smacked him. "I'd hope so. You okay."

"Am I dying inside? Is that what you're wondering?"

Victoria laughed. "You? No. I doubt me marrying Sonny is breaking your heart. You seem very resilient. Hardly affected."

"Would you feel better if I cried?"

"I doubt you ever cry."

"Tears are useless." He leaned and cupped her hands in his. "I really do love you, but I know you love Sonny more than me. I will live with that. I am happy for the both of you. Really, I am."

"Thanks. Friends?"

"Always."

Victoria stood. "Well, I'm going to head up to bed."

"Night."

When she got to her room, she called Sonny. "I told Antony."

"How'd that go?" Sonny appeared genuinely concerned about his brother, not in a jealous sort of way.

"He begged me to reconsider."

"Really?"

"No. I can't be sure, but I thought I saw pain behind his tough exterior. I doubt he'd ever admit it. He said he understood and had no hard feelings."

"Guess I'll see about that in the morning. We have an early meeting," Sonny said.

"I'd better let you go, then. Love you."

"I love you, too."

TWENTY-NINE

SUSANNE SAT ON THE bench bouncing her knee, her eyes darting around the park wondering if Antony and Sonny would make it before Tabor. She thought the judge had changed the time to throw her protection off.

Agent Echo was on his way, too, but she wasn't putting bets on his help. His sincerity wasn't in question, but his lack of survival skills worried her.

Doc stood at her side, his hand resting on his gun. He checked his phone again.

"Are they close?" Susanne chewed her thumbnail.

"On their way. I've got a couple guys around the park." He glanced at his phone. "Dwyer just texted. Tabor's here. He's by himself."

"I'd still feel better if Antony and Sonny were here."

Doc nodded. "Me, too."

She was thankful he didn't start another lecture about how stupid it was to go along with the time change because of less security. When Tabor called, her protection didn't matter, she had just wanted it to end. Now, she was second guessing herself.

Tabor approached. He'd gotten older and looked greyer than she last remembered. He opened his arms to give her a hug.

Doc jumped between them and pushed on Tabor's chest. "That's close enough. You have a gun? I'd like to pat you down."

Tabor looked past him at Susanne. "Who's this?"

"Bodyguard."

Tabor nodded and took a step back. "You will not pat me down unless you can prove you don't have a wire, which would mean I'm checking you both."

"He's fine, Doc. Judge Tabor, neither one of us is wired." Susanne shoed Doc back.

Doc took one step aside then stood, glaring at Tabor, his gun at his side.

Tabor motioned to the bench. When Susanne nodded, he sat next to her. "We'll talk about your indiscretions too, just in case."

"Doesn't matter to me. I'm not wired," Susanne said.

Susanne glanced at Doc then back at Tabor. She would say what needed to be said and get out. "I wanted to let you know I'm tired of hiding. I've lost my husband already because of this. I don't want to lose my girls. You win. I'll keep my mouth shut if I have your word we are safe."

Tabor rested his arm on the back of the bench. "We had some good times."

"We had a business arrangement. I needed money. You helped me out."

"You still gambling?"

"No. I paid my bookie off and haven't gambled since my husband was killed. I know it was my fault."

"You should've never gone to the Feds."

"I learned my lesson. Please, can we end this?" Susanne looked around the park and still no Sonny or Antony.

"We call it over how do I know you'll never testify?"

"If I did, I know you would come after me or my girls. I won't. I promise."

"Okay. We'll call it over." He stood.

She stared at his eyes, unable to tell if he was lying. Standing, she held out her hand.

He shook it and pulled her into a hug.

Doc pried his way between them.

The muffled gunshot shocked her as the pain of the bullet ripped through her stomach.

Tabor spun around and started walking away as Susanne fell on the bench. Tears filled her eyes and her body went numb. Warm blood rushed between her fingers as she pressed the wound on her stomach.

* * *

Doc ignored the bullet wound in his arm, raised his gun and double-tapped Tabor—once in the head, once in the back. "Now, it's over."

Doc placed his hand over Susanne's and pushed.

Susanne shrieked.

"Sorry. Gotta try and stop the bleeding." He put the phone to his ear. "You here yet? Susanne's been shot. Tabor's dead. We need an ambulance."

He slid the phone in his pocket. "Sonny and Antony are close."

Tears spilled from Susanne's eyes. "Why is your arm bleeding? Did he shoot you, too?"

"Bullet must've went through my arm into your stomach. Hopefully it slowed it down. It'll make it easier for them to fix you up."

Not that they could. He'd seen wounds like this on his tour. They could patch her up for a while, but she wasn't going to make it very long.

Agent Echo ran to them. "Ambulance is on its way." He ripped off his jacket and placed it over the wound. "I told you to do nothing without backup."

Doc took a step back, wiped his bloody hand on his pants, ripped the bottom of his shirt off and tied it around his arm using his mouth and one hand.

Antony and Sonny ran toward them. Antony stopped to check on Tabor.

* * *

Sonny leaned over Susanne as he slid his gun back in its holster and grabbed Susanne's hand. "Hang in there." It seemed like a useless command. Her pale face grimaced and body shook.

Agent Echo looked up. "Help is on the way."

Antony jogged to them, his gun still at his side. "Tabor's dead." He put his gun away.

Agent Echo pointed to Doc's arm. "Looks like he got you. What happened?"

"Yeah, Doc. What happened?" Antony glared.

Doc holstered his gun as Dwyer and Eddie joined them. "They talked. It seemed fine until he tried to hug her. I jumped between them. Gun must've been in his pocket. Bullet went through my arm and got her. Then, I shot him."

Susanne grabbed Sonny's arm. The blood on her hand soaked through his white shirt. "The Feds will get me out of here. If I die, let the girls think I'm back in hiding."

"You're going to be fine."

"I'd like to think so but…"

She pulled Sonny closer clutching his arm tighter. "I've got postcards and letters written to the girls in a box in the safe room. Send them every so often so the girls think I'm alive. Let them think I'm alive."

Sonny shook his head. "You can't ask me to spend the rest of my life lying to Victoria. I won't do it."

"You were there. You saw how she reacted to her father's death. You can't do that to her again. Promise me." Tears fell from Susanne's eyes.

"Victoria can handle the truth."

"Please."

Sonny looked back at Susanne. "I won't promise anything."

A man came running toward them carrying what looked like a tackle box. He rushed to Susanne, assessed the wound, then started an IV. He loaded a syringe with the contents of a small bottle and injected her. "It'll help with the pain."

"I don't want to see the girls. They can't see me like this." Susanne stared at the medic then at Agent Echo. She jammed a flash drive into Agent Echo's hand. "You want my confession, here it is. Get me out of here before my girls know. Please."

"We gotta move her." The medic pulled out gauze wraps and padded the wound to stop the bleeding.

"Get her to the hospital." Agent Echo slid the drive into his pocket and hugged his phone to his ear.

"What's going on? Who are you calling now?" Sonny ran his hand through his hair and paced. Everything was happening too fast.

"An ambulance is on its way. We'll get her the medical help she needs and I'll contact you."

"Listen to me." Sonny grabbed his arm and forced the agent back around. "I can't just tell Victoria and Zoë their mom is gone."

"Cops are on their way. They'll assist the Feds, but don't talk to them. Only talk to the Agents. We'll need that gun." He pointed to Doc. "And you'll need to go to the hospital."

Doc slapped his gun in Agent Echo's hand, then turned to Sonny. "You want me to go with them?"

"Yes. I'll go too."

"No," Echo pushed Sonny's chest. "Susanne needs surgery and she'll get it. I'll let you know where she is. The ambulance will take Doc as soon as he makes a statement. He'll need that arm checked."

In the distance a black boxed van and another car pulled up and two other men in suits got out.

"More Feds?" Antony asked.

"Yes. Just tell them what happened." Echo waved to the EMT and pointed at Susanne.

Sonny leaned into Antony. "Have someone follow that van. Get men at the hospitals, too."

Antony nodded, brought the phone to his ear and walked away.

The medic and EMT lifted Susanne onto the gurney and rolled it to the black van. The doors closed and it drove away.

Agent Echo waved an agent toward Doc. Another car pulled up, followed by the coroner. "I'll take your statement. You don't have to repeat it to the police. As soon as you tell us, we'll get you to the hospital."

The Feds invaded the scene like cockroaches, keeping the cops at bay. Even Martin and Zoë couldn't get past them.

Sonny rubbed his arm. Susanne's dried blood clung to his shirt and skin. The itching was driving him crazy.

"I want to know where you're taking her." Sonny got into Agent Echo's face. "It's your fault she's in this mess. Victoria and Zoë have a right to see her."

"She's not your concern anymore."

Sonny grabbed Echo's shirt collar. "Where is she?"

Antony grabbed Sonny and pulled him off. "Won't do Victoria any good if you get arrested for assaulting a federal agent.

"At least one of you understands." Echo straightened his shirt.

"Me, on the other hand, it doesn't matter." Antony grabbed Echo and threw him up against a tree. "Where is she?"

"Let me go."

Sonny yanked Antony off the agent.

Echo slid his sunglasses on and turned to Sonny. "Drop it. Tell Victoria and Zoë their mom will testify and she's back in hiding."

"Never," Sonny said.

Agent Echo pointed. "She trusted you. She wants to die in peace. I'm following through with her wishes. Take care of her daughters like she asked you too."

"You really think she's better off dying alone?" Sonny snapped.

"What I think doesn't matter. I promised her that I would do her wishes if she confessed on tape and met with Tabor. She held up her end of the bargain. I'll hold up mine."

"When have you Feds ever held up your end of a bargain?" Antony shouted. "You'll get the recording when you tell us where you're taking her."

Echo reached into his pocket and pulled out the jump drive. "I already got the recording." He spun around on his heel, climbed into a black car and sped away.

Sonny gave Bruno a nod to follow Echo. Bruno jumped in his SUV, but was blocked in by two other Fed cars.

Sonny dropped his head and rubbed the back of his neck. "I can't lie to Victoria again."

Antony slid his hands in his pockets. "I'm not sure you should, but it's your call."

Martin finally broke through the Feds and jogged to them. "What happened?"

"Nothing for you to worry about," Antony snapped.

Martin grabbed Sonny's arm. "Is it true? Susanne helped Tabor with those cases? She's a criminal, too?"

Sonny stared at Antony. He hadn't heard this one, but it could explain why she wanted to disappear and not let her daughters know.

"Say that again?" Sonny and Antony stepped closer.

"Pete said he found out that Susanne was working *with* Tabor. Lined her pockets pretty good, I hear. Not sure where that money is. The Feds were forcing her to testify or they'd prosecute her, too. When you found her last year, you saved her from both

Tabor and the Feds. That's why she let you hide her. She didn't want to testify, because everyone would know what she did." Martin crossed his arms over his chest.

Sonny's eyed widened as he looked at Antony. "It would explain why she doesn't want the girls to know where she's at."

Martin's brow furrowed. "She disappeared?"

Antony rubbed his chin. "Does Zoë know any of this?"

"No."

"Keep it that way." Antony looked at Sonny. "We can't do anything if they took her."

"Who took her?" Martin stepped closer.

"The Feds." Antony's eyes narrowed. "Now if you'll excuse us, we have to go tell Victoria that her mother has gone back into hiding. You can tell Zoë."

Martin nodded and walked off.

"You'd just give up and not look for Susanne?" Sonny scoffed. "That doesn't sound like you."

"You saw that wound. She won't make it through surgery if that's even where they're taking her."

"So, it's over. We just end it? Like the Feds told us to?" Sonny stared at his brother.

"It's your call."

"If I agree to tell Victoria and Zoë that Susanne is still alive and I mail those stupid letters like she asked, I have your word that it will never come out. Ever?"

"Yes."

Sonny rubbed his forehead and dragged a hand down his face. "I don't like it."

"Tell them the truth. Why do you care what her mother thinks? Victoria and Zoë can handle it."

"Yeah, maybe."

"Why are you hesitant?" Antony asked.

"You weren't there when Vic's dad died. She was comatose for a week. They had to put off the funeral because of it. I didn't know what to do. She wouldn't eat or drink."

"What snapped her out of it?"

"I threw her in a cold shower. Made her have to change. She went to the funeral with me but was mechanical for months. Then, every day got a little better."

"And it will with this, too, if you chose to tell her."

Sonny looked back to where Martin and Zoë had been. They were gone and he was glad. It gave him more time to think.

"Come on." They got to Antony's car and climbed in.

Antony started it up. "Where to?"

"Who's at the hospitals?"

"Sean and Max."

"Let me check with them." Sonny texted Sean. *You see them?*

Nope.

Sonny texted Max who was stationed outside another ER. *They show up there?*

No.

Sonny slid the phone in his pocket. "They didn't take her to any local hospitals."

His phone vibrated again. A text from Echo.

320 Monroe St. Only you and your brother.

We'll be right there.

Sonny looked at Antony. "320 Monroe. Echo wants us there."

Antony nodded. "You telling the girls?"

"Texting Bosco and Martin right now to get them there. I don't care what Echo or Susanne says. They'll see her before she dies." Sonny punched the address in and texted them.

"You telling Martin about Susanne wanting to pretend she's going to live?"

"Yes. If Zoë and Vic play along, Susanne can die in peace. Their call though."

Antony stepped on the gas.

THIRTY

SONNY AND ANTONY jogged into the office building where Echo pointed them to a room.

They walked into what looked like a makeshift hospital room. Susanne lay on a hospital bed. Her skin was pale.

Sonny took her hand and leaned in. "Susanne?"

Her eyes slowly opened. "You made it."

"How you feeling?"

"Not good. Promise me you'll let them think I'm alive."

"Susanne, please don't make me lie," Sonny said.

"If they find out and the truth gets out…"

"About how you worked *with* Tabor?" Sonny patted her hand.

"You know about that?"

"Yes. I'll keep your secret, but only if you let them see you. Say goodbye to them."

Echo stepped forward. "They would need to come pretty quick."

Sonny looked up. "They're on their way."

Susanne squeezed Sonny's hand. "Only if you promise. Let them think I'm alive."

Sonny nodded, knowing it was a promise he wouldn't keep. A lifetime of deceit was not in the cards.

The door to the building opened and shut. High heels clicked loudly on the tile floor. He left Susanne and walked to where Victoria, Zoë and Martin were.

Sonny grabbed Victoria's hand. "Your mother's been shot. She's alive and is very pale from blood loss."

Zoë pushed past him and went into the room. Martin gave him a nod then trailed behind her.

He pulled Victoria toward him so she wouldn't follow them.

"Sonny? What is it? Is she going to die?"

"Yes, but—"

"No….no…" Victoria shook and took a step back. "I can't go through that again."

Sonny cupped the back of her neck and drew her closer. "Yes, you can. We'll get through this. But there's more. She wanted me to tell you that she was going back into hiding. She made me promise. It was the only way she'd let you see her. But I can't lie to you anymore."

"She doesn't want me to know she's dying?"

"She wants you to think she's alive and in hiding. She's afraid if you know, you'll go back into a depression, like when your dad died."

"Oh, God. Not again."

"You're strong and you'll get through this. We'll get through this."

"What do I do?" Her tear-filled eyes looked at him. "I can't go in there and pretend."

"Yes, you can. For her sake. Go in there and say goodbye, but let her believe you think she's going to live."

Tears flooded Victoria's eyes. He pulled her into a hug and held her as she cried. "Make her believe it, Victoria. Let her die in peace." He cupped her cheeks in his hands. "You can do this. Take a couple of deep breaths."

When her composure was more normal, he took her hand and led her into the room. Zoë stood on the opposite side of the bed, holding Susanne's hand. Tears streaked her face.

Victoria touched her mother's arm. "Mom? I'm here. How are you feeling?"

Susanne opened her eyes and smiled. "Victoria. I was just telling Zoë how much I love you two." She grabbed her hand. "I know this is going to make you all mad, but I've agreed to testify. The Feds are going to put me back in witness protection until the trial. But I'll be able to write."

"I know you have to do what you think is best." Tears filled Victoria's eyes.

Zoë nodded.

Sonny had no doubt that Martin had told her what was going on.

"You'll miss my wedding," Victoria wiped a tear from her cheek.

"I know, Honey. I'm sorry."

Victoria hugged her. "It's okay."

Susanne wiped her eyes. "You girls should go."

"But we just got here," Victoria pleaded.

"Yes, but I need to rest."

"Antony," Sonny touched Victoria's arm, "Will you take Victoria out to the car? Martin?" Sonny motioned to Zoë.

Antony and Martin nodded.

Victoria leaned over and kissed her mom. "I love you. I'm going to miss you so much."

"Me, too, but I'll be in touch. Soon. I promise."

Antony rested his hand on Victoria's back and guided her out the door.

Zoë squeezed her mother's hand. "Love you, Mom."

"I love you, too. Be safe and love life like you always do."

"I will."

Martin led Zoë away.

"Thank you." Susanne took Sonny's hand. "You saw Victoria. You can't tell her I'm gone. Remember the letters." She pulled an envelope from under the blanket. "I was going to have Agent Echo give this to you…it's for Victoria, on her wedding day. Give the bracelet to Zoë."

Sonny opened the envelope. Out slid a necklace with a double stranded choker with a simple diamond pendant and a diamond tennis bracelet. "They'll love them."

"Take care of my girls."

"I will." He leaned in and gave Susanne a kiss on the forehead.

"We'd better get her out of here," Agent Echo said.

Sonny slid the blood-stained envelope in his pants pocket, then gave her hand one more squeeze before they pushed the bed away.

He grabbed Echo's arm. When Susanne was out of earshot, he leaned in, "We'd like her body when she's gone. The girls know and we'd like to give her a proper burial next to her husband."

"I can do that."

Sonny spun around and rubbed the back of his neck as he walked outside to Victoria, Antony, Zoë and Martin. He put arm around Victoria and forced a smile.

"She looked so pale." Victoria's arm went around Sonny's waist. "How much time do you think she'll have?

Zoë stared at Sonny. "Not long. They'll keep her comfortable."

Victoria went to Zoë and wrapped her arms around her sister. "How did you know?"

"Martin told me." Zoë wiped her eyes. "So, Doc killed Tabor?"

Antony nodded. "After Tabor shot Susanne."

"I'm glad it's over," Zoë tucked her blond hair behind her ears. "Even though we didn't get in on it. I would've like to have been the one who took Tabor down."

"I'm sure you would have." Antony patted her back.

"Mom would want us to go on. Be happy. Live our lives to the fullest." Zoë let out a long sigh. "Guess we're planning a wedding, huh, Sis?"

Victoria snuggled closer to Sonny. "Yes, we are."

"Then, we'll make it one she'd have been proud of."

Antony jiggled his keys. "You all have fun with that. I have a job and if Lorenzo calls me one more time and I don't answer, he'll send Vince after me." He pointed to Sonny. "You and Vic are with Clay?"

"Yep. Thanks. See you at the office in a bit."

Antony left.

Martin opened the car door. "We should go, too."

Zoë hugged Victoria. "See you later." She turned to Sonny. "Thanks, for everything."

"Sure." He walked Victoria to the car.

THIRTY-ONE

VICTORIA STOOD in front of the full-length mirror in the elegant Vera Wang mermaid wedding gown. Ivory and strapless, the ornate bodice was covered in crystals, and the romantic full skirt floated to the floor with layers upon layers of satin and tulle.

Zoë burst into the room. "Oh my, gosh, Victoria. I just saw Antony and, man does he look good in a tux. Lauren better hang on to him tonight. Every girl in the place is going to try and steal her man."

Victoria laughed.

"You look gorgeous." Zoë hugged her. "Now I wish Martin and I hadn't run off to Vegas."

"Did you see Sonny?"

"No." Zoë adjusted the crystal embellished veil. "Antony said he was in the dressing room. I'm sure he looks hot, too. I'll go see if they're ready for us." Zoë bounced out of the room like a two year old.

There was a tap on the door.

"Yes?"

Doc poked his head in. "This is from Sonny." He pushed a small box toward her.

Victoria opened the lid and held the small card. The words etched in her mother's handwriting. *I love you. Mom.*

"Can you help me?" She pulled out the double stranded choker with a simple diamond pendant and handed it to Doc. "I love it."

She lifted her hair and veil.

Doc clasped the necklace and stepped back.

Tears flooded Victoria's eyes as she looked in the mirror. The necklace topped the dress of perfectly.

Zoë rushed back in. Her eyes widened. "Oh my goodness. That is perfect. Sonny give you that?"

"It was from mom." Victoria felt the pendant.

"I love it." Zoë held up her wrist to show off the diamond tennis bracelet. "She gave me this."

"It's beautiful." They hugged.

Zoë backed away and grabbed Victoria's hand. "Come on. It's time."

Victoria picked up her bouquet, took a deep breath and followed Zoë.

The doors to the sanctuary opened and her heart quickened as she stared at Sonny. He looked deliciously handsome in his black Armani tuxedo.

A quick glance at Antony made her smile. She looked at Zoë, then got lost in Sonny's eyes. She'd give her entire being to him. Her heart pounded harder with each step towards her new life.

* * *

Antony was mesmerized by Victoria's beauty. She was about to give her whole heart to his brother, but when their eyes met, he could tell she longed for something Sonny could never give her. It gave him a glimmer of hope. She would be his someday. He believed that with his entire being.

Lauren sat in the pew of the small church. He winked at her. He'd bide his time until Victoria would be his.

The Luciano saga continues with

    ABSOLUTION, Book 1 in The Luciano Series

    MERCY, Book 2 in The Luciano Series

    EVERLASTING, Book 3 in The Luciano Series

    REDEMPTION, Book 4 in The Luciano Series

Also by Dana K. Ray

    A SECOND CHANCE

    THERE'S NO REASONING WITH LOVE

DANA K. RAY has been writing gutsy, true to life stories since her early teens. A full-time children's minister, she and her husband reside in the Midwest with their four children and four dogs. She loves to connect with her readers.

www.DanaKRay.com
danakray@yahoo.com
www.Facebook.com/danakray

Made in the USA
Columbia, SC
18 September 2018